THE MIDNIGHT DRESS

Also by Karen Foxlee

The Anatomy of Wings

THE MIDNIGHT DRESS

Karen Foxlee

Alfred A. Knopf
new york

THIS IS A BORZOI BOOK PUBLISHED BY ALFRED A. KNOPF

Visit us on the Web! randomhouse.com/teens

Educators and librarians, for a variety of teaching tools,
visit us at RHTeachersLibrarians.com

Library of Congress Cataloging-in-Publication Data
Foxlee, Karen.
The midnight dress / Karen Foxlee. — 1st ed.
p. cm.
Summary: Rose, nearly sixteen, is used to traveling around with her alcoholic father but connects with the people of a small, coastal Australian town, especially classmate Pearl and reclusive Edie, who teaches her to sew a magical dress for the harvest festival while a mystery unfolds around them.
ISBN 978-0-375-85645-7 (trade) — ISBN 978-0-375-95645-4 (lib. bdg.) —
ISBN 978-0-449-81821-3 (ebook)
[1. Eccentrics and eccentricities—Fiction. 2. Sewing—Fiction. 3. Friendship—Fiction. 4. Schools—Fiction. 5. Alcoholism—Fiction. 6. Single-parent families—Fiction. 7. Australia—Fiction. 8. Mystery and detective stories.] I. Title.
PZ7.F841223Mid 2013
[Fic]—dc23
2012029108

The text of this book is set in 11-point Goudy Old Style.

Printed in the United States of America

October 2013

10 9 8 7 6 5 4 3 2 1

First Edition

In memory of

Doris Winifred Foxlee

"Gone dancing"

*A*nchor Stitch ━━━━━━━━━━

Will you forgive me if I tell you the ending? There's a girl. She's standing where the park outgrows itself and the manicured lawn gives way to longer grass and the stubble of rocks. She's standing in no-man's-land, between the park and the place where the mill yards begin.

It's night and the cane trains are still.

It is unbearably humid and she feels the sweat sliding down her back and she presses her hands there into the fabric to stop the sensation, which is ticklishly unpleasant. She lifts up the midnight dress to fan her legs. It's true, the dress is a magical thing, it makes her look so heavenly.

The shoes she's wearing are too big. She's tripped once already walking in them, across the park, away from the town. She drank some wine earlier, cheap wine, behind the rotunda. She can still hear the harvest festival. A voice over a microphone proclaiming what a wonderful night it is, then music, a slow out-of-time waltz. She can hear the crowd too, the deep rumble of voices and the sudden shrieks of laughter.

She feels excited. The girl doesn't think she has ever felt so excited. It's been building in her for weeks, this breathless rushing sensation. She feels the gooseflesh rise on her arms just thinking of it. She's exactly where she is meant to be; that's what it is, it's like a homecoming. It's like her dreams. She puts a hand on her stomach because she has butterflies and, with the other, adjusts the coronet in her hair.

She doesn't know how she should stand when he arrives. She doesn't know if she should have one leg in front of the other like a beauty queen or legs side by side. Should she lean her back against something as though she isn't so excited, standing in that place, clutching the little black purse in her hands? What will she do with the purse? When he goes to hold her, how will she put it down—will she just drop it? She's trying to sort these things out in her mind.

What should she say? Her mind is perfectly blank when it comes to that. Usually she can think of words, but now she can't think of anything. Maybe something will come when he arrives. Something funny, maybe, or seductive, or both.

When she hears footsteps, her heart nearly jumps out her mouth. She laughs.

"Where are you?" she whispers, because she can't see him yet.

It's dark. Suddenly it feels darker, as though a cloud has passed over the moon. She looks up to check, but there is the moon, newly struck, white-hot. When she looks back, he's there. He looks as shocked as she, but then he smiles.

"What are you doing here?" she says.

Rose arrives one night in January when the barometer is dipping and there is not a breath of air in the wide empty streets. The palm trees along the main drag hang their despondent heads and women fan themselves in open doorways hoping for something, some little breeze. Old ladies watch the evening news, take hankies from their bra straps, and wipe their top lips; in public bars the sweat drips from chins. And already in countless darkened bedrooms, on beds beneath ceiling fans that thump and whir, girls lie dreaming of dresses.

The rain comes in sudden exhausted sighs and spontaneous shuddering downpours but does nothing to alleviate the discomfort. They drive down the main street and Rose thinks it looks like a shitty little place. She's an expert on such things. They could keep driving except there isn't enough petrol left. The service station is closed. That alone sums up the town. They turn across the train tracks where they see a sign proclaiming PARADISE JUST 7 KM AHEAD.

Paradise is a caravan park. Her father kills the engine and sits still, gripping the wheel. Rose can hear the ocean: the sudden intake of its breath, as though it has remembered something, something terrible, but finding there is nothing it can do, it breathes out again. The night is dark and starless.

"It's as good a place as any," he finally says.

She gets out and slams the door.

"Shit."

Toads leap before every step.

The kiosk is shut too. There's a bell for after-hours arrivals, which she rings, but no one comes. When she gets back to the car, her father is still sitting at the wheel. She reaches in and takes the keys from the ignition. He doesn't flinch. Typical. She knows exactly what will happen next. He will stay there all night thinking. He'll try to solve the problem as though it is a huge and complicated theorem, but in the morning he'll realize it is all very simple. He'll stumble from the car and into the caravan, pulling the little curtain around his bed, and his shaking will begin.

"I'm going to bed, Dad," she says.

"Okay," he says, staring out at the dark.

She can't attach the power until the kiosk is open, so she moves through the dark in the caravan until she reaches her own small bed. She opens the drawer beside her pillow, feels for her brush, undoes her hair. She brushes it out, seventy-one strokes, and ties it in a braid. She remembers her mother doing exactly the same thing. The memory is hazy, golden, like an overexposed photo. She presses both her eyes until the image burns and is replaced by tears.

Stupid. It's stupid to cry.

"Stupid," she says aloud.

It's raining lightly. It patters softly on the caravan roof. When she was small, her father said that was God drumming his fingertips. She can hear the sea very clearly, its sharp breaths and exhalations, the whole night around her, thinking. She lies down, presses her eyes again.

If she had a light, she'd write something in the little green notebook she keeps. The words would be clumsy as bricks, she knows it, and later she'd tear out the paper, ashamed. In the book, she keeps a column of words she hates. First is the word *grief*. She hates the sound of it. It reminds her of a small wound half healed. The word doesn't encompass at all the emotion, which has no edges. It rises, a giant cumulus cloud. It surrounds her, dark and magical. At night when she presses her eyes, she feels she could quite easily levitate, held up by that cloud, float out the little window above her bed. It would take her over the town, the truck stop, the highway, the cane fields, the paddocks, the bush. That is how she would like to describe grief. She wishes there were a word as powerful as all that.

She goes nowhere. Stays pressing her eyes. She listens to the rain until she falls asleep.

Pearl Kelly half listens to the others talking about the new girl in the seniors' bathroom. She sits on the bench with her legs stretched out while the others are huddled around the dull metal mirror staring at their smudgy reflections. She is half thinking about the kiss too, Jonah Pedersen's kiss, which was cool and wet and not at all what she was expecting. It was different from Tom Coyne's. His kisses had always been small and tight and dry. They had been rhythmical, as though he were beating out a tune with his lips. Tom Coyne had known how to kiss, even in grade seven.

It's disappointing, all of it, because she had waited so long for the Jonah Pedersen kiss when she needn't have. Everyone had been waiting. And now it's there, all messy on her lips, and she just wants to forget it. Worse than that, she could tell afterward that he was embarrassed. That he knew he was bad at it when everyone thought he was so perfect. It's an ugly secret.

She drifts back to the girls' conversation.

"She's really unusual," says Maxine Singh.

"Ugly unusual?" asks Vanessa Raine, who is the most beautiful girl in the school and likes to keep track of such things. "Or odd unusual?"

"I saw her in Mrs. D.'s office," says Shannon Fanelli. "I mean, just the side of her. I think she might have really bad skin, or maybe they were moles."

"Or warts?" says Mallory Johnson.

"I saw her from the front," says Maxine. "She's actually kind of an unusual pretty."

"Except for her hair," says Shannon. "She has this crazy hair in two buns tied up with about one thousand bobby pins."

"Hello," says Rose, entering the bathroom.

She doesn't have a bag. She's carrying just one pencil. Her uniform is way too big. She looks at the hem lengths, the hair, the way they are staring back at her with their lip-glossed mouths just a little open, calculates immediately, in a fraction of a second, that she will never fit in.

"Hi," they say in unison.

"Hi," Rose says again. She can tell she'll hate it. She always does. She touches her hair to make sure no stray curls have escaped.

Then Pearl jumps up from the bench, smiling.

"Geography or French?" she asks.

The truth is it should be geography because Rose has never taken French. Rose looks at Pearl and tries to think. The girl is a perfectly normal height, with perfectly proportioned limbs, and perfectly pretty in a golden-haired, sun-kissed kind of way. Exactly the kind of girl that Rose likes the least. But is she a geography or French kind of girl? She doesn't look exotic. *Exotic* is not the word for Pearl Kelly. She looks like she might like coloring in the layers of the earth. She'd take great pride in it. She looks like a girl who would feel quite at home with vile words like *tectonic* and *magma*. She would understand map scale.

"French," Rose says aloud.

"Excellent," says Pearl.

Rose's heart sinks.

The truth is she wasn't even going to go to school except that Mrs. Lamond, who runs the caravan park, vaguely threatened to go to the authorities. Mrs. Lamond is small and leathery. Sometimes she paints her eyebrows on and sometimes she forgets.

"Will you be here for long, then?" Mrs. Lamond had asked.

Mrs. Lamond can tell holidaymakers from drifters. This father-and-daughter outfit are drifters. Another sorry affair.

"Probably," Rose had said.

"Better enroll in school, then," she said.

"I'm fifteen, nearly sixteen," Rose informed her. "I don't have to go to school."

"School would be the best place for you."

Mrs. Lamond doesn't like the scrawny girl with the sad eyes who comes into the kiosk and thumbs through the magazines but never buys. "And while we're at it, this isn't a library."

Rose had put down the article SEVEN SEXY WAYS TO WEAR YOUR HAIR, touched her pinned-down curls.

The truth is the first morning she had discovered that the beach was in fact a paradise, a little cup-shaped bay fringed by rain forest. She had stepped out the caravan door and stared at it, rubbing her eyes. She had walked past the car, where her father still slept, all the way to the soft white sand. When she dipped her toes in the sea that morning, she broke its smooth olive-green skin. And when she turned, she saw the mountain, looming behind her, sitting sage in its skirt of clouds.

"Shit," she said.

Her father stumbled from the car into the caravan. He pulled the curtain to his own corner, stripped off, lay beneath his sheets. Over the next days the caravan filled up with the smell of his sweat. He grew oblivious. She wrote that word in her notebook. OBLIVIOUS. He was oblivious to the sea, which changed color through the day, green to blue to turquoise, the huge clouds that raked shadows across its surface and then flung them onto the mountain face. The waterfalls she could see, high up on the rocks. The startling eruptions of rainbow-colored birds.

Rose did exactly what she always did. She performed her ministrations. She made him toast, let it cool on the bench; it was all he could eat. She bought two-liter bottles of Coke from the kiosk, which seemed to soothe him. She wet a towel and he laid it over his body like a shroud.

She brought these things to him soundlessly, went on bare feet, sand still patterned on her legs, said nothing.

"Thanks," he said once.

Once, "I'm sorry."

Rose spent the rest of her time exploring. She climbed over the rocks at the right side of the bay and found another beach, exactly as perfect and completely deserted. She thought about moving her stuff there. A few items of clothing, her green notebook; she could empty out her little drawer into her little black plastic bag. She could build a shelter out of palm fronds. All she'd need was matches and a blanket. She would be able to find water somewhere. She fantasized about these things at length sitting on the beach or floating on her back in the sea. The clouds built all day and each night they burst and the rain that fell obliterated all other sounds: the sea, her breathing, her father's restless turnings.

"What's up with your dad, then?" Mrs. Lamond had asked. "Is he sick or something?"

"A bit," said Rose, running her fingers along the snow globes containing plastic reef scenes. "But he's getting better."

"I like your hair," says Pearl in first period, French.

Rose had used a black rinse. She'd walked all the way to town to buy the stuff and hitchhiked back with a man in a truck full of watermelons. It had cost her nearly twelve dollars on account of all her hair, money that could have been spent on food or petrol.

The rinse made her hair more coarse and wiry than ever.

"Serves you right," her father said, sitting on the edge of his bed tentatively, watching her with his long thin sorrowful face.

The first morning of school she ties her hair in two buns on either side of her head. It makes her look like she's wearing headphones, which makes her laugh. She walks to the caravan park showers and outlines her eyes in thick black eyeliner. There is nothing she can do about her thousand freckles. She examines herself in the mirrors.

"Ugly bitch," she says, then goes and waits at the place that Mrs. Lamond says the bus will pass.

She thinks at the school office they will make her wash off her makeup but the headmistress, Mrs. D'Addazio, doesn't even seem to notice.

"Lovely," she says, looking at Rose. "The girls will be so excited to have a new friend. We're a small school, very small, and how old are you, here, you're fifteen, so that's just lovely, you'll be able to take part in the Harvest Parade, that is on at the end of May, we have our very own float at Leonora High and all the girls are on it, you'll have to find a dress. All the girls have dresses made. We call it dress season here. It's a tradition, I guess you could call it that. Can your mother sew?"

"I don't have a mother," says Rose.

"Oh, darling," says Mrs. D'Addazio, "I'm so sorry, of course you don't. Well, don't worry, I'm sure we'll find someone who can help you."

Rose keeps her face implacable.

"I mean, it's a really nice color, your hair," Pearl adds in French.

Pearl's fluorescent highlighters have tumbled out of her pink pencil case and rolled across to Rose's side of the table. Pearl leans to retrieve them. She has no idea about the rules of personal space, Rose decides. Pearl Kelly smells of coconut and frangipani.

"I have a highlighter dependency," says Pearl.

Rose looks at her and away.

Pearl writes with the highlighters, mixing all the colors, big letters, tangerine and lime and lemon and cherry pink. She adds huge exclamation marks and instead of dots there are love hearts above each letter *i*. It makes Rose feel faintly queasy. She taps her black nails on the desk so that Pearl can see them.

"I think you're going to really love it here," says Pearl.

* * *

In French they have to form pairs so Madame Bonnick can hand out their group assignments.

"Just stay with me," whispers Pearl, which is *très* annoying.

She has arranged her highlighters *très* neatly.

"Good idea," says Madame Bonnick. She speaks French with a terribly nasal accent. "*Bonne idée.* Pearl will look after Rose. These are the roles that you will play for the assignment; you will pick them from the hat, and there will be no negotiation. For each role you will prepare two minutes of dialogue, and the more impressive you are with your roles, the more imaginative, the better. I am talking props, *mesdemoiselles et messieurs.* I am talking costumes."

Pearl picks a piece of paper from Madame Bonnick's hat.

"Oh goody," she says.

"No way," says Vanessa across the room, because she has picked the Hunchback of Notre-Dame. She flicks her long blond ponytail and starts to argue for a redraw.

At recess Pearl insists Rose sit with them.

"Honestly, where else are you going to sit?" Pearl says. "What are you eating?"

"Nothing," says Rose.

"Are you anorexic?" asks Shannon with a hint of excitement.

"Here, eat my apple," says Pearl. She hands it to Rose.

There are six girls in all: Vanessa, Pearl, Maxine, Mallory, Shannon, and now Rose. They begin to talk of dresses.

"Have you picked your color yet, Pearlie?" asks Vanessa. "The color of the year is aquamarine or hot pink or anything metallic. I'm not telling you what I'm having but it's along those lines. It is going to be the biggest surprise. I'm having sequins all across the bodice. My mother did my colors. She is totally psychic with colors. She can do yours if you want but I think you'd be an autumn. People who are autumn should never wear gold. There are lots of other colors that you can choose from."

"Are you going to eat that apple or just look at it?" Pearl asks Rose.

Pearl Kelly has brown eyes, very dark. She's nodding at Vanessa but her eyes are laughing. She winds her hair up on top of her head and sticks a pencil in it.

A boy comes over to the group. He's tall but slouches his shoulders. He peers out from beneath his shaggy bangs, talks very slowly.

"Hey, correct me if I'm wrong, but I didn't know there was a Star Wars convention on," he says, looking straight at Rose's hair buns. "Lucky I brung my light saber."

He gropes his crotch for effect.

"Fuck off, Murray," says Pearl. "Your light saber is the size of a peanut."

He lopes away, his work done. Rose ticks him off in her head as someone to hate passionately.

"Honestly, don't worry about him," says Pearl. "You'll get to know him; he just thinks he's really funny."

"Where were we?" says Vanessa.

"I don't know what color I'm going to wear," says Pearl. "I don't know what season I am. Maybe one of those weird seasons that isn't really a season, like Indian summer."

Vanessa flicks her bangs back with an angry twitch.

"This is serious," she says.

"What color are you going to wear, Rose?" asks Pearl.

"I don't even know what you're all talking about," says Rose, and her voice is husky from disuse and weeks of her own company clambering over rocks and pretending to be shipwrecked.

"It's the Harvest Parade," says Maxine, "and it's been going on for one hundred years or something. They burn the cane and then there's this big parade and all these floats and all the girls have to wear a dress and one of them gets to be the queen and some get to be a princess and then everyone kind of dances in the street."

"Weird," says Rose.

"It's not weird," says Vanessa.

"If you were a meteorological phenomenon, Rose, which would you be?" asks Pearl to annoy Vanessa even more.

"A summer hailstorm," says Rose quietly.

She takes a bite of the apple.

They had seen one, she and her father, phosphorescent green, coming across the downs. Her father had stopped the car and they stood watching it approach, lazily at first, then suddenly racing, whipping up the earth and bending trees, until they were scrambling for cover on the floor of the car.

Vanessa smooths down the already mirror-smooth surface of her blond hair.

"Are you saying you're going to wear green?" she asks.

"I'm not wearing any crummy dress," says Rose. "I'm only here for a little while."

"Good," says Vanessa, "because girls with red hair and freckles should never, ever wear green."

* * *

"I'd love to be shipwrecked," says Pearl after biology.

Rose has offered her the tiniest morsel about herself, told her about the hidden bay. She can't believe she has, it goes against all her ground rules, it's only half past one on the first day. She's been to too many schools to remember. She knows exactly how it all works. But Pearl has worn her down with all her kindness.

Damn. She kicks herself. Pearl is unstoppable.

"I know exactly which bay you mean. It's exactly like a place you would get shipwrecked on, like in a movie. Like Robinson Crusoe. Do you remember that show? I'd love to be marooned and just drink coconut milk and wear a grass skirt. I can't wait to travel. I'm going to go away as soon as school is over. That is exactly what my mum did. I'm going to Russia, first stop, that's where my father came from. No kidding. I never met him. Not yet. I am the result of a brief love affair. My father, he'll recognize me straightaway. We'll be in this crowded station. He'll put out his arms to me. He'll smell like snow and pinecones. I do care about school but I can't wait till it's finished. I don't know what I'm going to be. Do you know what you're going to be? How are we meant to know what we're going to be? My mother says life is the greatest educator. She danced in a chorus line in Paris when she was eighteen. And she was in the circus too. She could eat fire. I mean, she still can. She says love is the only thing in the world that really matters. Now, for this French assignment, I have this old froofy costume thing, I mean, I think it was when I was Little Bo Peep in ballet but it might still fit me, and I probably have a crown. So what I'm saying is I think I should be Marie Antoinette. And maybe you could be the executioner and you could

· 14 ·

make the guillotine. Do you ever have recurring dreams? I dream about this place. It's this big piece of sky over this town I don't know, I mean, a trillion stars. I don't know where it is and I've never been there before but it must be somewhere I'm meant to be. I'm always arriving there from somewhere else and I've been on a great journey. Do you believe in that sort of stuff?"

"Shit," says Rose. "I don't know."

"Sorry," says Pearl. "I talk too much."

Pearl shows Rose the way to art. The day has heated up, the afternoon clouds crowding the sky. It will rain soon. Already Rose can tell from the way everything has grown breathless and still, the air is right up close and personal, it's like walking through honey.

"But do you know what you want to be?" says Pearl.

Rose bites her bottom lip. She thinks of climbing on the rocks at the beach, which is her favorite thing but hardly a career choice. And her green notebook, where she writes her stories, her stupid embarrassing stories, as if she'd mention that.

"God, Rose," says Pearl. "It's just a question. Don't look so scared."

The caravan seems even smaller after school. Her father is sitting on the step waiting for her. It's the first time he's been up. Really up. His eyes have cleared.

"Nice beard," says Rose.

"Thank you," he replies.

He always grows a beard. Sitting there without a shirt, he has a biblical air with that beard. He might stand up and proclaim something, point a stick at the water and part the sea. He is always freshly chastened when he gives up drinking. His forehead is smooth; there is none of the treacherous twinkle in his eyes.

"How was it?" he says.

"How do you think?" says Rose.

"I made you some pancakes," he says.

"That's weird," says Rose.

"Come on, now," he says. "Can't I be kind?"

"It doesn't really suit you."

She goes inside and sees he's taken out his sketchbook and one pencil. Soon he'll draw again. Hesitantly, as though he can't remember how. He'll start to notice the world. He'll say, "Will you look at that sky, what do you think of that, Rose?" He'll think aloud about paints.

On the bus home, light-saber boy had sat in front of her. It was deliberate. She'd narrowed her eyes and looked out the window. He seemed newly grown tall, didn't know what to do with his great lengths of legs and arms. He smelt. He needed to wash his shaggy brown hair. Rose ignored him as hard as she could, stared right through him as he turned to her.

"I was only mucking about," he had said. "Today, you know. The whole Star Wars thing."

"It's all right," she had replied, glancing at him, not smiling.

He played the drums with his fingers on the back of his seat. She ignored him until he turned back and put his earphones on.

"There was this girl who never shut up," Rose tells her father. "And these other girls. They're all going in some parade. Everyone goes in a parade here. It's like some pagan thing. Something to do with harvesting the cane. Everyone has to buy a dress."

Her father raises his dark eyebrows.

"Don't worry," she says. "I won't be doing it."

"You can do it if you want," says her father.

"Have you ever seen me wear a dress?"

Later she goes to the beach and draws her name in the sand. ROSE LOVELL. Large curved running writing with loops and petals. ROSE LOVELL. Rose Lovell does not wear dresses. Rose Lovell does not need friends. Yet all she can smell, even with the huge sky and the evening storm clouds brewing, is coconut oil and frangipani.

Oyster Stitch ━━━━━━━━━━━

The second morning, when the girl is gone, the mountain seems to watch over the town. Skein after skein of birds unravels from the forest canopy into the clear blue sky. The air is heavy with the smell of molasses and the ground is littered with cane ash. There are still paper flowers decorating the telephone poles, streamers hanging from shop windows.

The town is fidgety. Schoolgirls and women meet in restless huddles the length of Main Street, disband, band again anew. The topic remains unchanged. Something is wrong. Something isn't right. She's run away. Would she run away? She's disappeared, clean disappeared, leaving not a trace behind.

Mrs. Rendell, the newsagent and postmistress, cannot sit still. She goes up and down the two aisles of the shop, nylon stockings shishing, straightening magazines, talking to anyone who will listen.

"She's gone, she is, I know it in my bones," she says, then whispers, "It's a murder, I don't want to say it, but I know it. I feel it."

Her only son, Paul, comes out from behind the curtain that leads to his little Blue Moon Book Exchange. He leans against the wall, folds his arms, watches her with watercolor-blue eyes.

He'll join a shambolic search of the cane fields closest to the mill alongside fifty or so agitated men. They'll search for her first where the cane has been cut, a long line of them spread out, trampling down the stalk with their boots. Then later in the fields not yet harvested, in the rows. They'll peer through the leaf, which has grown tall and lush in the wet. They'll search the ditches that run beside the fields, all the smaller streams.

They will take boats out on the flat green river. Ride haphazardly without a plan. They'll break the surface, send out a display of ripples that reaches those who have come to watch on the old bridge in town. When the ripples pass and the river grows flat again, the townsfolk see their own reflections there. They will look into the river's mirror at each other.

They will search until the sun goes down and then stand on Main Street, bereft, speaking but their voices drowned by the wild gossiping of flying foxes settling for the night. There will be nothing to say something terrible has happened, but they will know it all the same. Nothing will be found. Not a trace of the girl in the midnight dress.

"Oh my God," says Pearl.

"I'm sorry," says Rose.

The rain pummeling on the shop roof is deafening, cascading off the awning in a fountain. There are crystals everywhere, shelves and shelves of them, lumps of amethyst, agate, amber amulets hanging in neat lines. Tiger's-eyes and chalcedony, rose quartz, carnelian, citrine, jasper. Every inch of the ceiling has something hanging from it, glass beads and glittering mobiles and wind chimes and tinkling bells. There are candles burning in colored-glass candleholders in the windows, the flames reflected in a thousand other shiny things. It figures, Rose thinks, that Pearl would live in such a place.

Rose has been invited there to complete the French assignment. She has a drawing of a guillotine in her black jeans pocket, a soggy mess.

"Come in," says Pearl.

"I'll wet your floor."

"Oh my goodness," says Pattie Kelly, Pearl's mother. "You look half drowned. Quickly, Pearlie, get a towel."

"Did you walk all the way?" asks Pearl, not moving.

"It's not that far," says Rose.

"She walked from the bay," says Pearl.

"The bay!" shouts her mother.

"I found a shortcut through the cane," says Rose.

"The cane!" cries Pattie. "You can't walk through the cane; it's full up with taipans and browns."

"It was kind of a road," says Rose, and then looks down at her feet. "It was a bit muddy."

Pearl's mother is nothing like Pearl. She is short and curvy and dark-haired. She has a huge patchouli-scented bosom. She grabs Rose and presses her there, and when released, Rose is horrified to see the wet imprint of herself.

"Aren't you just gorgeous?" says Pattie. "Isn't she gorgeous, Pearlie?"

Rose's bangs are stuck to her head and her eyeliner has run down her cheeks. Her school shoes are caked with mud. Why has she come? She should have said no. Why didn't she say no? She just keeps making these same stupid mistakes.

"Go into the bathroom, darling, and get changed. Pearlie, get Rose a kurta off the rack, no, not the white one, that red one, yes, and we'll put this stuff in the dryer," says Pattie.

"I didn't know you didn't have a lift," says Pearl through the bathroom door. "You should have said."

Rose takes off her clothes and looks at herself in the full-length mirror. They don't have a mirror in the caravan, so she's shocked to see herself, so thin, really thin, with tiny little breasts. She puts her freckly hands up to the outline of her rib cage. She has freckles covering her arms and face and legs but none on her stomach, which is the color of cream. The beach has turned her arms a little pink.

"It isn't that bad," says Rose. "I didn't know it was going to rain so hard."

"Welcome to the Big Wet," says Pearl.

Pearl rips off the price tag and passes the kurta through the door. It's like a caftan that reaches her knees. It's ruby-red cotton, half see-through and covered in sequins. Rose has never worn anything like it in her life. She has always worn black jeans and flannel shirts and, now that she is in the tropics, an old black T-shirt flung over a pair of cutoff shorts. She stares at herself in the mirror for a long time.

"Aren't you coming out?" asks Pearl at last. "We need to blow-dry your hair."

"I don't think that will be necessary," says Rose.

Pattie Kelly gets the hair dryer and sits Rose down on a chair in the middle of the shop. Pearl turns over the Open sign to Closed. They go to work removing all the bobby pins and elastic bands that Rose has tethered down her hair with, placing them one by one into her open palm. They are both laughing as though it is the most fun they've ever had. Rose can see where Pearl has got it from, all her words. Pattie Kelly never stops talking either. They interrupt each other and argue and laugh constantly.

"Do it straight, with a round brush," says Pearl.

"No, I'm scrunching it," says her mother. "I want curls."

"Go and put some music on."

"No, you go and put some music on."

Rose is not used to being touched. She cuts her own hair with the scissors that live in the drawer beside her bed. Now Pearl's mother is massaging her head. She would like to get up and run out of the shop, only she's wearing a small see-through dress. She tries to slow her breathing. Pattie has put a record on. It's someone singing in sighs. Rose closes her eyes. She doesn't know what she should do. She wishes she knew where they put her clothes. Will she have to pay for the red shirt? She doesn't have any money. Not a cent. Plus the drawing of the guillotine is in the dryer now too.

"You think too much, young lady," says Pattie when she turns off the hair dryer.

"Come on, Rose," says Pearl, and Rose follows her to the bedroom, already tying down her hair as she goes, feeling with her fingers for curls, slicing through them, anchoring them with her pins.

Pearl's bedroom is as small as a cupboard, with a slanting roof, and every section of wall covered in something, pictures of models and famous paintings and fragments of poems and constellations of stars and photocopies of stone statues and maps of countries like Brazil and cities like Paris and even a diagram of the Moscow underground. Rose doesn't know where to look. *Do not go gentle into the night*, she reads on a scrap of paper, tacked down, then looks quickly away because it seems a private thing. She looks at the Moscow Metro instead. Pearl sits on her bed with legs crossed, waiting.

"I'm not very good at French," says Rose. "I actually haven't done it since, well, not ever."

"I'll make it up," says Pearl. "Don't worry. Let's do it quickly so we can talk about other things."

She hands Rose the French-English dictionary and asks her to find the words. Pearl cobbles them together on a piece of paper. Rose isn't sure if they make sense but Pearl says them with such conviction that they sound truthful enough. Pearl holds her heart and kneels down on the floor in her spangly, incense-scented bedroom and lowers her neck onto the footstool.

"I'd hate to get beheaded," she says when she stands up. "Or eaten by a tiger. But maybe it would be more exciting than just getting a disease."

Rose tries to think of something interesting to say but can't.

"I think you should do the whole dress thing," says Pearl. "The Harvest Parade thing, I mean. It's really fun. I'm the secretary of the Leonora High float. We're going to make a really big fiberglass fruit bowl with fruit and all the girls will be standing inside. I mean, next to really big bananas and apples and everything."

"I'm not really a fiberglass fruit sort of person," says Rose.

"There's heaps of time," says Pearl, ignoring her. "You could buy a dress or get one made. There's a couple of dressmakers in town. Or lots of the girls go to Cairns. It's bigger than formal night. No kidding. And you can probably get to be a princess. The queen is nearly always in year twelve, but you never know. But a princess is just as good."

"I don't have . . . ," says Rose. "We mightn't stay in town that long."

"I know someone who could make you a dress!" shouts Pearl. "Of course. Of course. Of course. There's this old lady who is a dressmaker; she lives right at the end of Hansen Road."

"I'm fine."

"No, you'll love her. There's all these stories about her, Rose. She made all these dresses with her mother when she was small and the dresses were amazingly beautiful and kind of magical or something; well, I don't know about the magical actually, but she's really unusual, weird like, and she lives in this really crazy house full of stuff. And she doesn't even have electricity or something. And quite possibly she's, you know . . ."

"What?"

Pearl doesn't say anything then. Rose waits. She doesn't know why her heart is beating a little faster.

"End of Hansen Road," says Pearl eventually. She smiles and nods at Rose. See, she says with her eyes, there is a dressmaker for you. A mysterious one who will entirely suit your needs.

"Still not that interested," says Rose, expressionless.

There are long silences between them. The silences make Rose twitchy but Pearl doesn't seem to notice them. She lies back on her bed and smiles right into them.

"My father's last name is Orlov. It's very common. There are about one hundred of them living in Moscow." She reaches under her bed and pulls out several pieces of paper stapled together. "My mum got them from a man on a bus who knew someone in the embassy. The buses stop here every day; you wouldn't believe the kinds of people we meet. She said she got the addresses because I wouldn't shut up about trying to find him even though it's probably a crime or something, to have the addresses, I mean. I've written to all the A. Orlovs."

"Has anyone written back?"

"Not yet," says Pearl. "I only sent them a week ago. It takes weeks and weeks for the letters to get to Moscow."

"What do you say?"

"I say, 'Hello, my name is Pearl Kelly and I'm looking for my father, Bear Orlov.'"

"Bear?"

"That was his nickname; that was all my mother knew him as. She only knew him for a night."

Pearl rests back again, closes her eyes, leaves Rose sitting there holding the Muscovite Orlovs.

"My mother was a dancer and he met her in the night; she says he had to bow his head to get through doorways. He was really handsome, and even though he didn't speak much English, they talked and talked and talked all that night. It was love at first sight. They talked at the bar and then the café; they talked on the Metro. They talked beneath the Eiffel Tower, and finally they talked outside her little apartment until the sun came up.

"He was going back that day, he was an attaché or something, something to do with the government, but she can't remember what anymore and it didn't really matter at the time. My mother wrote down her address on the back of a napkin and he put it in his coat pocket but it must have fallen out on the train or on the platform of the Gare du Nord because he never wrote to her. She waited for him and everything, like the whole nine months, but he never came back, so she came home with me."

Pearl opens her eyes, sits up.

"I kissed Jonah Pedersen on the Friday night before he went away for rep football," she says. "He wants to go out with me. I mean a permanent kind of thing."

Rose bites her bottom lip.

"I mean, I like him. He's the best-looking boy in the school and in grade twelve but, can I tell you a secret, he's a really bad kisser. I mean, it was like he was drooling or something. It didn't . . . excite me."

Still trying to think of something interesting.

Rose listens to her own heartbeat.

"But it's kind of expected. Everyone says it was meant to be."

"Oh" is all Rose manages.

Pearl thinks of her other secret. It's much bigger, and when she thinks it, she feels fluttery and breathless. She won't tell Rose now; the other secret will blow Rose away.

"You look full of secrets," Pearl says. "You're a real closed book."

"No I'm not," says Rose.

It's almost dark when Rose gets dressed in the bathroom again. She folds up the kurta neatly and tries to give it back to Pearl's mother.

"Oh no, darling, you keep it; it's a welcoming gift to you."

Rose holds it in her hands and imagines it in the caravan, like a bright slash of blood. Pattie insists on driving her home and

Pearl sits in the back beside Rose. The rain is so heavy that twice Pattie has to pull over.

"Rose is getting her dress made by that old lady on Hansen Road," says Pearl when they are stopped and waiting for the rain to ease.

"Edie Baker?" says Pattie. "How do you know about her?"

"They talk about her at school."

"Still?"

"Still," says Pearl with a sidelong smile at Rose.

"I don't know, is she even still alive?" says Pattie.

Rose ignores them and stares out at the rain. She asks to be dropped off at the kiosk. She doesn't want them to see the caravan or her father, who will be sitting on the step beneath the awning staring at the sea.

"Thank you, Mrs. Kelly," says Rose.

"You call me Pattie," says Pattie.

"Okay," says Rose, although she knows she won't.

"And I'll call you Ruby Heart Rose," says Pattie. "Because your aura is such a beautiful red. That's why I chose that kurta."

"Oh," says Rose.

"Mum reads auras," says Pearl. "Mine's yellow."

"Really, Rose," says Pattie. "Yours is just the color of a Ceylon ruby."

"Thanks," says Rose.

But after the car has driven away, she feels angry because she knows Mrs. Kelly can't see anything at all. She's just making it up. If she could really see inside her, she'd know her aura is black. Onyx black. Tar black. Black as the burnt-out insides of a scorched tree.

$\mathcal{C}$atch Stitch ━━━━━━━━━

On the third day they find the blue diamanté shoes in the mill yards, lying on the tracks beneath a cane bin, the coronet as well. An officer raises his hand and calls, then a silence quickly settles as he goes down on his hands and knees. He treats the objects with reverence, holds the small crown in his gloved hand as though it were the real thing, something precious, not tinfoil. The shoes are bagged.

The bigwigs have arrived from Cairns, Detective Glass himself, who caught the killer of the girl up on the range and solved the baby-in-the-backyard case. The crush is stopped. The mill exclaims its anger, snorts steam as the tippler and the crushers and the centrifuges grind to a halt. The last of the stack smoke dissipates in the cloudless sky.

Glass emerges creased and frowning from the patrol car, sees where the yards have been trampled, where the mill workers have walked across the tracks and taken up a vigil in the park, sighs. The yards are searched again under his direction. Each cane bin, each cane

train, each holding barrel, the vacuum pans, the sugar dryers, the boiler
rooms, each demountable, the bathrooms.

In the park, people sit on the grass or in the rotunda. Clumps of
crying schoolgirls form. The sun burns their faces. On Main Street
some shopkeepers shut their shops and join the crowd. They stay in
the park until late in the afternoon, when the sky turns the color of a
lightning opal. They stay and do not seem to want to leave.

A rumor grows, there in the first evening shadows, and gathers
speed. A patchy, slippery, taffeta rumor. She was wearing a dress. A
dark blue dress. And this dress was made by a witch.

The strange thing is that Rose doesn't need to knock at Edie
Baker's back door; Edie Baker is waiting for her. Or that's how
it seems. She's standing with her arms crossed at the top of her
back steps, looking at the mountain, the foot of which begins in
the far back paddock. She smiles when she sees Rose come round
the corner.

"Hello," she says.

Rose has looked at the front steps and decided against them
on account of the great fig tree growing through them. The fig
has lifted the steps, and the house from its stumps a little too. The
tree brazenly embraces the front of the house with its dark limbs
and peers inside.

It's a huge house, rambling, uneven. It's a house of tiltings
and leanings. It's holding itself together through sheer determi-
nation. Beneath the house a row of battens has slumped to one
side, and as if to correct the situation, clusters of stumps have
braced themselves knock-kneed. The verandas are boarded over

with cheap wood that has swollen and rotted in the rain. Through gaps Rose glimpses rusted garlands and fretwork vines. There are banks of filthy louvres and rows of colored casements, all shut, all cracked and crazed.

"Are you Miss Baker?" says Rose at the bottom of the steps.

"Edie will do."

"Someone said you make dresses," says Rose.

"I do," says Edie. "You better come inside."

Rose still isn't sure why she's come. The normal Rose would have refused to entertain the idea of a dress, a parade, fiberglass fruit. The sensible certain angry Rose would have said, "I'm not wearing a dress. I'm not. You can take your Harvest Parade and stick it right where it fits."

But this is another Rose. A coconut-frangipani-enchanted Rose who keeps imagining a dress no matter how hard she tries not to. It's a solemn dress, a seriously gothic dress, dangerously blue-black. She has imagined it at night in the caravan dark. She has imagined it on her way to school, Murray Falconer playing the air drums beside her with his fingertips. She has imagined it even though she has tried to erase the imaginings each time.

It's late in the afternoon and the day is pulsing with the shrill chant of cicadas and the first strains of the frogs' evening choir. It is impossibly, insufferably humid. Rose wipes at the sweat that keeps forming at her hairline.

"I wondered if someone would want a dress this year," says Edie. "I had a feeling. I had a feeling you'd come."

Rose follows the old woman up the stairs and across a veranda cluttered with old chairs and old beds and piles of stones, neatly heaped, and sheets hanging on a sagging line and large boxes filled with leaves. They enter a long kitchen, painted yellow, its walls covered with ceramic bluebirds, whole flocks of them, twenty, thirty maybe, flying in formation toward the closed windows. As soon as they're inside, the rain begins.

It is a monumental downpour, dulling the sounds of Edie putting on the kettle, their footsteps on the wooden floor, the scrape of the chair that she pulls out for Rose. When it passes, the day is left speechless until finally the frogs start up again.

"I haven't made a dress for many years," says Edie, moving a pile of newspapers from a chair so she can sit down. "There are other women now, I hear, and big shops where the dresses come from China."

Edie is small and old but Rose can't tell how old, not really. Her silver hair is worn short, roughly cut, like a little skullcap, and the skin on her face is very fair and remarkably unlined. Her arms look ancient, though; they are speckled with age spots, and her feet puff up over her slippers like rising dough. She wears a simple cotton sundress, straight up and down with two large pockets at the front. A revolting green. The material sags, empty, in the space where her breasts should be. Rose looks quickly away.

The table is covered in envelopes and jars of pins and two cat-shaped ceramic salt and pepper shakers in the process of being repaired and a huge caterer's-size pickle jar containing a floating dead brown snake. There are boxes filled with letters and pages of magazines tied together with ribbons and a vase filled with what looks like plum pips. Edie slides a scalding-hot cup of tea toward Rose, motions to a sugar bowl riddled with ants.

"I just want a dark dress," says Rose. "Maybe black. I like dark things."

"When I was young," says Edie, ignoring her, "all the girls made their own dresses; what do you think of that?"

Rose shrugs, bites her bottom lip.

"Girls sewed for weeks before a big dance. We imagined our dresses right out of our heads."

Rose taps her black fingernails very lightly on the table.

"I have rules," says Edie. "The thing is if a girl asks me to make a dress, I always ask the girl to help me with it. I think it's only fair, as I don't charge a fee."

"I could get money," says Rose. "I mean, a bit. How much do you need?"

"I don't want money," says Edie. "I want you to look a great beauty."

Rose wipes the sweat from her forehead again and tries to take a sip of scalding tea. The sun has come out after the shower and the room is struck suddenly aglow.

"If you are prepared to help, then we will make this dress. It will be a magnificent thing. I only work at night after six because of the heat. I will let you think about it, and if you decide yes, you can come back next week on Wednesday and we can begin."

"But I don't know how to sew," says Rose.

"I will teach you everything," says Edie.

$\mathcal{S}$traight Stitch ----------

The paper flowers and the streamers have been taken down in the street but the offerings on the front steps of the Catholic church remain. The flowers have wilted and the insides of the pumpkins have grown moldy and the bananas' skins have shriveled and turned black. The Harvest Queen's crown has been placed back inside its box in the mayor's office. All the princess coronets too, bar one.

Detective Glass, with his weary crumpled face, has commandeered the school gymnasium. All day long he and his officers interview girls who have waited in line on wooden chairs. For hours at a time there is nothing but the solemn steadiness of words like rain, then suddenly a salvo of tears. The sobs echo in that place. The detective and the officers look uncomfortable, write down their useless notes, run fingers through their hair.

Glass thinks it's a waste of time. She's a missing person, simple as that. There's no body. He's seen small towns like this before, working themselves up into a froth over a pair of shoes and a plastic crown. Girls are good at running away. It's a fact.

They have interviewed Maxine Singh, Shannon Fanelli, and Mallory Johnson. They have all been asked the same questions. They all return again and again to the dress.

"It was deep blue, so blue it was almost black," said Mallory, "and it had all this lace in it and all these bits of glass. Do you want me to draw you a picture?"

"It was magical," said Maxine. "I mean, it must have been."

"It hurt your eyes to look at it," said Shannon. "It made whoever wore it turn completely beautiful. But . . ."

She pauses. Bites her bottom lip. Glass raises his rumpled face to wait. Only she says nothing. She buries her head in her hands and begins to cry.

Murray Falconer has size 12 feet. Rose looks at his muddy footprints on the bus floor and marvels at how small hers are in comparison. He has dyed his hair blue and it's caused a commotion with all the younger boys. They're shouting, "Now you're going to get expelled, Falco," with glee. He takes his position in front of Rose and jiggles his leg nervously. He's done a bad job. There's still a lot of dark hair along the back of his neck. She can tell he wants her to say something but she sighs and looks away from him instead.

Murray lives just after the turnoff to the bay, through the cane. There's a creek that runs across his land, and sometimes when it's running high, he can't get to school. Rose tries to see his house but all she can see is the roof behind the crop. She has a strange fascination with how other people live even though she wouldn't like to admit it. Has he always lived there? Ever since he was just a baby in a crib? Does he know every part of that house, all the cracks in the walls and the way shadows fall at windows?

"I like your nails," he says.

Rose ignores him.

"What is it like having the word *love* in your last name?" he asks. He pronounces *love* in a stupid voice.

"Shut up," says Rose.

"I'm only making conversation," he says.

"Well, don't." She touches her hair to make sure no curls have escaped.

"I went fishing with my old man at the bay on Saturday," he says. "I saw you there on the rocks."

"So," she says. There were boats everywhere on Saturday.

"You looked like a mermaid."

Wildfire breaks out on her cheeks.

"Do you like fishing?" he asks.

"No."

"Do you like long walks on the beach?"

"No."

"Do you want to go out with me?"

"Shut up, Murray."

"I'm only joking," he says.

Murray's reception at school is rowdy. He tries to appear like he doesn't care, walks with his hands in his pockets, pretending not to hear, but he looks at himself in all the windows. He smiles happily when Mrs. Bonnick suggests he accompany her on a little visit to Mrs. D.

The hullabaloo is only outclassed by the arrival of Jonah Pedersen, who is home from a representative football tour of New South Wales. He strides into the school flanked by the lesser demigods Peter Tuvalu and Ronnie Cartwright. Jonah Pedersen is still wearing his rep tracksuit jumper even though it is high summer. He is tall and muscular, it's true, good-looking in a homogeneous toothpaste-ad way. He has impossibly smooth brown skin, walks as though he is about to break into a sprint, walks as though he is about to score a try, all tensed up and vibrating. People can't help but look at him.

Rose sees Pearl grow quiet. She shrinks back inside herself. She bends down outside the science block and pretends to be very interested in finding something in her bag. Jonah Pedersen passes like visiting royalty.

After he is gone, Vanessa whispers in Pearl's ear.

"He looked at you," she says, which makes Pearl smile.

"I've started learning Russian," Pearl whispers to Rose in Modern History while Mrs. Bonnick is sorting her handouts. Her alter ego, Madame Bonnick, has been put away. She is no-nonsense in Modern History, Mrs. Bonnick.

"It's for when I meet my father," says Pearl.

She takes a little pocket Russian dictionary from her backpack.

"I'm going to write to the B. Orlovs in Russian. Do you think that's a good idea? I mean, I wrote to all the As but maybe they couldn't read English."

"What if he doesn't live in Moscow?" says Rose, which seems a more practical question.

Pearl ignores her.

"I think the Bs are going to be lucky," she says. "I'm translating this little book. I think it's about two brothers."

She holds up a Russian novel. Rose isn't sure about Pearl

Kelly. Sometimes she seems really, really dumb, then the next minute she starts reciting the names of Russian Metro stations, writing them at the same time in pink highlighter pen. It's strange that she is so pretty and weird at the same time.

"In Russia you can get your legs stretched if you like," adds Pearl. "They take extra bits of bone from your ribs and put them in your legs and then all these metal screws and stuff. A lot of the models get it done. It's very gruesome. Sometimes it goes wrong and they can never walk again."

"Now you're talking," says Rose.

A type of dark fairy-tale story is lurking there. She'll write it down in her notebook when she gets home.

"I knew you'd like that," says Pearl.

"Listen up," says Mrs. Bonnick. "I don't want a peep out of any of you."

She starts talking about Adolf Hitler and the Third Reich. Adolf Hitler is her favorite topic. She could talk about Adolf Hitler for a year.

"She totally gets off on Adolf," whispers Pearl. "It's so boring. Have you been to see Miss Baker about a dress?"

"No," says Rose.

"Sure you haven't," whispers Pearl, laughing.

She takes a lavender highlighter and writes on Rose's arm. Rose keeps her arm still, doesn't want to look down, breath catching in her throat.

I WANT TO SHOW YOU SOMETHING. It takes up her whole forearm.

"What?" says Rose.

Pearl turns Rose's hand over and writes on her palm.

A SECRET.

"What?"

IT'S A SURPRISE on the other palm.

"I don't like surprises," says Rose.

Rose knows her father won't be worried, not really, he never is. He might wonder where she is briefly and then go back to thinking about his drawings. He'll light his cigarettes back to back, staring out to sea, drink coffee after coffee until by night he's wired, arguing with himself under his breath.

Rose and Pearl walk down Main Street after school.

"I can't believe the main street is called Main Street," says Rose.

"I know, isn't it *très* boring here?"

Main Street is wide, ridiculously wide, as though when it was built, the town was expecting something amazing to arrive, a thousand people to stake their claim to a patch of soggy green land, a huge boat, *Titanic*-sized, on the back of a truck. Instead there's nothing, a few parked cars, four pubs, a handful of shops. Rendell's News, Crystal Corner, A Hint of Class Hair Salon, Hommel's Convenience Store, where all the packets look as though they have been on the shelves for years and Mr. Hommel still makes and sells his own soft drinks and frozen cordials in containers shaped like kangaroos.

"I'm so glad you came to town," says Pearl. "I can't wait till I leave home. I feel like I can't breathe in this town. I'm going to leave and only come back like once in a blue moon. Where are you from? I feel like you're from everywhere. You know where I want to live? I want to live in Paris. Mum says it is the best city in all the world that she ever went to. I would definitely live on the Rive Gauche because that is where all the artists live. You could live there too. You look like a poet or something. Do you write poetry? I could work in fashion and you could be a poet. We could have an apartment."

Rose thinks of the words she keeps in her notebook. She loves them and hates them at exactly the same time. They aren't exactly poems; she's not sure what they are. She has no control over the words. Those words control her. She imagines herself in the Paris apartment but it's like looking into a coin-operated telescope, all tunnel vision.

"I don't write poetry," Rose says.

"Sure you don't," says Pearl in a disbelieving voice, standing before a shop window examining her hair. "How do I look?"

"Where are we going?"

"I'm just showing you something."

They go into the news agency, which is also the post office and the book exchange. Mrs. Rendell looks up from her chair behind the front counter.

"Hello, girls," she says, tilting her head so she can see over her reading glasses. Mrs. Rendell is sweating. Her hair is damp and she has a wet tea towel slung around her neck. She fans herself with a mold-speckled Japanese fan.

"Hi," says Pearl.

Pearl stops to look at the pens. She looks at the packets of highlighters and the sticky notes and the rulers with reef-scene holograms. She moves to the magazines.

"Is this it?" says Rose.

"No," whispers Pearl.

Cleo and *Cosmopolitan*. Pearl flashes the male centerfold at Rose, who rolls her eyes. *Woman's Weekly. Dolly.* Some very dusty issues of *Vogue* and *Vanity Fair* almost two years old. Pearl opens the magazines and shuts them one by one. Sighs dramatically.

"Not at all what I'm looking for," she says.

At the back of the shop, through a low arched door, there is the book exchange. The words above it are painted in an Eastern style—*The Blue Moon Book Exchange*—but the word *Exchange* doesn't fit very well. Whoever painted it had to cram the letters of that word together. Pearl motions for Rose to follow her through the bamboo-print-curtained door. She smiles back over her shoulder.

It's a tiny room, the Blue Moon Book Exchange, cramped and hot. It's a tight space, shelves everywhere, floor to ceiling around the perimeters and three of them down the middle of the room. The spaces between these shelves are narrow. Pearl rests her back against one shelf, brings one leg up and puts her foot on the shelf in front, starts trailing her finger along the titles.

Rose has never been claustrophobic but in this place she feels her chest constrict. She doesn't know why. It feels like a cave or a snake hole. It smells of yellowed pages, mildewy spines, rarely opened old books that, once opened, are pungent, ripe, shockingly sweet. Between the shelves there are more books spilling out from boxes or stacked in piles.

There in the V formed by Pearl's body and her arm, finger still moving languidly along the line, Rose catches a glimpse of Paul Rendell. He's sitting at a desk at the very back of the room, a pedestal fan in front of him, nodding its head slowly back and forward, ruffling the collar of his white peasant shirt with each turn.

Paul Rendell likes peasant shirts. He wears them very white. He favors faded blue jeans. Sometimes, to his mother's disgust as she sits at the front desk, he doesn't wear shoes. If he is feeling particularly bohemian, he puts on a leather necklace with an ankh charm, which means everlasting life. It makes him feel powerful, that necklace, but he would never wear it in front of his mother. He has a book open in front of him and one hand resting on his cheek.

"Hello, Pearlie," he says without looking up.

"Hello, Paulie," she says, still examining books.

Rose reads the titles on the spines in front of her, she reads them fast, it feels hard to breathe in that place: *Sky Pirates of Callisto*, *The Space Vampires*, *By the Light of the Green Star*, *Children of Tomorrow*, *The End of the Matter*, *The Unsleeping Eye*, *Where Late the Sweet Birds Sang*.

Pearl removes her hair tie and shakes out her hair. The smell of frangipani fills the little room. Paul Rendell closes his book.

"Blossomy as ever," he says.

He's handsome in a way, although old. As old as my father easily, thinks Rose. He has a pale face and his hair falls in a foppish way. He could be an English explorer or a visiting missionary, Rose isn't sure; whichever, he doesn't look like he belongs in Leonora. She watches him drum his fingers on the table, watching Pearl looking at books.

"This is my friend Rose," says Pearl, not looking at him.

"Pleased to meet you, Rose," says Paul, not looking at Rose.

"Hi," says Rose, looking back very closely at the books in front of her. She feels a droplet of sweat escape from the nape of her neck and travel the length of her back. She would like to get out of this cruel little space.

"What book are you looking for now, then, Pearl?" he asks.

"I want more . . . romance," says Pearl.

"Of course," he says. "Well, you know you've come to the right place."

Pearl laughs, a little breathy nervous laugh. She pulls a book from the shelf, studies it for an eternity.

"Can we go now?" whispers Rose.

Pearl shushes her.

"*A Virgin in Paris*," he says very slowly when Pearl hands him the book. "My, my."

Pearl runs a hand through her hair. Paul Rendell leans back in his chair, arms behind his head, smiling. Rose thinks he has too many teeth.

"How much is it?" Pearl asks.

"For you, fifty cents," he says.

Pearl looks nervous now, once she's in front of him. She looks only at the book. She takes fifty cents from her uniform pocket and drops it into his outstretched hand without touching him.

"Well," she says, "I guess we better be going."

Paul smiles but doesn't say anything.

Outside they walk along the street without speaking, Pearl looking at the book, half smiling, barely breathing.

"What were you showing me?" asks Rose.

"Him," whispers Pearl. "Him."

$\mathcal{B}$inding Stitch ━━━━━━━

Will I show you Vanessa Raine's face, which is crumpled up with crying? It isn't a pretty sight. She's pulling at her renowned golden hair and forgetting to wipe her nose. Detective Glass is interviewing her.

"What about this place?" he's asked her. "This place that the two girls went to, Rose Lovell and Pearl Kelly? Do you know about that? This secret place up in the trees?"

He's not losing his patience. He lets her cry. I need a smoke, is what he thinks; he's sick of crying teenage girls who won't tell the truth. He's sick of teenage girls in general; he's interviewed ten of them that morning. He's sick of their scrawny little bodies and their oversized heads. He's sick of trying to get to the bottom of it.

"It isn't about that," says Vanessa Raine. She's sobbing when there's no need to sob. It's only a question, he thinks. Only a question. "You've got it all wrong. I don't even think that place was true. They talked about this hidden house up on the mountain but they were always talking like that, making things up."

"It's just I've heard it from a few other people. Parents, you see. It could be important. If you can think of anything you heard Pearl or Rose say about this place—"

Vanessa's mother, Mrs. Raine, the color psychic, Harvest Queen 1969, interrupts then. She looks like an older version of Vanessa preserved in formaldehyde. Her hair is bottle-blond and her tan skin is beginning to crease. She stretches open her painted pink lips and explodes.

"I think we've had just about enough," she says, getting up. Her hot-pink heels click on the gymnasium floor. "Vanessa has said what she knows and I think we'll leave it at that. Come on, Vanessa, stand up. We all know where you should really be looking; you want some answers, you just need to go down Hansen Road and pay a visit to that woman because we all know—and I'm telling you this right now, if you don't, you're idiots—she had something to do with this."

The dress again.

"Right," he says, picking up his pencil. "Tell me about this woman."

"The house at the end of Hansen Road," says Mrs. Raine. "Very end, old house up against the mountain, looks like a dump. Her name is Miss Edith Baker."

"And how is she related to all this?"

"She made the dress," wails Vanessa. "She made the dress."

The same creek that runs through the Falconer cane bends backward on itself, then up toward the mountain from where it sprang. It crosses some way behind Edie's strange house, where the paddock gives way to bush. Rose can hear its rushing behind the trees. She stares up at the mountain, which fills the sky from the old woman's back steps.

"It's a beauty, isn't it?" says Edie.

"It's okay," says Rose, even though there is something about it that makes her feel dizzy. She wonders what it would be like beneath its mysterious green pelt that grows dark with the shadows of clouds and silvery in the sunshine, that releases startling sprays of parrots, that veils and unveils itself all day long. She imagines all the mossy groves and caves and hidden things.

"Full of secret places," says Edie, which makes Rose look at her and cross her arms.

"Has it got a name?"

"Well, that rock there, the big bluff, is called Weeping Rock, of course, because it always weeps even in the dry season. And the middle part, where the mountain dips, was always called the Saddle Back. There is a lookout there, and on the other side of that, the seaboard side, you can't see it from here but from the bay, that bluff is called the Leap. They're all easy to get to from the town side, big tracks, but really only places for visitors. Day-trippers, we used to call them. See above those trees? I would climb all the way to there when I was a child with just the old paths that have been here a thousand years. I didn't know if you'd come back. You must really want a dress, which is a good thing; dresses are the best medicine for young girls."

Rose keeps her face very still.

"I can already see it," says Edie, turning up the stairs.

Rose isn't so sure. She's argued with herself the whole way. She doesn't know whether she likes the old woman with the small dark eyes and skullcap of hair. The house is falling apart. There's a tree growing through the front stairs. Everywhere there's the detritus of the forest. The leaves drying in small piles in the corners of rooms and seedpods jammed in the floorboards. The curtains are dappled with mildew and festooned with spider-webs.

"Is Miss Baker as strange as they say?" Pearl has asked her, painting her nails in lavender highlighter.

"Yes." She hasn't lied.

"Tell me."

"Where should I start?"

In Edie Baker's house it's almost six o'clock. Outside there are hours of sunshine left but inside is already filling up with shadows.

"I open the windows along the back now," says Edie. "At night a breeze comes down off the mountain and it's good to catch it. I close all the windows again in the morning and it stays cool all day. When I was a girl, my mother called it the mountain's breath."

She goes about opening up all the colored-glass casements and the louvres in the long back kitchen, and the afternoon light dances on the bluebirds. She wears a sleeveless sundress and her pale arms are the color of pastry, and when she raises them to release the catches, two little wings of fat hang down.

She walks with a limp, as though one hip hurts, and she makes a small humming noise in her throat. Rose stands watching; there's still time to go.

"Now," says Edie, "what dress will we make?"

"A lot of girls are having strapless or one-shoulder," says Rose.

"Strapless is for hussies," says Edie, fixing her with her bright dark eyes. Then she waves for Rose to follow her and they go down the hallway into the gloom.

The house is as vast and creaking as a museum and each room they pass through is filled to the brim with dusty collections of things. Tallboys and faded settees and velvet chaises gone lumpy. Boxes filled with bits of paper and others crowded with leaves and large crystal vases sitting on the floor overflowing with twigs and dressmaker busts lying down on beds and hatboxes stacked in towers. In corners there are sudden surprising piles of stones. And in every room there is paint peeling from the walls, emerald green or turquoise or scarlet, and immense constellations of mold spreading across the ceilings.

Edie turns lights on in each room and huge blank-faced wardrobes loom. She opens their doors and rifles through their musty interiors, holds up old clothes, opens trunks, pulls suitcases out from beneath beds. She gathers up an embroidered shawl and a armful of men's coats.

"Oh yes, this is good lace," Edie says when she comes upon a small black dress, a deflated thing, with black rose lace sleeves. When she lifts it, a shower of dust tumbles from the ancient petticoats.

In another room she approaches a small lamp with a black glass-beaded shade.

"What do you think of this?" she asks.

But before Rose can answer, Edie has unplugged it from the wall and tucked it under her arm. They go down a narrow corridor, where the house drops away beneath their feet and the floorboards plink and plonk like piano keys. Edie opens a stiff wooden door.

"Here," she says.

There is natural light in the room and Rose realizes they must have traveled from the back of the house to the front. A grimy sash window displays the overgrown yard and a small patch of cloud-filled sky.

In that room there is material: cupboards with opened doors filled with material, boxes filled with material, bolts tilting in piles. Taffetas, failles, velvets, satins. Gingham haphazardly folded, summer cottons stuffed into boxes, rolls of organdy leaning. Tartans, brocades, damasks, satin crepe, voile, crepe de chine.

The room smells nasty. Old. Fusty. It smells like the bottom of an old lady's handbag, perfumed, powdery, dusty. When Rose looks closer, she sees much of the material is spotted with mildew and the bolts have gone black along the edges.

Her heart sinks.

There are dresses there too. Some hanging on dressmaker mannequins and others on coat hangers. Beautiful dresses: an ivory satin dress with an organza skirt crumbling at the hem, a red gown eaten away by moths, a wedding dress turned yellow slung across the back of a chair.

Rose chews on the end of a black fingernail.

"Do you see any colors that you like?" asks the old woman.

"Not really," says Rose. She's looking for black and she can tell Edie knows it.

"What about this turquoise?" Edie says instead. "Turquoise was the color worn by Cretan princesses. Or this pink? This pink organza is always very popular with girls."

"It's got holes in it," says Rose.

"We would use something else as well, to go with it," says

Edie. "Or what about this yellow? Queens in England wore yellow to their coronations."

"No one would ever wear yellow to a dance," says Rose.

"It probably wouldn't suit your coloring anyway. Redheads are best in emeralds and deep blues and of course the darker shades of red. But you're young and these colors aren't really for girls but women."

"I'm nearly sixteen," says Rose. "And I'm not a redhead."

Edie makes the small humming noise in her throat.

"I don't think you understand," says Rose.

"I understand perfectly well," says Edie.

"There is something there for you; it's only a matter of finding it," Edie says as she leaves her in the room. "You can use anything you like."

Rose hears the house creaking away beneath the old woman's feet, stands still in the room thinking. She could climb out the sash window and run away. She pushes a dusty dress, gold brocade, out of the way and tries the window but it's jammed. She reaches her hand up to smooth down her hair; a pin is removed and replaced.

She moves slowly from pile to pile, pulls down boxes from the cupboards, opens up suitcases on the floor. She touches speckled linen, stiff lawn, gabardine disintegrating where it has been folded. She holds up tattered tweed, ragged serge, shabby shalloon. Georgette shredded by silverfish. Threadbare velvet. She touches dimity, gingham, chintz, and Holland silk. She knows none of the names, of course, only that all is ruined.

It's a joke. Why did she listen to Pearl Kelly? Pearl bloody frangipani Kelly, who knows everything and nothing, going through her Moscow addresses, how has she persuaded her to have a dress made? Pearl bloody Kelly is probably getting a brand-new dress from a brand-new shop on a brand-new street in a brand-new town. She'll shine like one of the baubles in her mother's crystal shop.

Rose Lovell will have a dress made out of rags.

Now she's crying. It's unexpected.

I don't care about the stupid dress, she tells herself. But she does. It's dark and beautiful. It's a mystery inside herself. She can't work it out.

They're painful tears, the sort that swell in the throat. She feels enraged. She's going to march out of that room, march over the plinking plonking floorboards; the house will rattle with her steps; she's going to march past Edie. She'll tell her to fuck off if she has to.

But there's one more wardrobe. A tall narrow one with laughing kookaburras painted on the doors. Rose wipes her eyes. Afterward, in dreams, she'll open that door again and again, return again and again to that moment, turn that little dark key.

She leans forward. There's a sudden applause of rain on the roof.

"Oh," she says.

There is one dress hanging inside the cupboard. It smells like dirt, Rose thinks, dirt and rain and sky. She touches the dress hanging there on its plain wooden coat hanger. It is made of the most lustrous midnight-blue silk taffeta. It makes a soft sound, as though it is glad to be touched after all these years.

She takes it out and holds it up in front of her and immediately sees it's damaged. There's a long violent tear across the full skirt and it has separated in parts from the bodice. The taffeta is brittle and in places stained a shimmery brown.

"I'm not sure about that dress," says Edie. "What about the orange organdy? We could lay it over the turquoise."

Rose hasn't heard her come to the door to stand quietly with her hands held together in front of her.

"I like this color," says Rose. "This is exactly the color I've been thinking of."

"What about the red taffeta? Did you look at that?"

"You said I could choose whatever I wanted." She's trying to keep the anger out of her voice. "Is there any material left over from this dress?"

Edie hesitates. She looks at the midnight-blue dress, takes it from Rose and holds it across her arms, feels the dreadful weight of it.

"There is a dress inside, yes," says Edie. "I can see it. There is a dress in here."

She holds the dress across her arms, cradling it; it makes Rose feel uncomfortable.

"We'd have to unpick what we have here, it has a lot extra in the seams and in the hem; I remember making it that way."

"I don't want to wear something that looks . . . secondhand," says Rose.

"Old things can become new things," says Edie.

It's late when Rose gets home but there is Mrs. Lamond sitting with her father on the foldout chairs, her Lycra-clad legs crossed daintily, her gold scuffs hanging on her leathery feet. She has makeup on; Rose can see it even in the dark.

Only three days before, Mrs. Lamond had summoned Patrick Lovell to the kiosk via Rose.

"The thing is," Mrs. Lamond said to Rose, "your father's going to have to pay some rent in advance. I know there is no one here now, but you wait till after April, the place is packed, people will start booking soon, I get letters from all over the country wanting a space booked; it isn't called Paradise for nothing."

Patrick Lovell showed up, of course, bare-chested, bearded, shoeless. He leaned on the counter and sorted out Mrs. Lamond in a matter of minutes.

"You've got a beautiful place here," he said. "It must be the best place in the world, I reckon. Rose said I've got to pay up front. I'm going to walk into town this morning to get some petrol, then I can get to the dole office. Does Mr. Lamond do all the handiwork around here? I'm only asking because the sign is very faded and I'm good with paints. I don't want money."

"There's no Mr. Lamond," said Mrs. Lamond, lowering her tone, trying to sound sad about it. "He died ten years ago; cancer it was, cancer of the stomach."

"No good," said Patrick.

"I tell you what," said Mrs. Lamond, taking a long drag on her Holiday, "why don't I give you enough petrol for the trip to town and you can pick up some paints to do the sign. That can be our agreement for now. I'm sure there are a few other jobs around the place as well."

Rose shook a snow globe, listening. When she looked up,

Mrs. Lamond flashed her large yellow-toothed smile. Rose's father whistled all the way back to the caravan.

And now here Mrs. Lamond is sitting in Rose's chair.

"Your father's been worrying about you," she says.

"I didn't think you'd be doing sewing classes until midnight," says her father.

He can't meet her eyes. Mrs. Lamond nurses a coffee cup, holding it like it's an alien thing; there is leftover food between them. Mrs. Lamond smiles, crinkles her eyes as though she cares; her yellow teeth glow in the dark. There is something Rose would like to say but she doesn't. She goes inside, slamming the metal screen door.

"Teenagers," Rose hears her say.

Rose brushes her teeth, sits on her bed and brushes out her hair, seventy-one strokes, presses her eyes until they burn. She lies down, tries to build her dream house inside her mind. It's a game she plays to fall asleep. It isn't a grand house, a cottage really, all slanted ceilings and wooden floors. There is only one bedroom. Her bed is a four-poster with dark velvet drapes; it's so soft, like sleeping on a wave. There is a round porthole window that looks out to sea. The house is filled with all her black things. Black nail polishes. Black lipsticks. Black jeans. Black shirts. Black notebooks filled with black words. She has a black cat called Blackie.

Mrs. Lamond is laughing at something hilarious. Rose covers her head with a pillow. She has to start building the place again now; one interruption and it all falls apart.

Edie.

She thinks of the woman's creaking house, even though she tries not to.

That night Edie had cleared the table and lit four hurricane lamps. She took the jar with the snake and the cat-shaped salt and pepper shakers and the piles of newspapers and the vase filled with plum pips and placed them all on the floor beside the old daybed in the far corner of the long kitchen. On the bare table she laid out the strange collection: the midnight-blue dress, the embroidered shawl, the old black dress with the rose lace sleeves, the lampshade with the black glass beads.

"We'll need black tulle, of course," said Edie. "Did you see tulle in the sewing room?"

"I don't know," said Rose. "What's tulle?"

"Don't worry," Edie said, "I'll find some. I think there are some old confirmation dresses with petticoats somewhere; we can unpick them."

Rose bit her bottom lip.

"I can see it again," said Edie, her hands hovering over the table in a way that made Rose feel uncomfortable.

"What does it look like?"

"It looks like a creek tumbling over falls, with the beads falling across the bodice and down here through the skirt. It's like a dark sky."

Rose looked at the dress, the jagged tear across its skirt.

Edie sat down at the table; she patted the chair beside her. Rose sat down tentatively.

"Do you want to hear a story?" Edie said, holding up a seam ripper.

"Not really," said Rose.

"I come from a long line of tailors and dressmakers," said Edie. "My great-great-great-great-great-grandfather on my mother's side was a tailor on the rue Saint-Honoré. Now, his name was Jean-Claude Mercier and he was trying to make ends meet with six sons and his wife dead with the last. He made thread buttons like many of the other tailors, which was illegal thanks to the button makers' guild, and one night when he was closing up his shop and putting down milk for the alley cats at the back door, a man lunged out of the darkness shouting, *'Vive le bouton!'* and stabbed him in the neck. This is how seriously the French took buttons in that time. This was almost three hundred years ago.

"He was sliced here, all the way from the ear down to the collarbone, but didn't die. Somewhere a nerve must have been badly damaged, though, because when he recovered against all odds, very strange things began to happen.

"For starters, every noise became huge. A pin dropping, *crash*, like a cymbal; he could hear the dreadful passage of his thread through the cloth; his sons' voices were so loud and full of breath that he covered his ears with his hands and later took to wrapping his head in a scarf.

"And even stranger, he could hear, miles away, the coal being unloaded at the Place de la Grève, the bell ringer climbing the stairs at Saint-Gervais. He could hear, on a very still day, the Fair of the Holy Ghost, the clatter of feet and poor girls' fingers rifling through secondhand clothes. He could hear roses bending in the breeze at the gardens of the Palais-Royal and a mother whispering to her sick child on the rue de l'Arbre Sec and, in the dead of night, lovers everywhere whispering into each other's ears."

Rose tapped her fingernails lightly, looking as uninterested as she could. She picked up the hem of the deep blue dress, examining it.

"Have you unpicked before?" said Edie.

"No," said Rose.

"Here, I'll show you."

She took the midnight-blue dress and turned it inside out. She ran her fingers over the boning in the bodice and then the waist seam.

"We'll take off the skirt and start with that," said Edie.

She unpicked the skirt from the bodice, showing Rose how to break each stitch with the little hook; the skirt loosened from its large box pleats; the turned and hidden fabric was unturned. It shone with a magical luster in the yellow kitchen.

"See?" said Edie.

"I suppose," said Rose.

Edie handed Rose the emancipated skirt. Rose took her little hook and began to unpick. She opened up the hem and then the panel seams. The blue stitches fell to the floor. Each time she moved the dress, it sighed.

"Don't go too fast, it isn't a race," Edie said.

They didn't speak much then. Rose folded up each panel as instructed and laid them on the table between them. Money beetles crashed against the hurricane lamps. Frogs sang as the humidity built, and when the showers came, Edie took a handkerchief and wiped her forehead.

"Good," said Edie from time to time. "You're doing good."

The mango trees rubbed their fat wet leaves together and touched the house in an intimate way, creaking and sighing and breathing their rotten mango breath through the windows. Edie detached the sleeves and unpicked them open. She sectioned and split open the fabric from the bones of the bodice. She undid the darts and released the zipper.

"There," the old lady said when it was done.

"What happened to that crazy man?" Rose asked.

"He was taken away to an asylum, locked away. He'd taken to walking the streets with his head wrapped in bandages and telling anyone who'd listen about the things he heard whispered in heaven."

"Oh."

"Luckily he'd already apprenticed and taught his oldest son, so his fine needle skills were passed down. Everything I'll teach you, Jean-Claude Mercier taught his son."

Edie looked at Rose expectantly. Rose stared right through her at the windows and for effect put her hand up to suppress an imaginary yawn.

"Is it late?" she asked.

"Nearly eleven," said Edie. "You should go home. Will you come again next Wednesday?"

"Yep," said Rose. She didn't know if she was telling the truth, even with the old dress dismantled between them.

"Do you promise?" said Edie, which changed things.

She heard the steady steps of a possum making its way across the roof. The first of the evening breezes came down off the mountain. It was damp and cool against her burning skin.

"Yes," she said.

Stupid bloody promises, is what she thinks then, lying on her bed in the caravan. She can hear Mrs. Lamond cackling, right outside her window. Stupid bloody, stupid bloody, stupid bloody promises. She turns over, hugs the pillow to her head. She presses her eyes again.

Sometimes, if she's lucky, she gets to see her mother when she does that, just the outline of her in molten gold, briefly, a sudden flash. She's done that since she was very small. She presses her eyes until the tears come. She reprimands herself: Don't cry, don't cry, don't cry, you stupid thing. But there is something soothing once those tears have arrived, almost pleasurable, like a secret river inside her, down deep, released. She's so weak, that's what she thinks, turning herself over on the bed and sobbing into the sheets.

$\mathcal{S}$piderweb Stitch ━━━━━━━

You can see a small photo of the offending rain forest in the Cairns
Post. *All the other photos are of the girl, but the forest, it only appears
once. It's lost in acres of microfilm, easily passed. The headlines were
smaller by then, a week after the girl had gone. News marches on.*

*In the photo Detective Glass is standing on the path that leads up
through the trees behind the Baker house. It's unmistakably the Baker
back paddock. There is the carcass of a chair, an old chair, sitting like a
slumped throne in the long grass. The fence that runs at the very back
perimeter is the same fence, ornate rusted gate, wooden pickets, and
sagging barbed wire, an altogether pathetic attempt to keep the bush
out. Some of it has stepped inside already. There are lillypilly saplings
and a young bloodwood three meters high, standing boldly like a boy
with his hands on his hips.*

*The detective has already spoken to Edie by then, once, maybe
twice. Each time she is sitting on a kitchen chair with something in her
hand, a leaf, say, a butterfly wing, a broken piece of china that has lost
its other parts.*

Glass is confused by her house, its smell alone, which is dank and wet as a rain forest grove. All the kept things, there in the kitchen, all the paper, letters, pictures torn from magazines, patterns disintegrating in drawers, all the fabric turned moldy, turned to lace by silverfish, all the parts of the forest placed in boxes and pickle jars and baskets. The raindrops kept in teacups.

He thinks he hears footsteps. Faraway footsteps, deep in the house. But he can't be sure. Not long after, a shadow moves along the hallway wall. He gets up, looks down into the dimness, but sees nothing.

He has picked up the brown snake in the jar.

"That's a beauty," he says.

"My father killed it when I was a girl," Edie replies, "for no reason other than he wanted to hurt it."

She isn't intimidated by Glass. She stands with her hands on her hips in her sundress and her pea-green slippers. Or she is intimidated. She sits down, suddenly shocked by his presence. A man in her space. It brings back memories.

He asks her about the dress first.

"Oh yes," she says, "I'm a dressmaker. The best there is. From a long line of dressmakers. My great-great-great-great-great-grandfather was a tailor on the rue Saint-Honoré."

He looks at the bluebirds then, with their mended wings, flying across the kitchen wall. He thinks her house is grubby, overcrowded, falling apart, stinking. He thinks her strange and old. Harmlessly strange. Ridiculously old. She watches him coolly with her bright dark eyes.

The detective, he's a little fat. In the Cairns Post photograph he has hair business at the front, party at the back. He's wearing some

kind of light dress shirt with the silver top of a pen glinting in his pocket;
they're not climbing clothes but office clothes. He has one hand on a
tree, his side to the camera.

The photo was taken from some distance, you'll see, the trees are
huge and he is small. When the image is enlarged, it looks as though
he is peering into the spaces between them, which are dark. Darkness,
that's all that grainy photo shows of the rain forest. Not the red leaves
that fall like blood spots. Not the sudden vaults of space that make you
crouch and cry. Not the twisted architecture of the buttress roots. Not
the emerald-green python sleeping in a perfect coil.

Each year the wet season brings the monsoon, a vast system of
rain, continent-sized. The heat at the heart of the land, the dry
red center, pulls this cloud down over the top end like a shroud.
Sensing its arrival, the green ants build their nests and squeeze out
their eggs. The lowland forest trees burst into flower, the Leich-
hardt pines decorate themselves with pom-poms, and everywhere
there is the bright aching red of the native apple. Rat kangaroos
feast on wild plums, and wompoo pigeons eat the lillypilly seeds
and shit them down onto the forest floor, where they will begin
to grow again.

All this does not change.

It is the preordained nature of things.

And in the school yard of Leonora High, it is exactly the
same. All through the wet season, girls dream of the plumage of
dresses, and the prettiest girls are expected to go out with the
best-looking boys, and this has never changed. Jonah Pedersen
sends a message to Pearl Kelly. The message is this: Pearl should

sit with him at lunchtime. So Pearl Kelly does. She sits there beside Vanessa Raine, who has been summoned by Peter Tuvalu, and Rose sees her across the concrete sea, sometimes laughing but often with a strange fixed smile on her pretty face, as though she's wearing a mask.

The small group of girls is lost without Vanessa's command. Mallory tries to start up a conversation about the Harvest Parade; it's official, stop the press, she's wearing fuchsia, one-shouldered, Grecian. She explains to Rose exactly how it all works. How all the girls line up and the mayor introduces them one by one and they go down the stage into the crowd.

"It's kind of like a catwalk," says Mallory. "One of the girls is chosen."

"And sacrificed," says Rose.

Mallory looks at her. She doesn't get the joke.

"Silly," says Shannon.

"It's the one with the best dress that is chosen, actually," says Mallory. "She gets to be Harvest Queen. There are pictures of them all in the mayor's office. Going back for years. The queen gets to wear the crown and hold the sugarcane staff and lead the parade."

"Enthralling," says Rose.

"What color are you wearing, Rosie?" asks Shannon, who is sweet but, Rose suspects, as stupid as Mallory.

"I'm not wearing any color," says Rose. She thinks of the deep blue dress in pieces on Edie's kitchen table.

"I thought Pearl said you were getting your dress made by that lady, Mrs. Baker or whatever," says Shannon.

Rose thinks of the black lace dress and the cloud of dust.

"Not *the* Miss Baker," says Maxine. She widens her eyes in mock horror.

"Pearl said you went to see her," says Shannon. "I'm sure she did."

Rose thinks of all the creaking rooms and all the dreadful quiet whispery things.

"Well, I didn't," she says.

The conversation is exhausted. They sit in silence, listening to the thud of basketballs on the concrete floor. Rose looks at Pearl across the concrete; Pearl rolls her eyes in return.

"It's so boring there with Jonah," she says after school. "I mean, honestly. Football and more football. I'm trying to act interested."

"Why?" says Rose. "If it's boring, it's boring."

"You don't understand," says Pearl.

"Yes I do," says Rose. "I understand exactly."

Her fingers go up to check that no curls have escaped. She looks at Pearl with her perfect skin and her perfect hair, not a single freckle, completely unblemished, not a scrap of makeup. She looks at Pearl, daring her to keep arguing.

"Don't go on the bus," says Pearl, changing the subject. "Come with me to the post office."

She pulls her B. Orlov letters from her schoolbag. There are about fifteen of them. She's written the addresses in rainbow-colored highlighter. God knows what the Soviet officials will think of that.

"They probably have some law," says Rose. "About colors."

"I wanted them to stand out."

"Oh, they stand out," says Rose.

"How do I look?" asks Pearl when they are standing outside the news agency.

There's sweaty old Mrs. Rendell and her mold-speckled Japanese fan. She looks at Pearl and makes a face.

"Here's trouble," she says.

"I want to send these to Moscow, Russia, please," Pearl says.

"Do you just," says Mrs. Rendell. She leafs through the letters, scowling. "What are you doing anyway, writing all these letters? Pen pals?"

"Kind of," says Pearl.

"Kind of," huffs Mrs. Rendell, and she takes out her stamp book and starts breaking off stamps. "Can't guarantee they'll get there. The Soviet Union is a damned difficult place. And they can't stand anything fancy."

"Told you," whispers Rose.

When they have finished fixing the stamps, Pearl announces she has to return her book. She says it in a loud voice, as though she nearly forgot; Mrs. Rendell pays her no attention.

"Come on," says Pearl.

"You go," says Rose. "I'll wait outside."

"Oh, please," says Pearl. "Please, Ruby Heart Rose."

Passion's Fury, Love's Tender Fury, Savage Surrender. Bold Breathless Love. The Wayward Heart, Sweet Savage Love. Love's Avenging Heart, Captive Passions, Desire Me, Burned Fingers, The Men in Her Life, Rehearsal for Love.

"Why is love always savage?" whispers Rose. Pearl giggles. "Why is love always breathless?"

It's so quiet in that room, Rose thinks she can almost hear Paul Rendell breathing. Pearl undoes her hair; she studies the titles in front of her as though her life depends upon it. She chooses another Barbara Cartland at last, *A Serpent of Satan*.

"So, Pearlie," comes Paul's voice, "how was *A Virgin in Paris?*"

"I was up all night reading it," says Pearl, a little too quickly, Rose thinks.

"Of course," he says.

Pearl is standing in the safety of an aisle but she's dipping her school shoe into the tiny spit of linoleum that separates her from him. Rose moves away, looking for something else.

There are some old books at the very top of one shelf, brown spines crumbling, their fibrous innards escaping. She slips one from the shelf and is surprised to find it's called *The Art of Dressmaking*. She holds it up to her nose and inhales its tart, vinegary scent. She thinks of her little green notebook then. What it will look like in one hundred years' time. All her words there, her single words and groups of words that were meant to be sentences. Sentences that led nowhere.

PAIN. CHANDELIER. BLACK. DARK. DYING. COOLING. CRYING. UGLINESS.

WHAT WILL I DO? she had written.

PEARL, she had written.

She had been going to describe Pearl but even writing her name had seemed wrong. Like tacking down a live butterfly. She had crossed out the name, first with a pencil and then with an ink pen. Blacker and blacker and blacker until none of it remained.

Rose turns the pages of *The Art of Dressmaking*.

> *Large girls should never wear orange or stripes.*
> *Tall thin girls should not wear patterns.*

"And what was the story," Paul asks, "that kept you up all night?"

Pearl doesn't answer at first; she's gathering her thoughts.

"Well, there's this girl called Gardenia who goes to live with her aunt in Paris because her mother died. Her aunt has really wild parties. And there's this baron who's the aunt's lover and he's really bad and there's Lord Harcourt, who is really haughty and arrogant, and she really doesn't like either of them but she especially doesn't like Lord Harcourt because he is so, you know, arrogant. But in the end she falls in love with him."

"Ah, the arrogant man," says Paul.

"Gardenia was a good-enough heroine, although I don't really know what she saw in Lord Harcourt. I think I liked the baron better. He was kind of funny and sexy. And French."

Redheads should never wear warm colors.
There is nothing to fear when making a pocket.
Anyone can make a dress given time and patience.

A long pause. Paul laughs softly into the silence.

"Pearlie," he says. It's not a question. He's just saying her name. Rose is surprised at the tenderness in his voice.

Pearl steps out into the little space before him. Rose senses it more than hears it. She moves along the aisle, *The Art of Dressmaking* in her hands. She would like to buy it, she thinks, she could show it to Edie. That's a strange thought, she thinks. As though Edie is a friend. She shakes her head. Paul is leaning back in his office chair, arms slung behind his head. There are two large sweat stains beneath his armpits that look like matching maps of Africa. His hair is not really blond but dyed, brassy, going dark at the roots. His hairy feet are planted on the floor. The middle of him is hidden by the table, which is just as well, because without a doubt, Rose thinks, he would have a hard-on. He's like a spider. Exactly like a spider sitting there in his strange web of books.

Pearl seems lost for words now. She's holding *A Serpent of Satan* in her hands, trying to think of something to say.

"How much is this one?" Rose interrupts. Pearl jumps a little. Rose's voice seems loud in the cramped little shop. "There's no price on it."

Paul Rendell leans forward in his chair, retracts his spider arms, puts away his glistening teeth and his shining eyes.

"*The Art of Dressmaking,*" he says, holding the book. "This is a first edition and quite expensive. You can have it for seven dollars."

Rose doesn't have seven dollars. He looks her up and down, the way someone might glance at a statue in a museum and then move on.

"Now, what have we got here?" he says, holding out his hand for Pearl's book. "*A Serpent of Satan?*"

He flips the book over, reads the back, smiles.

"How much is it?" asks Pearl. She seems flustered now that Rose is beside her.

Paul waves his hand.

"A gift," he says.

For the first time ever, Rose sees Pearl blush.

Outside, the day has grown dark and oppressive. The palm

trees that line Main Street are violently green against the storm clouds.

"He reminds me of a spider," says Rose.

"Oh, Rose, don't say that," Pearl says, laughing. "That's so mean."

"No, really, it's so weird, this whole old-man-in-a-shop thing."

"He's not old," says Pearl. "He's only thirty."

"How do you know that?" Rose raises her eyebrows.

"I read it in the newspaper. He plays for the Leonora Lions. He's been to university. He studied literature. No one ever goes anywhere in this town. He knows so many different things."

Rose shakes her head.

"Oh, it's only a game anyway," says Pearl, exasperated. "He's only here until the end of the crush. He's just helping out his mother. His father died. It's so boring in this town. So boring I could die."

The first of the cold droplets hit their faces. Pearl closes her eyes and tilts her head skyward.

"I'm going home," says Rose.

She has drawn her eyeliner on *très* thick and painted black lipstick immaculately on her bow mouth. She has tried to powder over her freckles. She wants the effect to be startling, frightening even, although she doesn't know why she wants to scare Edie, of all people, who rescues ceramic bluebirds and keeps them in a flock on her kitchen wall. There is a box of them too, beneath the table, all their wings in pieces, waiting to be repaired.

Looking into that box makes Rose feel fidgety.

"You wouldn't believe how many of those birds are out there," says Edie. "You'd be surprised how many people own the things, then throw them out at the dump or give them to charity or sell them at garage sales. I don't go out much anymore of course, so I think my flock is nearly done."

Rose sits sullenly. Edie has not made one mention of her makeup.

"Did you come through the cane?"

"Yes," says Rose.

"You have to be careful of snakes," says Edie.

Everyone is always going on about snakes. Rose hasn't seen a single one. Leaving the caravan park, she started off on the road but then cut through a cane field along a row and then a vacant paddock rife with milk thistle. It cut almost fifteen minutes from the forty-minute walk. The afternoon clouds hung motionless in the sky, and when they moved, they were like huge ships un-moored, dragging their shadows behind them.

In the fields she was closer to the mountain, almost in its shade. She could see the places where the mountain folded in on itself and the open scrub turned to rain forest. When she left home, she could see the Leap, on the seaside, and as she walked, Weeping Rock came into view. That rock made her shiver, stirred something in her like a half-forgotten dream.

Edie hands Rose a pile of old confirmation dresses, once white, now yellow, heavily rust-stained. Rose sits staring at them on her lap until Edie lifts up one of the skirts.

"It's the tulle petticoats we want," says Edie, holding up the hook again.

Rose opens up the dress, carefully looks for the seam.

"Shall I tell you a love story?" says Edie.

"I hate love stories," says Rose.

"It involves the great-great-great-great-granddaughter of Jean-Claude Mercier—remember him?—and a Mr. Jonathan Baker, who was born right here in this very house in the very first room down the hallway. He nearly killed his mother coming out. She was very small, Lillian Baker, even smaller than me."

Rose starts to unpick. She gives the old woman nothing.

"The great-great-great-great-granddaughter's name was Florence and she was the only daughter of Herbert Mercier of Herbert Mercier and Sons Gentlemen's Outfitters, in George Street, Brisbane. There were three sons, Herbert, Frank, and Arthur, and not one of them good with a needle. Sloppy is what their father called them. They were never paying attention to their father's despair. But Florence, she was different, she knew all the mysteries of folding and draping and the pleasant secrets of pin-tucking. Her hand was fine. Her father loved to watch her stitch, her solemnness, which he thought was just as it should be.

"So Florence's brothers did the measuring and cutting and she sat in the back room, all day, every day, and sewed. It was a small, hot room with one window looking out over a laneway where crows sat on the awnings and their feet clicked and clacked on the tin roof.

"She had never been anywhere, Florence Mercier, not ever. Not counting the day trips they sometimes made to her uncle's house at Enoggera, where they swam in the creek. In the creek the current pulled against their legs. Her father had urged her to let go of the bank; he had shown her himself how there was nothing to fear, the waters would only take her to the river bend, where she could climb back out again. When she finally let go of the bank and floated away on the river's back, it had terrified her but also filled her with awe; the way the world was always leaning someway, draining someway, pulling someway. The tides, the moon rising above the rooftops, the water flowing from the mountains to the sea.

"Florence Mercier had a large and unsightly mole on her right cheek, the size of a fingernail, a dark velvety brown. She had a long calm face, a wide forehead, huge brown eyes. Her skin was smooth and very pale. She would have been a beauty were it not for the mole, and its presence was commented upon in all the shops up and down the street.

"She was pale from never going in the sun, Florence, fragile.

"She sewed and sewed and sewed. By hand often and then by machine. They had a very good machine, a Varley Medium that Herbert Mercier had imported from Yorkshire. The machine said *dig, dig, dig, diggity, dig* all day long and it lulled her almost to sleep. She traced her fingers over pinstripes, slid her nails through hand-stitched buttonholes, stood up, sat down, barely breathed.

"Jonathan Baker arrived the summer Florence turned twenty-two, which was very old in those days for a girl not to be married. Later she would say it was the heat, there was a heat wave at the time, you see, and the city was broiling in its own skin, all the shabby brown streets stinking with horseshit and the river turned gray. Horses hung their heads and dogs lay in shadows and women suffocated in their stays; no amount of fanning took that feeling of suffocation away.

"Jonathan Baker had a head of lustrous black hair and his skin was a burnt biscuity brown. He had bright blue eyes. Florence had never seen anyone like him. He was not like anyone from the city; he came into Herbert Mercier and Sons in his moleskins and a checkered shirt and his voice was so quiet that it could barely be heard. And it wasn't that she had never seen the sons of grazers or pastoralists before; she'd seen many, sewn them suits by the dozen, but this man was . . . what is the word she wanted? This man was gentle.

"That would be how she described him then.

"When she walked into the shop from the back room and saw him standing there, her heart leapt in her chest. That was always how she told the story. He was newly to the city and had money to burn. He was sorely in need of a new suit, being there to look at machinery and to find a wife, and was staying with the honorable member for Toowong himself, his pocket filled with other letters of introduction.

"Florence did her best to hide her mole. She was quite practiced in the fine art of turning away, very good at looking at things that didn't need to be looked at so that the horrible side of her face—that is how she thought of it—was hidden from view.

"'Florence, we'll make Mr. Baker tea,' said her father. Florence served it carefully, keeping the right side of her face averted.

"Her brothers slouched at their table, tape measures in their hands.

"'Where did you say you were from, north? Was it cattle you said? Or cane?' asked her father.

"'Cattle,' said Jonathan Baker very quietly. 'And cane.'

"But all of it was there in his eyes, the towering sky and carpet of fields, the lazy rivers and the crocodiles. Florence shivered and met his gaze.

"Who was this young lady with the disappointed face? Jonathan Baker thought. He watched her drift into the room and then out again, saw a large brown beauty spot just below her right eye. She kept hiding it from him, turning her face, again and again, almost as though she were playing a game. A faint breeze stirred the curtain in the front room and the whole of the small gathering watched in anticipation.

"It was the heat, Florence always said. It was the heat.

" 'Wild country up there, I've heard,' said her father.

" 'Wild enough,' said Jonathan.

" 'How interesting,' said Florence.

" 'Yes,' he replied.

"These were the only words they spoke to each other before she sewed the secret pocket into the lining of his suit jacket. She made the suit with her very own hands and sewed the secret pocket in the stifling sewing room behind the shop. Sitting before the sewing machine, she undid her blouse buttons and rested back in her chair. His trousers hung with a perfect crease over the stand and before her lay the pieces of his suit jacket. She took off her shoes. The clock ticked on the wall, and apart from her father moving in the next room, writing in his ledger, it was the only sound. She stood up and counted her steps around the perimeter of the room as though it were a cell. She cried, briefly, with her face in her hands, beside the window, but she could not stop what she knew she was about to do.

"The crows were calling out along the laneway and the city was hazy with heat and she could feel it thrumming, all the carriages and traps and the trams coming down George Street, through her bare feet pressed to the floor. She held the black satin lining in her hands.

"Her secret pocket she hid in the seam and she knew as she placed it there that he might never find it or her note to him. She wrote the note in pencil, very simply, and folded it with great care. It was a sack suit, coat and trousers and matching waist-coat in olive broadcloth, all the rage. Double-topstitched. Patch pockets. When her father went over the suit, each seam, each buttonhole, each cuff, she held her breath.

"'Very good' was all he said, though. 'Very good.'

"Jonathan Baker had decided he would no longer think of Florence Mercier. There were, after all, many other ladies he would meet at the dances. When he collected the suit, he did not look to see if she was standing in her doorway but kept his eyes on the tailor. But later, when he found the note, he realized he was very late and had to run. He sprinted out of Lennons Hotel onto George Street, shot across the intersection at Alice Street, hurdled the low hedges into the botanical gardens. He didn't stop running until he saw her standing there beside the fountain, frag-ile and luminous in the sun."

The parchment-colored petticoats are unfastened and the dresses lie in an exhausted pile. Rose's fingers ache from the work and she stretches them out in front of her. The frogs sing in the humid night air. She hasn't said a single word.

Edie looks at her with a half smile. She hauls herself up from her chair.

"You've done very well," she says. "Now, the next thing to do is to measure you up. There isn't much of you, is there?"

She takes the tape measure from the sewing box and asks

Rose to stand in front of her. When she sees Rose's face, she adds, "It'll only take a minute."

Edie has measured up countless girls, countless women, farmers' daughters and mayors' daughters and brides-to-be; she has measured fat women and rickety-thin old ladies, plump young girls whom she encased in confirmation dresses and slender belles she dressed in elegant ball gowns, but never in her life has she come across a girl who looked so terrified of a tape measure.

"What's wrong?" says Edie.

"Nothing," says Rose.

The old woman holds up the mildew-flecked tape measure. She lays it against Rose's shoulder tip and bends down to the floor. Her knees click. She wraps the tape measure around Rose's waist, her hips. She sees that the girl's eyes are squeezed closed.

"I suppose they got married and lived happily ever after, then," says Rose.

She doesn't like to encourage the old woman, but with her up close like that, she has to say something.

"Well," says Edie. She takes the pencil from behind her ear to write down a figure on the back of a brown paper bag. "In a fashion, I suppose.

"When Florence Mercier saw Jonathan Baker, her hand went to her throat. He held her note in his hand and the sight of it made her nearly faint. They walked along the river first, all the way to Customs House, not speaking, until Jonathan Baker couldn't contain himself any longer.

"'There is a leaf shaped like a love heart and just as red,' he said. 'It's not the only one. There are leaves like satin and others covered in thorns, there are flowers, purple, yellow, flowers in shapes you could never dream of, some trees drop pods like purses to the forest floor, inside there are seeds like gold, there are fruits so blue they hurt your eyes to look at them.'

"He took one from his pocket then, a little blue quandong, dried, held it out to her, placed it in her hand.

"Florence Mercier looked into his eyes.

"They caught the ferry, crossed the brown river, came back again.

"'There are waterfalls, the big ones that everyone knows about, but others too, smaller ones, secret ones. I could take you there.'

"Her cheeks colored, then paled.

"'In the forest there are trees as wide as trams, thousands of years old, and when you look up, you can't see the top, and all night you can hear the creeks telling stories.'

"'Is your house right there in the trees?' Florence asked, her first words; she was trembling.

"'No,' he said. 'The house is in a paddock, down below the mountain.'

"'Oh,' said Florence, and he thought she looked a little disappointed.

"'But I will build you a house,' he said, 'I promise. I could build you a house there, high among the trees.'

"They were by the fountain again, watching their silvery reflections in the water. He reached out and touched the velvety mole on her cheek. It was a bold act, right there in the sunlight, but she didn't pull away.

"'Yes' was what she said."

Edie writes down the measurements, puts them on the table, and places the lampshade on top. Rose isn't sure where the lampshade fits in; it makes her nervous. The first of the breezes comes again, she feels a tendril of it against her neck, and she closes her eyes.

"I better go home," she says.

"Yes, it's late and you have school," says Edie. "Are you scared of the walk?"

"No," says Rose. It's the truth.

"Good," says Edie. "There's no point in being frightened of the night."

They stand on the back steps. Rose can't see the mountain but she can sense it there, feels she could put her hands up and touch it, it's that close.

"Did he really build a house up there or was that a trick?"

"He did. It's still there. Or it was the last time I went. Now, that was many years ago."

"Do you know how to get there?"

"Of course."

Nothing then. Rose imagines it. Edie smiles in the dark.

"I could tell you how. It's a difficult climb but you might make it."

Rose shrugs.

"I'm okay," she says.

$\mathcal{S}$eed Stitch ━━━━━━━━━━━

"Do you know anything about some place up on the mountain?" Detective Glass asks Edie Baker in her kitchen. "It's some house of sorts or a hut, a dwelling anyway; there's talk of it, that Rose Lovell and Pearl Kelly went there. It was their place, their special place. A kind of hideaway place."

Edie still hasn't packed away the makings of the dress. The black thread, the needles, the old lampshade, the confirmation dresses sans their petticoats, the tulle remnants scattered on the floor like bits of cloud. The newspaper pattern is folded up there on a chair.

Detective Glass looks at the blue quandongs in pickle jars.

The peacock coverlet on the old daybed.

The shadowy opening of the hall. He shivers.

There in that house he knows suddenly the girl is dead. He's felt it before in other cases, without warning. He feels the knowledge settle in him like a stone falling to the bottom of a pond. Yes, she's dead. He shakes his head to clear away the thought.

"They keep talking about it, that's all," he says. It's almost an apology. "All the girls. That and the dress."

"Of course I know the place," says Edie, watching him carefully. Watching the gooseflesh rise on his arms. She's sitting at the table holding a leaf in her hand. "My father built it for my mother in the year 1913. It's near a waterfall. There were two men who helped him cut the wood but the rest he did himself. Carried the windows piece by piece. A hundred trips he must have made. It was when he could love, before the war knocked all the stuffing out of him. There's nothing really hidden about it; you just have to know where to find it, that's all."

"Did they go there, do you know?"

"Yes, I believe they did," says Edie. "Until Rose burnt it down."

"Burnt it down?"

"Yes, she burnt it down. Shall I give you directions?" says Edie. She pauses then, looks at the detective's beer gut for effect. "It's a bit of a walk."

"Fucking bananas," her father says on the way home from the dole office. "I knew it would be something ridiculous like that."

The dole office always wants to see the child. It's a technicality before they start making payments again. He keeps turning up in different places, this Patrick Lovell, and there has to be proof that he has the child with him. Hasn't just left her at a truck stop somewhere.

Rose has taken the day off school. The last thing she wants is for her father to arrive there to pick her up, for people to see the car, which has terrible suspension and bobs up and down like a ship at sea, her bearded father like Moses at the helm.

Rose couldn't stand another day at school anyway. Another day sitting in the circle talking about nothing. Pearl, all coconut-scented and crystal-shop sparkly, opening up her backpack and pulling out the latest romance novel, running her highlighter-painted fingernails over the cover.

The dole office is in the next town. The dole office madam has a name tag on; it says MARLENE.

"Marlene," says Rose's father, honey smooth. As though he is about to recite a poem. He strokes his beard, which has grown luxuriant.

"You were in Brisbane last," says Marlene. "And before that Theodore and before that Mullumbimby."

"Yes," says Patrick Lovell.

"Getting around?"

"Like to be on the road."

It was endless, that road. When Rose closed her eyes at night, it stretched out behind her. Her father drove with one hand on the wheel, an elbow on the window, a cigarette trailing a plume of smoke. He sang songs like "Love Me Tender" and "Heartbreak Hotel" in a quavering baritone. He said, "Where next, Rose?" "We're getting itchy feet, Rose." Sometimes he decided by tossing a coin. They would head inland or toward the coast. "Follow that bird," he would sometimes shout at the top of his lungs, then turn down the highway after a hawk that would lead them to the next town.

"And this is your dependent?" says the dole officer.

"Yes, madam," says her father.

"Enrolled in school?"

"Yes, madam."

"Can she step up to the counter, please?"

"Rose," says her father.

"What school are you enrolled in?" asks Marlene.

"The high school in Leonora."

"Not there today?"

"Obviously not," says Rose.

"Why?"

"I have a headache."

"Which school were you at before here?"

"Umm, Theodore State High."

"Before that?"

"I went to Mullumbimby State High but only for about a month."

The woman studies her closely and then looks back at her father.

"They need banana pickers and packers," she says.

In the car, Rose doesn't say anything about the bananas. At least they'll have a little money for a while. It won't be for long. It's all downhill from the first day of work. She knows exactly how it will pass. He'll get dressed and drive away in the car; he'll come home. He'll say, "You know, it wasn't too bad," or "It was a shit house but the men were good," or "I met this great guy called Reg, top bloke, salt of the earth."

Reg or Colin or Keith or Tom. Archie, Frank, Larry, Karl, Tony, Barry, Morrie. "I met this great bloke called Snow; he's got a boat and he said he'd take us out on the open water." "I met this great bloke called Harry and we got to talking and you wouldn't believe it but he's been to Africa and got chased by a lion." "I met this bloke called Frank, he has six girls, I'm not kidding, and he reckons he might have some clothes you could have a look at." A man called Blue with ginger hair, a tall man called Lofty, a small man called Shorty, a fat man called Tiny. Reg-oh, Dame-oh, John-oh.

In the beginning her father will present the easygoing version of himself. The happy, just-blew-into-town him, the traveling him with the quiet laugh, the looking-for-work him, the down-on-his-luck him, the father-with-a-daughter him, the she's-a-good-kid him, the we're-doing-our-best him.

Then he'll come home on the fifth or sixth day and say, "I'm just going out for a while. I won't be long." He'll go down the road, the lane, the track, the highway, to the pub and come back later merry and full of praise. But later, sometimes in days, other times weeks, he'll change. He'll grow louder, be full of bluster; his stories will grow more hilarious. He'll drink until he's staggering. He'll let down his disguise, he'll blow up in their faces like a storm. He'll argue with their words and ideas, pick apart their stories, he'll say, "What would you know, Harry, lions and Africa aside, have you ever actually fucking really ever been anywhere?"

Rose knows it and her father knows she knows it and it makes him nervous.

"It'll be different this time," he says after a long while in the car, cane field after cane field after cane field. "If it's bananas, then it has to be bananas; it'll all be good."

"I know," says Rose.

They buy groceries, a veritable feast, ice cream and soft white bread and a cooked chicken. He buys Rose two new packets of bobby pins. By the time they've driven down Main Street and turned across the train tracks, he's singing.

"Jesus," says Rose when they pull into the caravan park.

"Who's that?" says Patrick Lovell.

Because Pearl Kelly is waiting on their doorstep.

The problem with Pearl Kelly, thinks Rose, is that she never thinks things through. Not really. She can never tell when people don't want her around because she goes through life believing everyone in the whole goddamn world loves her.

"I walked," Pearl says, jumping up as they get out of the car. "Then I started freaking because you weren't here but this lady from the shop said you'd be back soon."

"Dad, this is Pearl," says Rose.

"Pearl," says Patrick. "I haven't heard that name for years."

"It's terrible, isn't it? I wish I was something else."

"What could you be?" says Patrick.

"Something much more romantic," says Pearl. "Persephone."

She looks at Mr. Lovell and smiles. It's exactly the same sweet sly smile she uses on Paul Rendell.

"Come on," says Rose. She can't believe Pearl is flirting with her father. She starts walking away toward the beach.

"See you, Mr. Lovell," says Pearl, laughing over her shoulder.

The problem with Pearl Kelly is that nothing bad has ever happened to her; okay, so what if she can't find her father, she lives in a shop full of crystals and listens to fucking panpipes all day and she doesn't understand anything. The problem with Pearl Kelly is that she lives in a dream world, thinks that she is going somewhere in life but one day she'll wake up and be in the same town still going out with Jonah Pedersen.

Rose walks ahead onto the sand and she is so angry she thinks she could die. The sea is as flat as a pond, gray-green; the dark clouds have tattered hems. Rose watches them unraveling their edges.

"Sorry," says Pearl. "I didn't know you'd be angry if I came."

"Don't worry about it," says Rose.

"I just wanted to say hello because you weren't at school."

"I was just busy," says Rose.

"Doing what?" says Pearl.

"Just stuff."

"Okay."

"You don't get it."

"I'll go."

"Don't," says Rose.

They climb up the rocks toward Rose's bay. Pearl is a hopeless climber. She has no sense of where to put her feet. She's laughing as though climbing is funny. As though finding footholds is a joke.

"Hang on," she laughs. "Hang on, you're going too fast. You're like a mountain goat."

Rose has to show her where to put her hands and where to put her feet. She has to offer her hand. When she lets go again, the imprint of Pearl's palm stays burning there. The fifteen-minute climb takes almost half an hour. When they reach the little bay, they sit down and dig their toes into the sand.

"Your dad's nice," says Pearl.

"Lovely," says Rose.

"I mean it. He's got really nice eyes."

"Thanks," says Rose. "I feel a lot better knowing you like my dad."

"What's wrong with you?"

"Nothing," says Rose. "Everything, probably."

"Did you go back to see Miss Baker?"

"Yes."

"Has she started making the dress?"

"Yes."

"What color is it?"

"Dark blue."

"That'd suit you."

Rose wants to say something about Edie. She wants to say something about her being weird and the huge lonely mildewy house that's so full but so empty, but she stops, stares out to sea.

"You should let your hair out," says Pearl.

"You saw it," says Rose. "It's an out-of-control Afro."

Pearl laughs.

"You're funny," she says.

"I'm not kidding," says Rose. "It really is. You saw it in the shop that day."

"It wasn't that bad."

"I need to dye it black again."

"I think you should just let it be red."

"Why?"

"Because it's beautiful," says Pearl. "And romantic."

She opens her little backpack and takes out *A Serpent of Satan*.

On the cover there is a woman with blond hair arranging flowers, a man standing behind her in a morning suit with an arrogant expression.

"Her name is Ophelia," says Pearl, "and that's the Earl of Rochester and he rescues her from where her evil stepmother, who is totally into black magic, is keeping her kind of like a slave and probably is going to sacrifice her because she's a virgin. And anyway the earl rescues her and he's been with so many women but he's never seen anyone as beautiful as Ophelia."

Rose takes the book and turns to a page that Pearl has dog-eared.

"'He bent his head as he spoke,'" Rose reads aloud, "'and his lips found hers. He could not imagine that any woman's mouth could be so soft, so yielding and yet so exciting.'"

Rose sighs for effect, pants gently.

"'For a moment he was very gentle, kissing her almost as if she was the child he sometimes thought her to be. Then as he felt her press her body a little closer to his, as he felt a sudden ecstasy make her respond to his kiss, he knew that this was different, very different from anything he had ever known before.'"

Pearl laughs, lies back on the sand, one arm flung across her eyes, listening. She's smiling.

"It's a good book," Pearl says. "Really it is. Have you kissed anyone?"

"Yes," says Rose, lying.

"Isn't it funny how I have no father and you have no mother. And your dad is called Patrick and my mum is Patricia."

"Hilarious."

"No, you know what I mean," she says. "I'm going to find my dad. It'll be hard but I'm going to find him. I think I might have sisters. I dream about them sometimes. They have long hair and faces like moonlight. What happened to your mum?"

"She died," says Rose.

"How?" says Pearl.

She has told girls before, in other schools, other towns, most often to shock them. The telling is always different from any other thought she has about her mother. She doesn't feel anything when she says the words. It's like a tape recording: "When you hear the bell tinkle, please turn the page." She tells the story and then waits in the silence for what they have to say.

The waves tiptoe on the sand.

"When I was five, she put me to bed one night," says Rose. "And when I woke up, she was gone, that's all. No one could find her for days and days. But then she washed up on the beach, which wasn't that far away."

"Are you joking?" says Pearl. She's just like all the others.

"Do I look like I'm joking?" Rose replies.

"What happened to her?"

"She liked doing crazy things, that's all. She said, 'I'm going for a skinny-dip.' She'd had some wine and some joints. She was a free soul, that's what Dad said; she painted and drew and made things all the time."

"God, that's terrible," says Pearl.

"It doesn't matter," says Rose.

She puts her hand up and catches the first of the evening raindrops in her open palm.

After Pearl has called her mother from the pay phone and been retrieved, Rose goes home. Her father is there in a foldout chair making excited marks in his notebooks. Broad, rough marks, working fast. He doesn't look up when Rose walks past.

"I know her from somewhere," he says.

"Who?"

"Pearl."

"From where?"

"I don't know," he says.

"Main Street?"

"No, not there," he says. "I think from a painting. She's in a famous painting."

"What?"

"Do you think she's Vermeer's Girl with a Pearl Earring? No, not that, that's too obvious. She's La Scapigliata. No."

He jumps up and goes to his bed and pulls out his art books from beneath and starts flipping through the pages: *Masters of the Twentieth Century, Renaissance Art, The Handbook to the London Museum of Modern Art, The Pre-Raphaelites*. He turns the pages quickly, stopping every so often, tracing his fingers over a woman's face.

"Look at this," he says. "Jane, Countess of Harrington."

Rose looks at the picture. He's really pissing her off.

"I think you need medication," she says.

"What about this one, Titian's Judith? There, look at that."

"She has brown hair."

"Hair, hair, I'm not talking about hair."

Rose goes inside, pulls the curtain, lies on her bed.

"Did you offer her a lift home?" he says at the caravan door.

"She rang her mother from the pay phone."

"Do you think she would sit for me?"

"Since when do you do portraits?"

"Do you think she would?"

"No," Rose says.

* * *

On Saturday they go to the John Parsons Oval. At first it doesn't seem purposeful. They start by walking to the small library beside the park on Main Street. They stand above the air conditioner vents cooling their legs, Pearl whispering, "Want to know an interesting fact about Jonah Pedersen? He can't spell. I mean, I've seen his writing, it's like he's a child. Even weirder, it made me feel really sad and really protective of him, like a mother."

Rose stares at Pearl, thinking. "Maybe you could teach him how to read and write," she says at last. "Kind of like Jane teaching Tarzan."

"Oh, Rose," says Pearl.

They drift back out the door again. They walk into Hommel's Convenience Store, dark and dry, and press soft drink cans to their faces, buy two, sarsaparilla for Rose, lemonade for Pearl, a packet of jelly beans, the blacks counted out into Rose's open palm. "Do you think it's bad to be born out of a one-night stand? Which is better, passion or boring love?" "If you had a choice of going somewhere, say, to another planet, only you could never come home again, would you do it?"

"What was the other choice?"

"Never going anywhere."

They walk through the park, in and out of the shadows of the great trees, lie on the rotunda bench seats; Pearl's hair hangs down in a golden swath. They go past the pool along Second Street.

"Where are *we* going?"

"Nowhere," says Pearl. "Just walking."

Past the small faded houses, overgrown lawns, agaves grown

monstrous in the wet; past the fish-and-chips shop, across cane train tracks. Through the railway proper. Past the quiet mill, not yet crushing. They can hear the football ground before they see it.

"I think Murray Falconer has the hots for you," says Pearl.

"Don't be stupid," says Rose.

"I see him looking at you all the time in English."

"Marveling at my grotesqueness," says Rose.

That makes Pearl laugh.

"Ruby Heart Rose," she says.

The Saturday football match is between the away Crushers and the Leonora Lions. A lazy crowd, drowsy with the heat, rests on blankets and in the half-full grandstand, watching the clash. Pearl stands against the fence first and then they go inside.

"What are we doing here?" asks Rose.

"Just looking," says Pearl.

Rose spots Paul Rendell almost immediately. He's taller than she imagined, since she's only ever seen him sitting behind the table in the Blue Moon Book Exchange. He's sweating, his blond hair stuck against his forehead, sweating the way an English schoolboy sweats, with rosy cheeks. He has very hairy legs.

Powerful legs, pale, covered in a pelt of curled white hair.

"Oh my God, look at his legs," whispers Rose.

"Shhh," says Pearl.

"Is Jonah playing?"

"He doesn't play Union, silly."

It seems they have arrived for the very end of the game; the whistle sounds minutes after they take their seats. The teams walk from the field and pass right beside where they sit. Paul sees Pearl, Rose sees him see her, but he looks away quickly, wiping sweat from his face. He laughs at something a teammate says. And when Rose looks back at Pearl, she is only staring up at the sky.

Stepped and Threaded Running Stitch ━━━━━━━━━━

I'll tell you another part of the ending. I don't want you to look if it hurts you. Close your eyes. She says, "What are you doing here?" He says, "It's you." Just as surprised. His words come out in a breath. He smiles, sways. "I'm waiting for someone," she says. Her heel catches on a stone; she wobbles, smiles in return. "Don't," he says. "Just stay." Even though she hasn't moved.

She begins to calculate briefly, distance first, if she has to run, then abandons her sums. That's silly. He can hardly stand up. She holds the dress out, looks down at it, then puts a hand on one hip, coils a finger in her hair, laughs.

The band stops playing momentarily, midbeat, a pause of several seconds; something has gone wrong, there's laughter from the crowd. They start again, a new song, a march; they've given up the other.

"We can just talk," he says. Like a boy.

* * *

It's only Monday. The week, which despite herself Rose measures from Wednesday to Wednesday, drags. The days move at an infuriating languid tropical speed; there is a whole week inside each day.

The air is hot and breathless, fans tilt full speed in shops; the swimming pool is so crowded after school there is not a patch left on the thick green grass. Not that Rose goes there. She wouldn't dream of it. After she catches the bus home, she walks down to the rocks and climbs there. She's good at it. Sure-footed. She climbs as high as she can up the point; it's almost as though she's sitting on the prow of a boat looking out to sea. It's the only place there is a breeze.

It's a welcome relief after the classrooms, so stuffy with body odor they make her feel drowsy, the teachers droning on and on with all the names and bloody moments in history: Stalin, Hitler, Mao Tse-tung, Gettysburg, Normandy, Waterloo. She hears the words for a while and then they drift away. She thinks of the table in Edie's kitchen and she thinks of the mountain.

Most of her doesn't want to go back. She doesn't like promises or agreements. It seems stupid to promise something to someone she barely knows. Each time she's in front of Edie, she feels exposed, like the old lady can see right inside of her, which is stupid; Rose shakes her head, there in Modern History, at the thought of it.

"Are you disagreeing, Rose Lovell?" says Mrs. Bonnick.

"Pardon," says Rose, coming to with all the sweaty pale faces staring back at her. "Sorry, Mrs. Bonnick."

Yet part of her wants to go back, a tiny part, which makes her uneasy, this part of herself that is disobeying all the rules. This part feels light, flighty, like a runaway balloon.

Pearl hasn't talked about her father since Rose told her about her mother. She hasn't said a single word about the letters, although Rose sees her writing one; she's gone back to writing them in English. She adds the letter to the other C. Orlovs in her bag, tied together with a rubber band. Sometimes she looks at Rose and smiles kindly.

"What?" Rose says a little harshly.

At lunchtime Pearl takes *Ashes in the Wind* from her bag and holds it on her lap, her hands folded over it neatly. She doesn't read it. Just holds it there, a charm.

"What about this one? Paul Rendell had said about it: 'A bewitching belle dressed as a lad, a doctor torn between love and duty, a thrilling tale of passion and promise. Let's hope there're some good bits in it, though. Really, Pearl, there was only kissing in *A Serpent of Satan*.'"

All the while Rose had stared at him from her cramped aisle, watching. He had his peasant shirt a little undone, his chest hair showing, very white. His watercolor-blue eyes.

Pearl sat on the floor going through a box, her hair undone, her frangipani scent rising like a cloud. She was chewing pink bubble gum.

"It's the getting to the kiss that's the good part, silly," she said.

She blew a bubble and let it pop. Paul Rendell laughed very loudly.

Pearl and Vanessa are back with the girls because the boys have started playing football over the lunch hour. They sit on the school oval to watch them. Jonah Pedersen takes off his shirt and easily sidesteps all of his opponents, scoring try after try. Pearl stifles a yawn. Murray Falconer plays as well; he's so scrawny beside Jonah Pedersen it makes Rose want to laugh. He nearly scores once before he is put down in the wet grass. He's trying really hard to impress someone, God knows who.

"My dad wants to paint your portrait, Pearl," Rose says. "He thinks you look like someone from a famous painting, except he can't remember which one."

Pearl laughs but the news makes Vanessa swish her ponytail like a horse annoyed by a fly.

"Is your father really a painter?" Vanessa demands.

"He's been to art college but he's not a portrait painter," says Rose. "He usually just paints weird things like washing machines with wings and fridges covered in scales."

"I don't think you should get involved with it, Pearlie," advises Vanessa.

"Yes, Mum," says Pearl.

As secretary for the Harvest Parade Float Committee of Leonora High, Pearl writes all the minutes in lime-green highlighter. The construction of fiberglass fruit is on track for the parade. Mr. Tate, who runs the fiberglass business near town, is making the fruit frames free of charge but the committee will have to paint almost fifty meters of calico: purple for grapes, yellow for bananas, red for apples.

"Maybe your dad could help with the painting," says Pearl.

Rose imagines it.

"Sorry, he hasn't had his community-spirit transplant yet," she replies.

"You could ask him anyway," says Pearl, never one to give up.

"Since when do grapes grow here anyway?" says Rose.

"It's symbolic," says Pearl.

"I wish I could dress up as a piece of fruit for the parade," says Rose.

"Which piece of fruit would you be?"

"I'd definitely be a black plum," says Rose. "All blood red inside."

Vanessa swishes her ponytail some more.

"So is it true, Rose?" Vanessa demands. "Are you getting your dress made by Miss Baker?"

Rose hesitates. "Yes."

Vanessa doesn't say anything. She smiles a little smile as though in pity.

"What?" says Rose.

"Nothing," says Vanessa.

Wednesday they make the dress pattern. Edie hauls herself up from the back steps and goes inside. She opens all the louvres and casements, ready for the night.

"It's in here, the dress," Edie says, tapping her head, "and now we'll get it out."

Rose sits at the table watching her.

"I can see it," Edie continues, eyes closed; it makes Rose chew her nail. "The way it will fall, the way the lines will flow."

It's a strange evening. For once there is no rain. The ceiling of the clouds has lifted suddenly, leaving a deep blue cathedral sky. Everything seems unsettled. Thousands of flying foxes swarm in a line across the cane fields. There is a gusty wind that silences the frogs. The coming night is fidgety, unsure of what to do with itself; the wind blows against the house; the mango trees drag their branches across the roof, making a noise like a hull hitting shallows. The flames in the hurricane lamps flicker and bend.

"I'm the best there is," says Edie.

Boring, thinks Rose. She's heard it all before.

"Unusual weather," says Edie, gathering up a pile of old newspapers from a box in the hallway. "Might be a late cyclone this year."

Along the windowsills black ants parade in millions. A line of them marches up the wall onto the ceiling. Rose sees that the lampshade has been removed from the lamp and the dark glass beads unpicked and the shade sits on the floor now, a newly plucked thing. The beads lie inside an old jar. Rose holds it up and looks inside.

Edie unfolds several of the newspapers on the table.

"I had some pattern paper somewhere," she says, "and now I can't find it."

It's no wonder, thinks Rose. The house is filled with so much junk it must be almost impossible to find anything. Small collections of useless things are everywhere: a shoe box filled with spectacles ("There's nothing so lonely as left-behind reading glasses," Edie says), a pile of electricity bills tied together with creeper vine ("I lived without electricity from 1965 until 1971; I'd encourage anyone to try it"), a pillowcase filled with blue quandongs ("You'd be surprised how often they come in handy"). Several flattened pillbox hats in a plastic bag, damask curtains folded half a century ago in a blanket box, wedding dress pearls in a coffee cup, dried yellow flowers in a dusty basket.

"In fact," says Edie, "I saw the pattern paper just the other day but I can't remember where. Anyway, newspapers will work just as well. Help me spread them out."

Edie separates the pages so they make one continuous piece that covers the table. She hands Rose the Scotch tape. Even the newspapers are old. Gough Whitlam is the prime minister on the front page of one. A headline reads VIETNAM SLAUGHTER. In another there is a picture of a train hanging off a bridge. Rose looks at it in horror. Leans closer. She tries to look into the windows; there are people inside, she is sure of it, not yet rescued.

"Granville," says Edie. "You might have been too young to remember it."

The page below Granville is from the *Courier-Mail*, dated 1977, the year Rose's mother died. Rose puts her hand out toward it but it's too late; Edie has decided there is enough paper and moves it away to the pile on the floor. She draws the skirt first, using the measuring tape and a blunt pencil.

"That's only half a skirt," says Rose.

"We cut it on the fold," says Edie. "Four of these will make the panels for the skirt."

"Four?" Now it seems too big. Four of the half skirts would fit two of Rose.

"Hang on," says Edie, bending down to retrieve the year Rose's mother died. "We'll need this for sleeves."

She hands the scissors to Rose. They feel heavy and important in her hands.

"Don't look so nervous," says Edie.

"What if I do it wrong?"

"There's no shortage of newspapers," says Edie.

She steps out of the way so that Rose can cut along the pencil lines.

"Will I tell you about the house up in the trees?" she says.

A big gust of wind comes through the back windows then. It lifts up the pattern and drops it again. The mended bluebirds rattle on the wall. The mango tree drags its fingernails along the roof.

"Yes," says Rose.

"My father did not bring home a bride befitting the house or the land. This house was grand; the parquetry was always gleaming and the colored glass was talked about up and down the coast. Lillian Baker, freshly widowed, ruled the place until my mother arrived, screeched all day at the black girls. Florence was not the daughter-in-law that Lillian had expected, not a girl with connections, not the daughter of the honorable member for Toowong, not the daughter of another landowner; there were any number of them in Brisbane at the time, she knew it, it was a fact, she had corresponded with their mothers. No, her son brought home the common daughter of a tailor. A little seamstress. Lillian Baker never forgave Florence for stealing my father's heart; she blamed everything on Florence: the falling price of cane, the downfall of the house, the cyclones, the outbreak of war.

"Florence was badly disoriented by the train trip. She had been so long in that little back room that she was disturbed by all the vast and empty spaces, the moon riding beside her window, the appearance and disappearance of small wild towns, knocked together, barely standing, the rivers, huge and sandy and half empty.

"Her knees nearly clean gave way at the grand entrance to

the house, where the floor was inlaid with golden birds. The dark furniture crowded, everywhere mirrors reflected her, and a carpet of flowers danced beneath her feet. Gold thread, acres of it, was stitched into everything. There was a coat stand with a brass lion's head, even though no one wore coats.

"Up north everyone was half dressed. No one buttoned up their shirts, men did not wear jackets, even the towns were half clothed, canvas where storefront walls should be, no tar on the roads, planks erected over mud puddles. Lillian Baker herself sat in the high-backed lilac-covered chair in the corner of the kitchen in just her petticoat and a silk dressing gown, angrily waving a bamboo fan.

"No, there was no large wedding. Florence wore a simple dress she'd made herself, ivory silk crepe, hand-tatted lace, but very plain. She wore no veil. It was a tea gown, really; that's what you would call it if you saw it now.

"Lillian Baker never forgave my mother, with her brown-spotted face and her calm quiet ways. When she spoke, it was to admonish her. What had she arranged for the evening meal? Well, no wonder Jonathan was just skin and bones. How had she got to be twenty-three, yes, twenty-three, and not known the first thing about keeping a house, how to keep it clean, how to keep down the insects, how to keep track of the silver—she should be counting it or having the head girl count it at the least—and which bedrooms should be turned out and on which day, the mattresses beat and the pillows hung out in the sun? Just look at the picture frames, they were dull as ditch water, she should be supervising such things but instead Florence didn't seem to notice. 'You've got your head in the clouds,' said Lillian Baker. 'And look at your hair, you don't wear it with so much as a single curl; you look like a girl just out of boarding school.'

"Now, all Florence knew of the outside world was Enoggera; she had imagined that the north might be much the same, only perhaps a little larger. There would be the forest, which Jonathan had described to her in detail, very green and tranquil, and she would be able to look out over fields dotted with cattle. But it was not like this at all. The land he took her to was close. It breathed right up against her skin. The cane was taller than two men, and all night long it sighed in susurrations; she couldn't walk without having her feet swallowed up in mud, everything clung, everything was damp, it rained and rained, and when it didn't rain, her hands swelled in the heat. The mountain was not tranquil; it leaned and twisted and was wild.

"'And why are you always disappearing, the two of you, like children, when now you have a house and land to run?' was what Lillian Baker shouted from her lilac-covered chair.

"At every opportunity Jonathan took Florence's hand, guided her across the house yard, across the back paddock, toward the place he called the hill. She tucked her skirt up and followed him.

"'You mustn't be afraid,' he said.

"He showed her the path that starts up in the open scrub right beside the fence, leads all the way to the gully and the first of the strangler figs. He helped her over the rocks and roots, down into the gully, and back out again by the rock shaped like a boat. There were steps there, not man-made steps, but a series of rocks placed as though by the mountain itself. He taught her how all she needed to do when the path disappeared was look for the stand of ancient rose gums. Oh, the skin of those trees. He taught her how she must listen for the falls.

"He took a fallen sassafras flower and placed it behind her ear.

"The house, it was not really a house, more a cabin—a hut, you might call it—but still their place among the trees. He had built it during the dry season, all the while writing to her to describe his progress. The place was cut from one single turpentine—put up roughly, it was true—that in time turned a grayish color. He made it the way the settlers had made their first homes, forming dovetail joints, laying bark against the uprights, leaving spaces for windows. These windows he later fitted out with the colored casements from beneath the old house, amber, pink, green, blue. The first roof was made of fern leaves, but later he dragged iron up, one piece at a time. You could say it was a labor of love. It always leaned a little.

"They lay there together in that house, Rose. Florence watched the sky above the falls while he unbound her hair. He recited to her poems, the well-known ones, and some of his own. He shouted at the edge of the gorge, shouted over the roar of the water, 'Love! Love! Love!' to make her laugh. Then evening came and they would have to make the climb back down. They would tumble into the kitchen, breathless, glowing, face to face with Lillian Baker scowling in her corner and the tea ruined on the table.

"'Fools,' she said to them one night when they arrived home in the twilight. 'You up there traipsing about like Gypsies when down here the war has come.'

"'War?' said Jonathan.

"He picked up the paper from the table, fire vine flowers raining from his shirtsleeves, and in less than a month he would be gone."

Rose cuts the pattern as Edie makes it. The old woman marks the paper—certain lines, arrows, a circle, letters, her very own hieroglyphics—across the face of a man walking on the moon, the prime minister Harold Holt lost at sea. When all the pieces are cut, Rose looks at the pile and bites her bottom lip. She has no idea how it will all fit together.

Edie smiles at her, waiting.

"What?" says Rose.

"No law against smiling, is there?" says Edie. Her hand moves toward the pincushion shaped like an echidna, then stops. "I think we'll call it quits for tonight. Start pinning out next Wednesday."

"The parade is the end of May."

"We've got plenty of time."

"It's only early, but . . . ," says Rose, motioning to the room, the night, the breeze lifting up the pattern paper.

Edie ignores her, starts walking toward the door.

"So how do you get to that place?" says Rose at the top of the back stairs.

"I told you," says Edie. "You mustn't have been listening."

"No you didn't, not really. I mean, you told me part but not in detail; wouldn't I need a map or something?"

"I never needed one," says Edie.

Sometimes the woman is infuriating. Seeing her standing there in her shapeless sundress and green slippers, Rose can hardly believe she has climbed anywhere at all. If truth be told, she probably doesn't even know how to sew.

"If you're going to try to find it, you have to promise to be careful in the gully," says Edie. "When it rains a lot, that creek really comes down and the thing is swamped. You can't even see the rocks. I got stuck on the other side many times. And you'll have to leave early or you can't get back in time before dark. It's not the best season to climb, but I know that when you want to do it, you can't help it, you just have to. It has a special pull, that mountain, a sort of gravity."

Rose doesn't like that the woman seems to understand these things about her.

"Do you really think it's still there?" asks Rose.

"I hope with all my heart it is," says Edie.

$\mathcal{F}$ern Stitch ----------------

So here's Detective Glass again standing on the path that leads up through the trees. I could show you him on the fallen tree too, the one that traverses the gully; that's a real crack. He isn't a bush walker, hates bush-walking, but this is even worse. "Fuck" is what he says at every single rock. "Fuck."

He has a picture of the midnight dress inside his trouser pocket. The one that Mallory Johnson drew for him and insisted he have. He's kept it like a talisman. That's what it feels like. If he keeps it, he'll find the girl. He'll find her body. That's what he thinks. He's never been superstitious like this before. It leaves him feeling uncomfortable, itchy; the drawing burns inside his pocket. In the car he has felt compelled to take it out every so often, smooth out the creases gently, rest his hands over it. The shithole backwater town is getting to him.

He has employed an aboriginal tracker, well known, by the name of Waldron. When Waldron alights from the police car in Miss Baker's backyard, Glass thinks he looks too old to climb anything. He stands for a long time in his too-short trousers and his cowboy shirt tucked in.

But when he starts, Glass is amazed to see he is like a wallaby, springing across the rocks in the creeks, cupping them with his bare feet. He can see a nest fallen from a tree and the shallow twisted valley left behind by a snake.

"Don't like the bush?" Waldron asks.

"No, mate, don't like the bush," Glass replies.

He likes a flat patch of mown lawn, a neatly trimmed hedge; he doesn't like the way the rain forest crowds in along the path, nothing holding it back but the thin strip of mud. It's all too messy, without edges, one minute quiet, the next igniting with birdsong. He hates that he can't see the end of it. Standing there on a rock in the gully, he feels a wave of hopelessness roll over him. He sways.

All the time the tracker can see everyone who has come and gone that way. The sandshoe girl and the sandal girl and the man. Even the old lady once with a stick, as far as the word tree. On the path, in places, the rain has washed away their presence, but here, through the leaves, leading away in front of him, they are obvious, glaring as a set of train tracks.

There are the marks of a pademelon that has been startled, a small ant nest caved in by a careless foot, which makes him drop to his haunches, cigarette dangling from his mouth.

He already smells the ash of the ruin.

Glass follows the tracker, tries to imitate the man's footsteps, but the rocks close up their faces to him and he stumbles and swears. Somewhere, farther away, there is the tremulous rushing voice of water.

"Is there another creek?"

"There are creeks everywhere up here," says Waldron. "Magic water. Comes right out of the rocks."

Glass thinks it possible that he will have a heart attack. He's always prided himself on his levelheadedness. He's seen terrible things. Sorted out terrible business. But up here he feels momentarily lost. It takes his breath away. Waldron shows him where the fallen tree has been used many times as a way out of the gully.

"You've got to be shitting me," Glass says.

Waldron laughs around his smoke, crinkles up his eyes.

Fat old bastard copper, he thinks.

In the end, when they have climbed until he thinks his legs will crumple beneath him, Glass feels the land curve away beneath his feet. He doesn't like it; it feels as though it is slipping away, dropping off into nothing. The trees begin to thin. There is a jumble of great rocks, iron-colored, patterned with moss, and when Glass looks up from his feet, he sees that the earth gives way in front of them to a small gorge where a waterfall roars. There is dazzling sunlight in the rift, the land laid out before them startling in this white glow. Glass's hand goes up to his eyes.

He shakes his head.

He hasn't really expected to see such a thing up here.

There it is, the burnt-out smear of a dwelling, just a little back from the lip of the gorge, a small place, a hut really, all hardwood and colored glass, the tin roof collapsed across the charred stumps. The trees surrounding the tiny clearing are blackened too, but not burnt. Rain must have stopped the blaze. Glass looks out at the falls, at Waldron, who seems spooked by the place. The detective picks up a pink stone from the ground, holds it in his hand thinking, then walks toward the ruin.

Patrick Lovell goes to work at half past five each morning, six days a week. Rose hears him, his feet hitting the floor, the scratch of his zipper, the rustle of his raincoat, the flick of his lighter. He pinches her as he passes. Ruffles her hair.

"See you, Rose," he says. "Behave yourself."

She turns on her side and ignores him.

The cool blue morning light creeps through the little caravan window. It's Saturday and she's thinking of the house in the trees. It's the perfect type of day to go. She should get up right now, get dressed, start walking, but she doesn't. When she thinks about the mountain and finding that place, part of her lifts, inflates, soars. She must try to push that part down. It's like trying to fit a hot-air balloon back inside a tiny pocket. It's a stupid idea, she tells herself.

Stupid idea, stupid idea, stupid idea.

She's angry with her father. He's not his normal self. Something has happened to him. He's mad with not drinking. He's permanently wired. As if he's been electrocuted, his hair stands on end, his black eyes burn. In the evenings, when he fillets a fish, he says, "I'm the best banana picker this place has ever seen. I'm a gun banana picker, darling," he says, "I am a master banana picker; till now I've missed my calling in life." She knows where such sarcasm usually leads but the words never come. There is no "I'm just going out for a while."

Whenever Mrs. Lamond sees Rose's father, she smiles at him, her face puckering up like the folds in a handbag. She smells of rubbing alcohol and fish and chips. She's taken to wearing low-cut tops and leaning forward ever so slightly when she speaks to him.

But it isn't just that. Rose is really angry with her father because of the problem with Pearl. She came to the caravan yesterday to work on their French project. Rose suggested they climb to the cove but Pearl said no.

"Perhaps secret coves aren't your thing," said Rose. "Perhaps you prefer small book exchanges run by dirty old men."

"He's not a dirty old man. He's not even old," Pearl protested. "He's completely . . . cultured. He's been everywhere."

Rose closed her eyes and sighed.

"Anyway, I'm *très* bored," Pearl said. "We really do need to make this guillotine if we're going to pass French."

"A guillotine?" said Rose's father, hovering too close. "Now, that sounds interesting."

He collected cardboard from the back of Mrs. Lamond's kiosk and laid it out on the ground in front of the caravan.

"Now, let's think, girls," he said.

I wish you'd fuck off, Rose thought.

Her father couldn't stop looking at Pearl and Pearl was aware of it. She just kept talking and talking, though, in true Pearl fashion. "Did you know that Marie Antoinette was only fourteen years old when she was married to the dauphin, that's younger than us, and when she became queen, she was only nineteen, which is not much older than us, can you imagine that, just going to another country right now and becoming a queen and having everything you ever wanted, jewels and shoes and dresses, I think it would go to your head, I mean, don't you, Rose? What would you do if you were in that situation?"

Rose wanted to say something but she didn't. It wasn't a very kind thing.

"Let them eat cake and all that," said Patrick Lovell, scratching his bare brown chest.

Rose closed her eyes. Her father's eyes were coal black, about to ignite. She'd never seen him so interested in one of her school friends. He didn't know where to look; his eyes settled on Pearl, he tore them away, they settled again.

But she'd never had a friend like Pearl either. Not one with such a face, who washed her hair in the rain and who read books in Russian and who constantly exploded with information, spouting it like a trail of stars, and who was so good and kind and utterly friendly. Rose felt like a thunderstorm beside her. Pearl just shone and shone and shone, and even after she'd left a room, some of her light remained.

"I think what we'll do is cut two frames whole and tape them together," said her father. "And into that we'll put the sliding blade; we can use a bit of baling twine and then we'll get some silver spray paint."

"Love your work, Mr. Lovell," said Pearl. "We knew you'd come up with something."

Rose had never heard her father called Mr. Lovell in her life. There was a pause. She could feel him thinking; he was going to ask her, she knew it, he was going to ask Pearl if he could draw her, sketch her, paint her. It was exactly the same as asking to touch her. The sea sighed up onto the shore and out again. He said nothing.

Rose gets out of bed, brushes her teeth at the tiny sink, dresses, walks down to the beach. The sea is almost still, reflecting the clouds. The soldier crabs have left their sand jewelry on the shore.

Hers are the first footprints; she looks back at them as she walks toward the rocks where she'll climb to her secret cove.

Rose could climb to the cove with her eyes closed. She leaps across the rocks, knows exactly where to put her feet. But the sense of satisfaction she felt in the beginning, of arriving at the perfect place and sitting alone, digging her toes into the sand, has vanished. She feels lonely there.

She thinks dangerous black thoughts about her father. She'd like to be away from him. She knows it's possible. She's seen kids her age before, on their own, washing at service stations and hitchhiking on the outskirts of cities.

The sound of a motor rouses her from her angry thoughts. A boat is making its way into the cove, the flat silver water breaking behind it. She sees it's Murray Falconer and shakes her head. He rides right up onto the sand, lifting the outboard in time, smiling broadly.

"I thought you'd be here," he says.

"What do you want?"

He comes across the sand toward her. He has ridiculously long legs, the hair on them golden, his board shorts wet. His hair is sticking every which way; none of the blue is left.

"I just thought I'd visit, that's all," he says. "And see if you wanted to go for a ride."

He motions to the old boat, which is the most dilapidated boat she has ever seen.

"It doesn't look very safe," says Rose.

"It's safe," says Murray.

"How old is it?"

"Dunno, it was my granddad's," he says.

"Shit."

"Come on," he says, "I can show you an even better beach than this one."

The sun is so bright on the boat that she sometimes has to close her eyes. She's in her worst clothes, her climbing clothes, a pair of baggy shorts and an old black T-shirt flung over her bikini top. Her feet stink inside her sneakers.

"Don't look so nervous," says Murray.

"I just don't want this thing to sink," she says.

She hasn't tied back her hair completely. Tendrils escape and blow across her face.

"How come you never smile?" he says.

That question hurts her. It's been asked before and the hurt makes her angry. An old bruise touched.

"It isn't in my nature," she says.

"Bullshit," says Murray, laughing, and he cranks the outboard motor full throttle. The prow of the boat leaps out of the water and slams down again as he turns out to open sea.

"You're a wanker," she shouts.

He guides the boat out around the rocks and toward the next bay, which is even smaller, a tiny deepwater inlet without sand. The rain forest reaches right down to the sea. The boat rocks gently on the waves, making her drowsy. The surface of the water is alive with twisting ribbons of light and she trails her finger through them. A huge turtle swims beneath the boat and she peers over the edge until it has disappeared. Murray points up to the rocks, where there is the shimmer of a waterfall.

"Have you ever climbed on the mountain?" she asks.

"To Weeping Rock? Yeah. Why?"

"I'd like to climb there," she says.

"It can be arranged," he says in his Terminator voice.

She shakes her head and tries not to laugh.

"Have you heard the legends?" he asks.

"No," she says.

"About the rock and why it cries, even when there's no rain?"

"No."

"There's this story that the rock is this mother and she lost her children in a flood; they got swept away and she turned all bitter, and each year she takes a child back, or an adult, whoever she can get her hands on, as a revenge. Heaps of people go missing up there."

"Every year?"

"Well . . . ," says Murray. "Maybe not every year."

"How many in your lifetime?"

"Colin Atkinson's father hit his head on a rock in the big falls. And this other guy, a tourist, he went off the track and never came back; that was years ago."

"Hardly an annual event," says Rose.

"This mountain will take you," says Murray in a German accent.

Rose shakes her head but this time she laughs. He runs his hand through his hair, laughs in return, infinitely pleased.

The rain starts when they are out on the boat. It comes from the horizon, a vast bank of clouds, drenching them to the skin. Rose is embarrassed by her shirt, the way it clings to her; Murray tries not to look. She takes the hand he offers, though, when he is helping her from the boat.

"Sorry," he says.

She supposes he is apologizing for the rain. "It's not like you control the weather," she says.

The rain doesn't stop for three days. It falls and falls and does not end. It fills up the agaves' rubbery throats and fills the potholes and ditches to the brim. It nullifies every sound. It thunders on the caravan roof, floods the creek on Murray's land so he can't get to school. He is there waving behind the water when the bus stops at his turnoff, a wave of celebration. Rose is careful not to look at him for too long.

On Wednesday there is a clearing. The sun comes out and shines with a feverish intensity. The wet land is limp and breathless, still frosted with raindrops, the tinfoil sky repeated in countless puddles. At school teachers sweat where they stand, delirious-eyed, the fans thump, thump, thump. The girls sit in the shade on the cool concrete, but even Vanessa, so perfect, has tiny beads of sweat along her perfect top lip, which she wipes away with distaste.

"Are you having sequins, Rose?" Vanessa asks, although it's also a demand. It will be an unspeakable crime to say no.

"I think I'm having antique glass beads," says Rose.

That shuts her up for a while. Pearl smiles at Rose with her eyes.

When Rose arrives in the afternoon, Edie is collecting the blue quandongs that have fallen to the ground. She has two full buckets beside her and in the house she places the brilliant fruit inside two huge pickle jars. Rose is wearing a black T-shirt with a devil riding a horse. She bought it at the thrift shop for fifty cents. She's annoyed when Edie doesn't even glance at it.

"What are you going to do with those things?" Rose asks.

"Nothing," says Edie. "I just can't bear to leave them out there."

Edie puts the pickle jars on the floor and Rose guesses they'll stay there forever. She looks at them while Edie opens up the back windows and lights the hurricane lamps and the mosquito coils.

"Why have you got so much stuff?"

"I like stuff, I suppose," Edie replies.

"What do you like about it?"

"I like the magic within such things; the sadness and the joy, it's very strong," says Edie simply. Then she adds, "You'd understand what I mean."

"No I wouldn't," says Rose.

Edie ignores that. She doesn't say, "Yes you would." She puts part of the midnight-blue material out on the table and lays a section of the newspaper pattern on top.

"Pinning," she says.

She produces the dusty echidna-shaped pincushion and hands it to Rose. Shows her where to pin the pattern. How far apart to space the pins. The paper feels fragile beneath her hands. While Rose is pinning, Edie sits down and begins unpicking the old black lace dress; she separates the black rose lace from the yoke and from the cuffs of the sleeves and from the edge of the skirt.

"When you've finished pinning, you can cut out," she says.

"I'm not sure," says Rose.

"It's only a pair of scissors," says Edie.

"I could make a mistake, cut somewhere I'm not supposed to."

"Good Lord," says the old lady. "You'd think I was asking you to perform surgery. You know where the scissors are."

The scissors feel even more dangerous this time. Rose places the blade to the fabric and begins. The silk taffeta makes a satisfying noise as she cuts out the shapes of the skirt. A sighing, releasing sound. She lays the pieces pinned to the pattern over the back of a chair. She cuts out the small delicate parts of the bodice.

"Where's the rest of it?" Rose asks. "I mean the back of the top and the sleeves?"

Those pieces of newspaper pattern still lie unused on the edge of the table.

Edie holds up the unpicked tatters of the old black lace dress.

"Mourning lace," she says.

A smile breaks out on Rose's face.

"Now I think we should practice our stitching," says Edie. She threads a needle, lightning fast, damp tongue, a flick of her fingers.

She hands Rose the thread and another needle.

"Go on," she says.

It takes Rose five attempts. Edie says nothing, waits patiently.

"Which bit do I sew first?"

"We won't touch the dress yet," says Edie. "Not until you have a fine even stitch."

She hands Rose an old pillowcase.

"You can practice on this; I'll show you. Know which side of the fabric is the back and which is the front; there is a right side and a wrong side to every piece of material. Now go in like this."

"I have sewed before, you know," Rose says. "I mean, mending things."

"It's not the same as a perfect dressmaker's stitch," says Edie. "You must learn to sew a straight line. In dressmaking that's everything. And you'll find that there is nothing better or more calming than a straight and proper line stitched by hand. Every stitch matters. When you're hand-stitching, you must never think ahead; worry only about the needle coming up and going down again. My mother taught me how to sew and her father taught her and so on and so on all the way back into the past and this is how it goes."

Blah, blah, blah, says Rose in her head while she makes her first stitches.

"Too big," says Edie. "Try this, this is what my mother taught me when I was a girl. Give thanks with each stitch. Thank you for this old house, thank you for the roof that doesn't leak, thank you for the creek, thank you for the possums, thank you for the fat mangoes on the trees. You try that."

"I don't really feel like it."

"Go on, just do it inside your head."

Thank you for the rocks, thinks Rose. The big ones and the ones with places for my hands. Thanks for the footholds. That's stupid. Thank you for . . . Pearl. Stupid, stupid, stupid. Thank you for that turtle that swam under the boat.

"Too fast," says Edie. "Or each stitch can be a memory. Try that. Here, this is me when I'm a girl. This is my pink floral bedspread. Here's my father's glass eye in the teacup on the second shelf of the kitchen cupboard. Here is me walking up to the trees. Go on, you try."

Rose sighs and picks up the pillowcase again.

Here is me lying in my bed. Stitch. Faraway house. Stitch. Way back in the beginning. Stitch. Here is my mother singing in the kitchen. Stitch. Here is my mother saying something, I can't hear what it is. Stitch. "Do you want to draw while I make dinner? Here is some paper." Stitch. Did she ever say that? Stitch. Here is my mother putting me to bed. Stitch. She's kissing me on the head. Stitch.

"You're doing well," says Edie. "You're a fast learner. Keep trying."

"This pillowcase is made from some kind of stupid slippery stuff."

"All the same."

Rose pricks her finger. She examines her bright blood.

"I'm bleeding," she says, holding up her finger.

"Exactly why we couldn't start on the dress."

"I thought you'd have a sewing machine or something," says Rose sullenly.

"I did have one," says Edie, "but for this kind of dress, we must make it with our hands."

Rose sighs dramatically.

"You never said Jonathan Baker had a glass eye," she says.

"He didn't," says Edie, "not in the beginning, but then he went away to the war and came back and nothing was ever the same again."

Edie holds the mourning lace. Rose closes up her face, keeps very still. More story is about to tumble from the old woman. Rose won't let it show she's waiting.

"I was born while he was away, of course, if you wondered when I would turn up in the picture, Jonathan and Florence being my parents. My grandmother was raging all day. She was fury in a black dress. Perhaps I was not the child of my father but some other man was what Granny Baker said. My mother was common as mud and she wouldn't put it past her. My grandmother wouldn't hold me, not even for a second. All my years she sat in the corner lilac chair and leapt out of it from time to time to hiss and howl at people like a cat with a stepped-on tail. She was terrible to us. And my father, he came back from the war with all the poetry and gentleness banged right out of him."

Rose takes another needle, threads it, pricks herself again.

"Shit," she says.

"Yes, shit, exactly," says Edie.

Edie touches the black rose lace, tracing the old flowers.

"He wouldn't wear his glass eye they'd made for him; it's still in the teacup up there but I haven't looked at it for a very long time. My mother and I, we used to divine his mood by looking at the eye. Sometimes it looked angry and sometimes forlorn. Sometimes it looked defiant from the bottom of the cup.

"'Gloomy,' my mother might say.

"'Miserable,' I might suggest.

"'Vicious,' we would agree.

"No one mentioned the sunken crater where his eye had been, nor the pale pink slit like a rubbery lip. Not the neighbors, not visitors, not Mother, not Granny Baker. When he first came home, he was like a man underwater. People spoke to him and he looked at them for a long time as though he couldn't understand.

He turned his right ear toward them, shook his head. He was hearing other things. If a pan was dropped in the kitchen, he leapt up in the air.

"Then he began to wake angry, which was a new development; he banged my nursery door and swore at the dogs and cursed the weather and spat off the back steps. Most days he was coiled whip-tight and we stepped carefully around him. If Mother asked me to take him a cup of tea, my hands shook. I had to decide whether to look at him and speak, or place the cup down quietly and retreat. It was a difficult decision; sometimes a cup placed down without a word enraged him, sometimes to engage him in conversation was even worse.

"'What would you know about good mornings?' he would shout. I was only very small. Other mornings he woke sad. He didn't put on a shirt but drifted from room to room in only his trousers. He had a scar on his chest, a bullet hole like a closed eye, and another beneath his armpit. He touched the scar on his chest, you know. All the time. Sometimes he lay for hours on the settee in the front room and didn't move at all. The only sign of life would be the small tremor of a pulse at his neck. He was not biscuity-brown anymore; he was blue-white like a corpse. It was my mother and I who went then, up into the trees.

"Any moment away from this place was like a small miracle.

"I grew up climbing there. First tied to my mother the way the black women did with their babies. Then, later, taking steps by myself. The sky was so huge, and when we were inside the forest, the trees towered over us and the cool air evaporated our tears. My mother's toes had grown curled and hardened from climbing, and by the time I went to school, I was already the same; of course my mother combed my hair and washed my face and I had shoes, but on the inside, Rose, I was . . . untamed."

Rose looks up at Edie. Her gray hair shines in the light and she looks back at Rose with a half smile on her lips.

"Do you understand?" Edie asks.

Rose looks at her own stitching. It staggers and sways across the pillowcase. She doesn't know what to say. What can she say?

"It must be getting late," she says.

*F*ly Stitch ━━━━━━━━━━━━━━━━

"The car's behind the mill yards," he says, slurring. As if she's going to go with him. They're reading from two different scripts. She's trying to dazzle him with all her words. She's talking about the moon now. How everyone in the world tonight can see it. "Well, maybe not everyone; I mean, for some people it's daylight. God, that's amazing, isn't it?" she says. He drags his eyes from her, looks at the moon. "You're so beautiful," he says. "Do you have any idea how beautiful you are?" Even by moonlight she sees him color at his own words. Things he shouldn't say. She knows it, he knows it. It excites her, but there's a little prickle of fear too. It looks like he might cry. "Well, I better go," she says. "Don't," he says. "No, don't."

Rose doesn't take Pearl, not the first time, which is a Sunday. She knows she'll have to find the way first. Her heart races, just thinking that, as though she's an explorer. She's up before her father, putting on her climbing clothes, her shabby Dunlop sneakers, tying down her hair with the myriad bands and bobby pins.

"Where are you going?" he says from behind his curtain.

"To climb a mountain," she replies.

"Don't break your neck," he says.

"I'll try not to."

Rose has to walk across the back paddock behind the old house but she doesn't stop to see Edie, hopes that the old woman won't see her. She'd be full of instructions. "Don't touch this." "Don't touch that." "Look out for snakes." She'd be talking as if she owned the whole mountain range.

There's the gate at the back of the paddock, just as Edie said. A decorative gate, rusted now, the fence half falling down, a flimsy attempt at keeping what lies behind out. When she looks down toward the house, she can see an old chair, or what remains of one, sitting in the grass.

Behind the gate there's a path, a muddy overgrown path, but a path all the same. Easy, thinks Rose. Up the path until she gets to a gully and then across the gully and then climb out near a rock like a boat and then listen for the sound of water, look for the stand of rose gums, and there will be a path again. Rose looks up at the clear sky.

It's only eight in the morning but already the sun is white-hot. She feels it baking her scalp and wishes she'd brought a hat. She drinks some water from her small plastic bottle and wonders if it will be enough. In the open forest there are gums with skin like butter, towering bloodwoods, stringy barks. She touches these trees with her hands, takes a strip of bark from one, picks up a bright yellow seed with a fine fuzz of hair from the ground. There is a huge tree down across the track, desolate gray, riddled with the words of white ants; she isn't sure how long she stands there, but after that tree, as though it is the start line, the climbing grows gradually more difficult. The ground becomes more crowded with ferns and lawyer vines, the forest grows denser, there is a gradual dimming of things.

The strangler figs appear, first one, its grotesque lacework making her stop, smile, breathe a shuddering breath. The liana vines, corkscrew-tight, coil themselves up trees. The buttress roots grow huge, elaborate, twisted, washed smooth by rain. A gully opens up before her, the tree canopy above it pierced by halos of light.

She's too cocky at first. She clambers over rocks as though it's a race, finds herself halfway down with nowhere farther to go. When she's climbed back to her beginning point, she has to wipe the sweat from her eyes and is surprised to find her legs trembling.

There's a much easier route; she spots it almost immediately and begins her second attempt. How much time has she wasted? She moves from rock to rock, descending into the gully, trying not to think too far ahead, looking for one foothold after another.

At the bottom of the gully there is a small stream dotted with huge rocks. The heat of the day disappears there, a coolness brushes her cheeks. She looks up at the canopy stretched over the place and she feels suddenly as though she's in a church. There is a hushed silence. The forest watching her in return.

She doesn't know the time. She could have been climbing for an hour or two, or is it less? She's unsure. She squats and washes her face in the water. The creek croons over the rocks. She feels far from anywhere, even though she knows she could just stand up and climb back out the way she came in. She isn't lost.

A sudden burst of birds, parrots, screeching overhead shakes away her thoughts. She sits there beside the water looking for footholds on the other side. A rock shaped like the hull of a boat? A rock shaped like a boat? A boat?

There are many larger rocks on the opposite side of the gully and it looks much more difficult to climb. The rocks give nothing away. She can't see anything like a boat. What kind of boat, for God's sake? A big boat or a dinghy, the *Titanic* or a weekend runabout? She hadn't asked Edie a single question. Maybe there was no such rock. Maybe Edie was making things up.

"No," whispers Rose in the dim gully, and her voice sounds foreign in that quiet place.

High up along the gully she sees a large granite boulder partially concealed by a tangle of fallen trees. It's been many years since the old woman has been this way; things might have changed. Rose picks her way up the creek, rock-hopping, until she stands beneath the place.

It could be a boat, if she uses her imagination. She tilts her head to one side. It seems the rock slipped at some point, bringing down several great trees, one of which traverses the gully floor. The rock is tilted down but it has a sharpish edge, now facing toward the stream. Where the trees have fallen, a little piece of the canopy has opened up and there is a proliferation of ferns.

She stands in front of the mess, looking for a way.

She places her feet gingerly on the fallen tree that runs like a bridge across the gully, tests her weight. She begins to walk along its length as it rises toward the rocks. It's solid. She bends down once to regain her balance, finds she can't stand again; she looks down at the stream meters below her. The tree is rotting. Already parts of it are eaten away; through a hole she sees a coil of orange fungus, so bright that she freezes in her tracks. There are colonies of pale mushrooms and lurid green moss that looks wet, but when she touches it, she finds it is papery, dry. She listens to her own ragged breathing.

The fallen tree takes her almost to the top of the gully, almost five meters above the stream. It's audacious, she knows it, climbing that way. The thing could collapse or move. Almost at the lip of the gully the tree becomes wedged between the sinking boat rock and another. Her view from the bottom was distorted; it is a small space she finds she must press herself through.

The rock beneath her hands is cool; the space smells of stone, damp stone and earth and leaves. She presses her nose to the place and breathes. Black moss and cave, the dank green breath of the mountain. She's breathing in something intimate, something she shouldn't have knowledge of, something secret.

When she finally clambers over the ledge, she whoops with joy and her voice sings out in the forest. She squats again to steady herself. The forest crowds in at the top, hushed, as though it has been waiting to see if she would make it.

"God," she says. Doesn't know why.

She feels herself sob in the face of it.

She stands, takes tentative steps. On this side of the gully the forest seems even dimmer. The canopy is so thick that the floor is almost empty of plant life, clear but for the mulch of fallen leaves. She listens to her feet moving through these leaves, picks some up as she walks. A red leaf. Blood red, exactly like the ones she's seen in Edie's house. A leaf shaped like a star. The skeleton of a leaf, perfectly preserved, frail as a spiderweb. She puts them in her shirt pocket, runs her hands along the trees.

Which direction, she's unsure.

A general upward direction seems right.

There's a tree as wide as a car, its buttress roots as tall as her. Edie hadn't mentioned it. Surely she would have mentioned it. She hesitates. Turns in a circle. A stand of rose gums. A stand of rose gums? She feels her skin then, the gooseflesh prickle; it falls away, prickles again, the cool tremor of fear. She doesn't even know what a rose gum looks like.

It's okay, she calms herself, it's a gum and it might be the color of a rose. Or it might have flowers like roses. It will be different from the other trees. Yes, all she has to do is walk and look for a different type of tree.

She can't tell the time. That's the problem. Next time she'll have to bring a watch. Has she been gone minutes or hours? She looks up at the canopy but there is only the same dim light. Upward is what Rose Lovell says to herself. Upward. One foot in front of the other. She wishes there were rocks. She's good at rocks, not these leaves, this whispering unsettling carpet of leaves. The rose gums she finds soon after. A stand of them, seven or eight, so giant that she forgets to breathe; they wear russet-red skirts at their bases and their skin is the color of quartz.

"There you are," she says, looking up, unable to see where they end.

She stands for a long time, listening to the sound of falling water.

When Rose comes down through the scrub again, the day has grown dark with clouds and the remnants of the sun have dipped behind the old house. She is running because a storm is settling over the mountain, a huge thunderstorm, so close that she can taste the sulfur.

It was small, the house she found, and half reclaimed by the rain forest. It sat cradled by the trees at the edge of a clearing. The waterfall plunged past, only meters before it. The sudden aching chasm of light made her dizzy. She bent down, held her head, felt wild. It was bright with moss, that house, and, when she stood and pushed open the front door, filled up to her knees with leaves. She ran her fingers over the colored-glass windows dark with mold.

"Hello," she said as though it were a living, breathing thing.

She needed a broom, that was her first coherent thought. She kicked at the leaves carefully, in case of snakes, pushed them in piles out the door. It was a single room, tiny, not a stitch of furniture. She imagined Florence and Jonathan Baker there and later Edie. Edie as a girl. Edie her age. Edie climbing the same path she had taken.

She sat on the front step, drank from her water bottle, leaned against the wood that Jonathan Baker had cut with his bare hands, closed her eyes. She felt her heartbeat and the friction of the sun on her skin, her muscles quivering from the exertion, sweat falling in rivulets down her neck. She felt more alive than ever before. Her heart beating in her chest and in her ears, tuning out the other sounds of the day.

She explored. She searched for the base of the waterfall first, moving away from the house, down through the trees again. She climbed over trees and rocks, caught glimpses of the pool, which was small, circular, so precise and perfect it could almost have been man-made. She could see the thing but was unable to find a way down.

It took her another hour at least, although she wasn't sure, to find the path and wash her face there. Afterward she lay down on her back, on the flat rocks warmed by the sun, cried openly into her hands.

The clouds began to pile up in the small jagged patch of sky above the little falls. She watched them, at first lazily, through half-shut eyes, and then suddenly with concern. She stood up. Listened. The day thrummed with the sounds of the forest, the rhythmical drone of cicadas, the ringing of insects, the chatter of birds. But something had changed.

She began to make her way back down the mountain through the trees, at first walking, then running. By the time she was descending crouched on the fallen tree across the gully, she heard the thunder, looked down and saw some of the rocks already swallowed up by the new swell in the creek. In the scrub the huge cool raindrops hit her face and bare arms, her hair sprang loose from its bobby pins, curled into a frenzy by the humidity.

Now in the paddock she is running full pelt, the rain so heavy she is half blinded by it, but all the time letting out yelps of pleasure. She races up Edie Baker's back steps and bangs on the lattice veranda door.

"I did it!" she shouts when it's opened and Edie is standing before her with hands on hips.

"Well," says Edie, "I don't doubt it going by the state of you. Quick into the bathroom or you'll die of cold."

Only then does Rose realize that she's shivering. Shivering so hard she is shaking. And that she is wet through, hands bleeding, leeches stuck to her lower legs, sending out spiderwebs of stinging blood.

Edie leads her to an ancient bathroom, sits her on the edge of the bath, picks the leeches off one by one with a pair of tweezers and throws them into the sink. She runs warm water into the bath, taps grumbling and hiccuping, and hands two towels to Rose.

"I'll find you something dry to put on," she says, "and leave it outside the door."

Rose sinks down into the bath, every cut and scratch on fire, her legs aching. She sees that a vine has grown in through the louvres and stretched its way across the ceiling and in the summer hothouse atmosphere erupted with yellow blooms. The rain pummels the roof, a deafening downpour; Rose lies there, legs drawn up to her chin, until her shivering subsides.

Edie Baker leaves her a sundress on the doorknob. It's bright green with white piping and at least fifty years old. Rose shakes her head but puts it on. The pieces of the midnight dress are there hanging over the back of the chair.

"Can you believe I did it?" she says to Edie, who is in the kitchen, cooking pancakes on the stove.

Edie turns and looks at her. The slip of a girl with the angry face. She remembers what it was like in her own childhood, how when she went outside and up that path, the sun filled her to the brim. How she ran her hands over the bare limbs of trees. How she kept raindrops in glass jars and wished she could distill the power of such things.

"My girl, of course I can," she says very tenderly. "Of course I can."

"Here," says Rose. "I found these for you."

The red leaf is wet, glossy. The skeleton leaf a pulpy mess. She places the strip of bark on the table between them. Edie's hands tremble over them. She picks up the red leaf and places it against her cheek.

"The gully?" she says eventually. "Did you find the rock?"

"I think it's fallen down. There was a rock but it was like a sinking ship, the point facing down."

"It's slipped?"

"I climbed along a log; it was the only way I could see out."

"That could be a risky business."

"It was hard to tell the time. I didn't know how long I'd been."

"I can teach you that."

"But I just kept walking. Until I found the house."

Edie's eyes dark, expectant, she hunches forward on her chair.

"It's still there," says Rose. "It's filled up with leaves but still there."

$\mathcal{S}$lip Stitch —————————

Near the burnt-out hut Glass finds a singed water bottle and the wrapper from a packet of biscuits. He bags them. He lifts up part of the roof, then lets it go again. The sound echoes in the silence. It's quiet, too quiet. The hairs rise on his neck. He has an uncomfortable ache in his chest, feels suddenly nauseated. He lifts another part of the roof, then another. There's nothing underneath. He can't smell death. The only smell is ash and the forest.

He should have brought more officers.

Up there he senses someone watching. He wants to turn quickly, catch them out, but he resists the urge, turns slowly, full circle, peers into the trees and vines. Even when he's looked, the feeling stays.

"Can you tell if she's been here lately? I mean, what can you tell?" he says to Waldron, who is squatting beside the rift.

"A week ago maybe, maybe less," says Waldron. "Sandshoe girl, she came last. Sandal girl, she doesn't climb good; she came only a few times. Once with the man. He only came once."

"Who's the man?" thinks Glass aloud.

"Big fella," says Waldron.

"Big fella?" says Glass. Well, that narrows it down. Sandshoe girl, sandal girl, big fella.

Older boy? Man? Check the boyfriends again, past, present. Love triangle? Never underestimate the power of a love triangle. Potent shit. He mentally notes these things. Touches the drawing of the dress in his pocket. The water courses over the falls, into the sunlight.

"What do you think?" he asks Waldron.

"No good. I reckon not here but somewhere here. You got to search the whole place. Take you years," says Waldron. He motions to the trees, means the whole of the rain forest, the mountain range.

Which makes Glass laugh. At the hopelessness of it all.

"Yes," says Glass, realizing he still has the pink stone in his left hand. He looks at it, then shoots it up at that sky above the falls, over the edge into the abyss.

"What the hell is that thing?" says Murray, sitting slumped in the bus.

"It's a guillotine, you moron," says Rose.

"Fatal," he replies.

Rose sits and looks out the window. It's raining, a fine misty rain, and the cardboard is damp and already starting to sag. Murray sits, half turned toward her, his legs stretched out on the seat. The bus floor is a mire of mud.

She doesn't know how to look at him, not really, not since she went in his boat. Not that anything happened. It was just a boat ride, Rose tells herself, a simple boat ride. If he liked her, he would have tried something.

At the little bay where the rain forest meets the sea,

Murray had opened a small cooler at his feet and removed a beer can.

"Drink?" he said.

"I don't drink," said Rose.

"Everyone drinks," said Murray.

"I've never had a drink," said Rose, getting angry. "Not once."

"Curious," said Murray in his best mad professor voice, and he put the beer away.

On the bus Rose holds the soggy cardboard guillotine and her cheeks burn.

"Does it ever stop raining here?" she says. She has to; she can't stand the silence.

"Never," he says in his best foreign accent, and then he laughs a Count Dracula laugh.

Pearl wears the Little Bo Peep costume and a powdered wig that her mother once wore to a ball. She speaks what sounds like perfect French in front of the class, though Rose can't understand a word she says. She pauses when it is Rose's turn to reply. Rose reads from her piece of paper, pronouncing the words clumsily, then motions for Pearl to bend down. When her neck is resting in the frame, she releases the cardboard guillotine blade.

"Bravo," says Madame Bonnick. "Excellent. *Fantastique*."

Pearl Kelly and Rose Lovell take a bow.

"What if you'd taken geography?" Pearl whispers when they take their seats. "Would we still be friends? I mean, what if your dad had decided to go somewhere else, not here, what if you'd had enough petrol and you'd just kept going? Do you believe in fate like that? Even if we hadn't met now, we would have met some other time?

"Do you believe in fate?" she asks again when Rose doesn't answer, just keeps twirling a sky-blue highlighter in her hand.

"I don't understand fate," says Rose.

"It's like everything is already written," says Pearl. "Everything. Everything we ever did in our lives is already set out somewhere."

Rose thinks of it. All her baby steps, her mother with her long hair and glowing face turning away from the bedroom door, all the roads, all the hills, all the sudden startling lines of coast, the way they followed the birds to choose their paths, the way her father wept inside the car beneath a billion stars. Edie climbing the paths, first on small feet, then on teenage feet, then on grown-up feet. The dress. The midnight dress.

Until then Rose has not once thought of who that dress was made for. The original dress with the torn skirt and half-ripped-away bodice. Who had that dress belonged to?

Pearl's still waiting for an answer.

"I found another secret place," Rose says.

"What kind of secret place?"

"It's a little house built up in the trees, way up, near a waterfall, that no one knows about."

"How'd you find it?"

"Edie, that lady who is making my dress. She told me how to get there."

"Can I come?"

"Do you want to?"

"Of course I do," says Pearl. "You know how I love mysterious things."

That afternoon Pearl begs Rose to walk down Main Street but she says no. She knows exactly how it will go. Pearl will examine herself in a shop window. She'll say, "How do I look?" She'll undo the top button of her uniform. She'll let out her hair. She'll take *Ashes in the Wind* from her schoolbag, or *A Virgin in Paris*, or *Neptune's Daughter*; she'll slip past Mrs. Rendell at her counter and dip her head to pass beneath the crappy Blue Moon Book Exchange sign.

And even inside it will be exactly the same. Paul Rendell's pupils will dilate, he'll sniff the air, he'll smile. He'll ask perfectly ordinary questions, Pearl will make perfectly ordinary replies. He'll put his hands behind his head, watch her, no one will dare make a move.

He'll think, I can't. She'll think, He won't. He'll think, I want to. She'll think, I shouldn't. He'll think, I won't, I definitely won't, I never will. She'll smile, drop the coins into his hand, say, "Well, I better be going, then."

Rose goes back to Edie's house. It's a Monday, not a Wednesday, but somehow, as if she knows, Edie is waiting for her.

"Come to practice your stitch, have you?"

The question makes Rose bristle but she doesn't say anything. Near the doorway she looks at one of the many boxes that fill the long yellow kitchen with its flock of bluebirds on the wall. She sees the red leaves from the rain forest, picks one up and holds it by the stem.

"When I was a child, my mother got me a book about the leaves," says Edie. "I knew every single one. That is the bleeding heart leaf, of course, always my mother's favorite. Each time I went, I brought one back. The one you brought me was from the quandong."

"I like them," says Rose. Feels stupid. "I wouldn't put them in a box, but I think they belong where they fall."

"Do you?" says Edie. "You might be right."

They sit at the table and Rose threads her needle and begins practicing on her pillowcase. Edie hums beneath her breath. She hasn't performed her opening of the windows because it's not yet six o'clock. The house is shadowy closed up like that.

"There was a really big tree, giant, you could fit a whole car through it," says Rose.

"Oh yes, the big tree, the red cedar; there's hardly any of those left in this part of the world, they came looking for them specifically, the loggers. That one is a beauty. There are bigger, though."

Rose looks up from her work.

"Another place. I'll tell you about it one day."

Rose pricks her finger, sticks the tip in her mouth to taste the blood.

"Shall I tell you the story of my magpie?" says Edie.

Rose looks at the closed windows and, as if sensing the time, stands with the old woman, who has already begun to tell. They open the casements, the cracked and crazed louvres, throw open the door to the coming night.

"Now, I was twelve the year Granny Baker died. The house was already falling apart then. My father was never the same after the war, I told you that; you might have heard of such things, but to live with it, each day, it was like walking through a minefield. Still. I'm sure there are worse things. The farm fell apart, you see, because he refused to work it, and the more he refused to work it, the more Granny Baker blamed my mother. It was all her fault, the ruin of the farm, the ruin of the house, the war, everything. The cane was cut down and not planted again but still grew wild; the big fields filled up with weeds. The tree that grows through the front steps, well, it was just a sapling then. A big blow came one year and lifted a part of the roof up and carried it away, so we had canvas there instead, waiting for the new tin, which now my father couldn't afford; sometimes we'd be sitting there, eating our lunch, say, and the canvas would lift with a big wind and let in such sunshine that we all shone like angels and the clouds rolled over us.

"A lot of the weather came in. There were other parts of the roof that had started to leak, you see. The paintings buckled in their frames and the settees grew moldy, and sometimes sitting at the table, you would feel a little rain, just a sprinkle on your head.

"It wasn't the Depression yet but already there was a steady procession of men that went past the front gate—swaggies, we called them. Some stopped here, asked for just a little tea. I'd run back up the road and ask and Mother would measure out spoonfuls into a tin and some flour and wrap up biscuits in newspaper. These men always took off their hats to say thanks. Some said little, others more; they told you just where they'd been. Easy country, hard country, wet country, dry country. Country with work, country without.

"The year I was twelve, Granny Baker had a cough that wouldn't go away; all night it echoed through the house, she coughed and hawked and choked and gasped. She turned the color of old paper. Even when she was dying, she was full of spite.

Sometimes I had to go and help my mother turn her in the bed; she was as small as a child, I could feel the bones beneath her skin. My mother was gentle with her. Always gentle with her in return. She combed back Granny's hair and made it rest on the pillow like a gray cloud.

"Her old chair, the lilac-covered one, well, it was put outside when Granny Baker departed, by Mother herself, and it was the only thing my mother ever did that seemed in defiance. She put it out in the grass that had grown long as though she were putting out Granny from the house itself. When my mother put it outside, my father didn't say a thing. He never said a thing anymore. She sat down at the table and wrote a list. She read it out to me.

"'We'll need this many yards of duchess satin and this many spools of thread and so much bias binding and so many packets of pearl buttons and this amount of soft tulle,' she said. That list is still here somewhere.

"She counted the money into my hand and folded the note in half and I walked into town to buy these things."

"I thought you were going to tell me about a magpie," says Rose.

"I am," says Edie. "Show me how you're doing there."

Rose holds up her pillowcase.

"Not too bad," says Edie.

"I brought home all those yards of satin and those pearl buttons and the makings of veils. My mother went to work sewing wedding dresses. The first were very plain. Straight up and down, drop-waisted, which was the style then. Not even any lace at first, but later more, lace she found in the house, the edges of pillowcases and on the good curtains, which, I might add, had come all the way from France. She made them and I knew she could do better, I knew she could, but I didn't say anything then and I didn't know my talent yet.

"That came one morning when she handed me a length of silk satin, just to hold while she was opening up her pin box, and I told her exactly the dress that was sleeping inside. The bride-to-be who wore that dress was standing right there. Her name was Sophia Fanelli; you might go to school with some of them, they're thick on the ground around here, they always grew big cane, good cane, the Italians, and produce hundreds of babies.

"Sophia only died last year. I think she was six or seven years older than me.

"She took off her day dress in our kitchen, right here, and I can still see the way her black hair fell against her cheek when she bent down to pull up her stockings. Her breast was milk white against her yellow petticoat. Sophia Fanelli was very pretty.

"I held the silk, felt its weight, closed my eyes. I could see every part of the sleeping dress.

"I said, 'It should be fitted at the bodice.'

"My mother looked at me. She was going to put a finger to her lips but stopped.

"I said, 'The bodice should join the dress here.'

"I touched Sophia Fanelli's natural waist; she was a slender thing.

"'There are two panels for the skirt, but the hip yoke is pointed, here and here; the skirt will move so beautifully.'

"My mother had her hand still raised in the air, halfway up to her lips.

"'There should be ribbons,' I said, 'here, sort of floating down.

The veil should be gossamer, with only two roses on the right. You'll look a dream.'

"After she was gone, my mother said, 'Edith Emerald Baker, you are my little mystery.'

"We became quite renowned for her wedding dresses then. They would all come to stand in our kitchen and be measured this way. They would wait for what I had to say; so would my mother, with her long calm face and the velvety mole on her cheek. Sleeping box pleats, the inserted godet, three-tuck ruching waiting to be released. There was never a bride who wasn't happy. We became known far and wide in the district.

"In return she taught me all the secrets of stitching, my mother. Sewing is in our blood, you see."

"Magpie?" says Rose.

"I'm getting there," says Edie.

"My father started to kill trees. Did I already tell you that? He poisoned them. All along the path up to the gully. You might have seen some of them; for a while he was winning, but the place fought back over the years. He became a master at ring-barking. 'Why?' my mother asked him. 'Why not?' was what he replied. He was making inroads into the forest. That was what it felt like. He would get rid of the whole lot of it. We stared at his glass eye in the teacup.

"'Murderous,' I suggested.

"Mother shook her head.

"'Despairing' was what she said.

"He killed animals too. Wallabies. Pademelons. Possums. Snakes. Goannas. Skinks, crushed under foot, beetles, bugs, butterflies.

"He sat on the back steps watching quietly for hours, rifle in his hands, and then fired a single shot up into the trees.

"We jumped in our seats where we were sewing, calmed ourselves, proceeded.

"The magpie I got the year I was thirteen. My mother said it was a foolish thing and maybe it should go back to the wild—there were no doubt other magpies that would take it in—but secretly she was terrified my father would dispose of it. The magpie's mother was a pile of black and white feathers in the middle of the road beside Hansen's corner and the ditch.

"Now, Karl Hansen—he owned the farm next door, where the Falconers are now—had taken a train to Brisbane and driven back in a Vauxhall tourer, the whole way collecting wildlife on the shining front fender with great enthusiasm.

"The juvenile magpie was calling out to the pile of feathers and walking back and forward across the road and there were others about singing in the gum trees, calling to the bird, but soon enough they left it to its own end. I found it there on my way to school, raced home to fetch something for it to eat, right in past my mother, who had pins in her mouth, standing before a bride-to-be. I brought bread and dropped it all the way to school and the bird hopped behind, swallowing each piece and crying out between.

"That first day in the classroom we were sweating in our seats and the teacher, Miss Collier, was fanning herself with the *Cairns Post* and the storm towers were growing out over the sea and the only sound was that magpie calling outside the classroom. She went out and clapped her hands at it.

"'Stupid bird,' said Miss Collier.

"'It's Edie's bird,' they said in the class, which made the teacher angry.

"Miss Collier didn't think much of me. She didn't like my needle-pricked fingers and my creek-washed hair. She didn't like my knotted toes, she didn't like my quietness. Stupid Edie, strange Edie; I could tell that's what she thought of me. Always-climbing-hills Edie, Edie-from-the-falling-down-house, magic-wedding-dress Edie. Miss Collier wasn't married and never likely to be. She had a face all bumpy like a pickled cucumber and just as shiny.

"'Don't bring it back tomorrow, Edith Baker,' she said.

"At lunchtime I fed the magpie my mandarins and begged Peter Hansen for half his biscuit for the trip home. He said he would oblige if I promised to kiss him on the way home. There was much talk of what sort of kiss it would be, short or long, on the lips or on the cheek, and he made me commit to his specifications, which I did because I wanted his biscuit for the bird, which was all feathers and misery at my feet.

"Peter Hansen was an oaf of a boy, a head taller than everyone else in the class, and his head was bigger too, block-shaped, with a big thatch of blond hair that stood up like a scarecrow's. He had wet his pants once in first form and I never forgot it. The incident didn't make him sad, only enraged, and when the teacher tried to stand him up, he clung to the edge of his table and turned the color of uncooked sausage, yelling through his gritted teeth. I remember it right now, like I'm there. He got his way by using his fists.

"Peter Hansen was the eldest of the five Hansen brothers and the four others were present for the kiss and they were equally blond and block-headed and they were all equally stupid. They stood with their arms crossed and ribbed each other with their elbows and their faces grew bright red when Peter kissed me.

"Now, I kissed him beside the ditch not far from where the pile of feathers lay. His lips tasted of the grease from his dripping sandwich and we both kept our eyes open and we laughed, I remember, and he counted the seconds with his fingers, which must have taken away even more of the pleasure, but he removed his lips all the same when the time was up. He leapt back like he'd been holding his breath underwater and he was a dusky color, oh, the color of him. He shouted, 'One day I'll be marrying you,' and then he ran down the road between the cane with his younger brothers following him.

"And to tell you the truth, I began to cry. It might have been the kiss, because suddenly my cheeks burnt, but also it was the way that baby magpie walked right by the pile of feathers on the road and didn't recognize its own mother anymore. Each day after, it would pass that place and never stop again. And that place remained until the rains came, filling up the streams until they roared on the mountain and made Weeping Rock weep. That place remained until the rain washed away the last traces of the mother, wiped the road clean.

"But that magpie stayed with me for three whole years.

"It's strange how life turns out. That day is threaded all the way to here and me sitting with you. If I pulled that thread right now, I would see the places that day has touched my life, gathered up in folds. You won't understand it now."

"Who did this blue dress belong to?" asks Rose.

"It belonged to me. I sewed it a long time ago."

"Why was it so ripped?"

Edie doesn't reply; she picks up a jar and looks at her collected beads.

"I've been thinking," she says. "Why don't you take one of the bicycles from under the house? You could ride then and the trip here wouldn't be so far."

She's up before Rose can say anything. Rose follows her, stuffing the pillowcase and thread inside her schoolbag. Under the house Edie feels for a switch and sighs, as though satisfied, when a new and altogether rustier sea of junk is revealed. There are casements in piles and several wooden doors; a stroller, very old, minus its wheels; saddles resting on wooden sawhorses; umbrellas hanging in lines from hooks; bed frames; chair frames; wooden crates containing milk bottles; a guitar hanging enigmatically from a piece of string. There are at least five bike carcasses.

Edie points out a bike without a scrap of its original color. Despite the rust, its two tires are pumped up and in working order.

"I rode it until not that long ago," Edie says.

Rose bites her bottom lip.

"It isn't a gift," says Edie. "I want it back. I just thought it'd make it easier for you."

"Okay," Rose says. The bike squeaks as she wheels it out from under the house. "But you still never told me what happened to that dress."

"I've already started to," says Edie.

Rose looks at the old lady; the old lady looks back at her.

Rose rolls her eyes and feigns a yawn.

It's just getting dark when she arrives home.

"Nice bike," says her father by the campfire.

"Shut up," says Rose.

"I'm just saying," he says.

"Well, don't."

"Pearl came here today looking for you."

"Did she?"

"She was in a bit of a state."

"What kind of state?"

"Well, she looked like she'd been crying. I offered her a cup of tea."

"Did she stay?"

"We sat for a while out on the deck chairs but she didn't want any tea. She's very upset about this Chernobyl thing."

"What's a Chernobyl thing?"

"There's been a nuclear meltdown in Russia somewhere, some place called Chernobyl."

"Oh," says Rose.

"She was really upset about it. I said I'd drive her home but she said she'd be all right."

Rose goes inside to get changed and sees her father's sketchbook on the kitchenette bench. She opens it to the first page. She's expecting to see his usual fare, a spectacular invasion of flying vacuum cleaners, but instead there's a pencil drawing of Pearl. Unmistakably Pearl. Pensive Pearl. Beautiful Pearl. Pearl looking down, hair falling across her cheek.

"Did you do this today?" she asks him from the caravan door.

"I did," he says.

"While she was here?"

"No, after she left. I still had her in my mind."

She hates the way he says that.

"Don't draw my fucking friends," she says very slowly.

"I don't like your fucking language," he replies.

"I hate you," she says.

She does. This new him. The other him is much better. The larrikin him. The drunk him. The drunk him just blusters, breaks, barges; the drunk him just up and leaves. This new him terrifies her. He's too quiet, too controlled; he's always thinking.

"Don't be like that, Rose," he's shouting, but she's already pushed past him, she's already halfway across the sand, walking into the night.

$\mathcal{T}$wisted Stitch ••••••••••••••••

Glass is in his motel room. He's lying flat on the bed, arms out-stretched, fully clothed. His legs are still aching from yesterday's climb. He thinks about mountains, how they're formed by cataclysmic events. Every single one of them. Earthquakes and volcanoes, huge shudder-ing, earth-wrenching moments. Tectonic plates, or whatever they're called, crushing blindly against each other, lifting, splitting, crumbling.

Suffering.

He should have a shower but he just can't get up. The motel room is almost completely beige. Beige carpet. Beige curtains. Beige bed-spread. Mustard-colored walls. There is a faded print of the rain forest, a generic misty creek, all gentle water and mossy rocks. He knows it's nothing like that. Getting there would be a nightmare; that much itchy vine and slippery rock, it could kill a man.

"Okay," he says aloud into the room. "Think."

The phone rings instead. He can just reach it without rolling over. "What you got?" he asks.

He takes his notebook from his pocket. His pen. Closes his eyes to *listen. There's a good print on the back of the biscuit wrapper, somehow survived the rain. Belongs to a young man who was once done for possession of cannabis as a twenty-two-year-old in Cairns. Nothing since. No other record. Address is in the town.*

"Say the name again," says Glass.

He knows it from somewhere. He puts down the phone and goes through the file. Someone said that name. Right back in the beginning. First interviews. First day. Before he arrived. He's seen that name or heard it; he doesn't know which.

He flicks through the pages, swearing softly under his breath; there it is. Paul Rendell. "You should ask Paul Rendell."

PAUL RENDELL, he writes, 18 MAIN STREET, LEONORA.

Relief. It soothes his aching muscles. He circles the name. Circles it again. Doesn't stop until the page is awash with pond ripples.

There is something about Chernobyl that excites Rose. She knows it shouldn't. It's wrong to be excited by a catastrophe but it feels so much like the end of the world. She opens her green notebook and writes while she half listens to the voices on the radio. The voices sound excited too; they speak faster, argue with each other; of course the nuclear cloud will drift down, they say, it's already drifting out of the USSR and into Germany, it's only a matter of time.

Mrs. Bonnick wheels the TV into Modern History and makes them watch the news. There's a building burning, people in protective suits, and everywhere in Europe people terrified of the fallout. They're putting on layers of clothes and masks; everything is contaminated. It is such a dark thing. With unlimited dark possibilities.

"You see," says Mrs. Bonnick, trembling slightly and in need of a cigarette. "You are watching history unfold."

Pearlie isn't there. She hasn't been for three days.

"*Où est Pearl Kelly?*" says Madame Bonnick in French.

Rose shrugs.

"It isn't like her," says Vanessa. "She comes to school even if she has a cold. She can't bear to be away from people."

Vanessa has been to the hairdresser's for a trial run with her Harvest Parade hair. She describes it in intricate and excruciating detail while the other girls listen, enraptured. There are several pieces of hair that will be swept up and several pieces that will cross over these pieces, creating a basket effect. The basket effect of her hair will be laced with baby's breath and diamanté pins.

"You're going to look so beautiful," shrieks Shannon.

"Like a model," says Mallory.

"Don't be stupid," says Vanessa, although she is splitting at the seams with pride. "Is your dress nearly finished, Rose?"

"Not really," says Rose. "It's only been cut out."

Vanessa thinks for a while; it's obvious she's thinking up something nasty, just planning the best way to word it. The other girls wait. Rose is unprotected without Pearl, her flesh exposed. She waits too.

"Did you know," says Vanessa, quite slowly, quite stealthily, like a venomous snake preparing to strike, "that Miss Baker collects things out of bins?"

"Don't tell her that," squeals Maxine.

The words paralyze Rose. Afterward she can't say why. They are stupid words, just words. All the same, a huge shame rises inside her like a mushroom cloud. It affects her limbs and her speech. She smiles along with the other girls, some laughing; no words come. There is a small noise that comes out of her throat, perhaps the beginning of tears, but she swallows it down, swallows and swallows until it is gone.

Vanessa turns away and returns to the subject of hair.

Large thoughts loom inside Rose, thoughts that don't fit inside her head. They are monstrous and black and they bump against the ceiling of her brain. It's a grave injustice that she has to have her dress made by someone who is so strange and who lets a tree grow through her front door. But worse, it doesn't seem fair that now she should feel so protective of Edie alone in her big old creaking house with all her collections and clinking teapots and teaspoons and the rustling dying lost sound of things.

"I was only joking, Rosie," says Vanessa outside English class.

"No you weren't," says Rose, her voice finally recovered.

"Well, it's just the truth," says Vanessa. "I mean, Miss Baker has this, this reputation; there's kind of like these rumors, that's all. Bubble, bubble, toil and trouble. You know?"

"No, I don't know," says Rose.

"Anyway, she's the last person in the world I would have got to make my dress," says Vanessa. "Even a dress from Kmart would have been better."

Now, Edie would only have been going through a rubbish bin to rescue something. Something discarded, lost, left behind. An unusual jar or an old newspaper. A piece of something without its other part. Rose knows it but she still feels ashamed each time she thinks it. That's the worst. She knows Edie will know it too.

Edie will sense her new shame as soon as she walks through the door.

Sitting on her caravan bed, she sews small perfectly formed stitches on her pillowcase. It's Wednesday night but she isn't going to the old house. She can't. The rusty bike leans against the caravan, an accusation.

"Not sewing tonight?" asks her father.

"Shut up."

He laughs, whistles under his breath.

"I can buy you a dress, you know," he says. "Now we've got money. Elaine says she'll come with us, help look for one."

Elaine. That's what he calls Mrs. Lamond now.

"I'd rather jump from the Leap," says Rose.

"Bit dramatic," says her father.

"Will we be going soon?" Rose asks.

They've been in Leonora for two months. It's a record of sorts.

"Don't you like it here?" he says. "In paradise."

She closes her eyes. What will Edie think if she never goes back? What will she do with the dress? Will she fold up all the pieces and place them in a box? The rustling midnight-blue taffeta. All the thread. The black mourning lace. Will she hold the glass beads in her old hands? Will she wait each Wednesday on the back steps looking up at the mountain?

"I'm going to see Pearl," says Rose to her father.

"Is she feeling any better?"

"She hasn't been back at school."

"Give her my warmest regards."

Rose stares at him.

"What?" he says.

* * *

Rose pushes open the door of the crystal shop and Pattie Kelly looks up from where she is making a charm bracelet. Her eyes are puffy, as though she's been crying.

"Oh, Ruby Heart Rose, I am so glad you are here," Pattie says.

She gets up and envelops Rose in a patchouli-scented hug.

"You're like a plank of wood," Pattie says, shaking Rose a little and hugging her again. "There. You need a hundred more of them. Now, come and knock on this little bugger's door and see what you can do to cheer her up. Honestly, she is beside herself."

"Okay," says Rose, even though she doesn't consider cheering up to be in her repertoire.

Pattie does the knocking.

"Pearlie," she whispers. "Ruby Heart Rose is here."

Rose opens the door when there's no answer and goes in. It's dim in the room, the curtains are pulled and the fluorescent stars glimmer on the ceiling. Rose looks at the walls, all the maps and poems and models with their pouting sultry faces. Pearl is curled up on the bed facing the wall.

"Hi," says Rose.

Pearl says nothing.

"Sorry about Chernobyl," Rose says.

Pearl lets out a wail and begins to sob.

"Shit," says Rose.

Pearl scrunches her legs up higher and wraps her head in her arms. She cries like a wild thing. It makes Rose's heart stampede, her mouth dry. It isn't right, not Pearl, source of all light, weeping in a bed. Rose sits down beside her tentatively and touches her arm. Pearl doesn't pull away.

"The thing is, Pearl," Rose says, looking at the map of the USSR, "you have to remember what Mrs. Bonnick said. The sun rises on one part of Russia while it sets on another, it's that big. There's nothing to say he's anywhere near Chernobyl, he could be thousands and thousands of miles away, say in Murmansk."

She looks at the map, strains her eyes in the gloomy room.

"Or Vladivostok."

Pearl says nothing, shudders on the bed.

"The acid rain or snow or whatever, it isn't even heading that way; it's going over the Ukraine, Belorussia, and heading toward Germany."

Rose hopes Pearl's father isn't in Belarus.

"It's not about that," whispers Pearl.

"What, then?" says Rose.

Pearl cries very loud then, a good five minutes of it. Each time she tries to speak, her voice dissolves into a high-pitched warble. She sits up, holds her face. Rose looks around for tissues, finds a T-shirt. Pearl dries her face on that.

"Try and say it," says Rose.

"It's just . . . ," says Pearl. "It's just I knew today that I was never, ever going to find him. And I only got up to the Cs."

Pearl falls forward then, slumps into Rose's arms. She cries onto Rose's shoulder, which is pointy and uncomfortable. Rose feels Pearl's tears pooling there. She doesn't know what to do. What should she do? She puts her arms around Pearl and touches her hair.

"It's all right, Pearl," she says. "Everything will be all right."

$\mathcal{K}$not Stitch ━━━━━━━━━━

I don't know whether you can guess how fast it happened. That whole night moved languidly, drifted, yet now their actions tumbled from them.

She won't listen to him. All he wants is for her to listen to him. He wants to say it. "Listen to me." But what will he say? What does he know? He staggers. She's turning away, one hand on her hip, looking back over her shoulder. Still smiling. "Silly," she's saying. He's reaching out; he's going to take her by the arm. He's going to touch her once. Just once. There's nothing wrong with that. It's as if she's made of sky, of stars, she's so beautiful she's shining. He's reaching out; she's moving out of his reach. There's no way to slow it down now it has begun.

In the Ukraine they are going to give the forest around Chernobyl a burial. They will dig trenches and bulldoze the trees into them, cover them up again. Pearl speaks about it on her bed, brushing out her hair. "It's all dead," she says. "Everything died. The trees turned red.

"Can you imagine it? Just nothing. Everything dying for miles and miles and miles," she says. She speaks of the forest as though she knows it. As though she's been there, has witnessed the flash. It's her own personal apocalypse.

She doesn't know that years later birds, huge birds, barn owls and eagles, will roost inside the reactor to lay their eggs. That the spruce trees, newly confused, will forget to grow upward, but will sprout pinecones the size of footballs, that the forest alleys will thunder with magnificent wild boar, that the stags, muscles brimming with strontium, will leap across the streams through light and into shadow.

"I'm going to change my name," Pearl says on her bed the first day they climb to the house in the trees. "Soon."

"What will you be?"

"I told you, Persephone."

"I like Pearl better," says Rose.

But it's as though Pearl is already shedding part of herself, Rose thinks; slipping out of the casing of her name, splitting it like a husk from the seed.

Now, when Jonah Pedersen sends the message that Pearl should sit with him at lunchtime, she doesn't go: she looks at her nails, shrugs, flinches, but doesn't look up when he kicks the wall.

"What's going on?" Jonah asked her after school near the bus stop two days ago. He was standing too close to her. He stunk in his tracksuit jumper. She didn't want to hurt him. He was all bravado and bad dance moves there on the footpath, but his eyes gave him away.

"Your loss, baby," he said. She hadn't spoken.

"Jonah," she said as he walked away.

In the bedroom Pearl brushes out her hair and stares at herself in the mirror. She looks at herself in wonder sometimes, as though she's never seen herself before.

"I felt it again, so protective of him. It hurts my heart. Maybe we *are* meant to be?" But she changes the subject almost immediately, before Rose can come up with a Tarzan comment. "What should I wear? I don't really have any bush-walking clothes."

She goes through her drawers, holds clothes against herself, tries on a pair of boots. When she's finally dressed, in an impractical white dress with bone-colored sandals and a denim vest, Rose is lying on the bed staring at the ceiling.

"How do I look?" she asks.

"It's a hard climb," says Rose. "I mean, are you sure you want to do it?"

"Of course I want to do it," says Pearl.

"You have to promise not to tell anyone," says Rose.

"It'll be our little secret," says Pearl.

They climb through the gums, Pearl talking endlessly. Rose is aware of the dark house watching them through the trees. She hopes that Edie won't see them, come rushing out, calling. But the old woman doesn't emerge. The house hunkers down beneath its vast dark roof, stares. There is a frantic bird calling; it sings out again and again, a warning cry that makes the skin on Rose's forearms prickle, but she shrugs off the half-formed thought. The sun is already high in the sky.

She can see Jonathan Baker's poisoned trees now, there on the slope; how could she have not seen them before? Their bases and jagged crowns, leafless, leaning, are all that is left of them. They are ghosts there among the other trees. Yet in places the forest has used these carcasses: tree ferns sprout from inside one, others are colonized by moss, vines use some as scaffolding in a vain attempt to reach the sun.

She's glad when the house disappears from view; when it's gone, Rose feels free. The land falls away sharply and the trees lay out their huge buttress roots. There's the hushing sound of water below, still unseen. The gully yawns into view.

"Now what?" says Pearl.

"We have to climb down," says Rose. "It's okay. I know the way."

Rose shows her where to squat, where to put her feet, where to turn, where to place her hands.

"This is ridiculous," says Pearl, suspended on a large boulder.

Rose feels momentarily panicked then as well. By herself it's different; she never doubts herself. She judges the distance between two rocks without stopping to think. She leaps out into air. She can tell if a rock is steady or not through her foot; she leans into the rock and the rock releases itself to her.

Pearl is no good at it.

"Just stay calm," says Rose. "All you have to do is move your foot about five centimeters to the left."

"There's nothing there," says Pearl.

"You're moving it to the right."

Pearl inches her way down with Rose's help until they both stand beside the creek. Pearl is breathing hard.

"Maybe we should go back," says Rose. "The next bit is harder."

Pearl sits down on a rock. She wets her face in the clear running stream.

"It's so beautiful," she says. "Isn't it?"

The trees rise up over the gully and the air is rarefied.

"Almost magical," says Rose. She looks at the already torn hem of Pearl's white dress.

"I think we should keep going," Pearl says.

Rose shows her the fallen tree bridge and Pearl laughs as though Rose is joking. She touches the iridescent moss with one finger. Rose shows her how to begin.

"This is a red quandong leaf," says Rose on the other side when Pearl can walk again and they have set off through the great trees, "and its fruit is blue."

Pearl holds the leaf in her hand.

"Okay," she says.

"Here," says Rose. "Look."

She plucks the blue fruits from the ground. Pours a handful into Pearl's hand.

"Look at this," says Rose. She dips again, this time to pick up two perfectly pink nuts. She gives one to Pearl, puts the other in her shorts pocket, hopes Pearl won't see.

"Pink," says Pearl, raising her eyebrows. "That's not like you."

"There's a vine in here, and if you touch it, you just about die from itching," says Rose.

"How do you know all this stuff?"

"I just know it," says Rose.

They stop in a space where a tree has fallen and the canopy is broken, step into a single shaft of light and laugh. Above them a blue Ulysses butterfly hovers.

"Look at your freckles," says Pearl.

"You mean they're terrible," says Rose.

"I mean they're beautiful," says Pearl.

At the hut the mist from the falls hangs in the air and wets their red faces. Pearl walks to the edge, covers her eyes to the sunlight, looks out over the view.

"I feel like I've been here before," Pearl says, and then shivers. She shows Rose the gooseflesh on her arms.

"I felt it too," says Rose. "The first time I came."

Rose pushes open the little door of the hut and Pearl walks inside. She looks about in awe at the little space with the pitched roof, the shadows of trees moving on the walls. The light from the casements, which Rose cleaned on her second trip, fills up the room like water.

"I love it," Pearl says.

"I could almost touch those clouds," Pearl says, lying on her back on the rocks beside the falls. "Look how they're hanging down, almost in the trees. I can't believe you found this place. It's exactly like in a dream. You can write about this, Rose. You should write a story about you and me, or some other girls that are like us, and we run away here to live."

Rose thinks of her green notebook, of Pearl's name hidden by black ink. They lie on the rocks beside the falls, the clouds passing right over them, lacing themselves through the trees, raining on them, misty rain that cools their skin. They hang their legs over the rocks, watch the water fall away beneath them. Between clouds there are sudden bright gaps of sunlight that burn into the clearing.

"Do you want to swim?" says Rose.

The climb to the base of the falls is difficult; the forest had been split down a seam by the creek, the sun allowed in; they have to move through a tangle of ferns and lawyer vines.

"It's worth it," says Rose. "You'll see."

The sunlight on the rock at the bottom of the falls renders them luminous. They hold their hands over their eyes. It is a perfect deep pool, the water roaring into it, the creek flowing away, down through the trees. Pearl is already bending down, unbuckling her sandals. She throws off her dress, picks her way over the stones into the water.

"It's freezing!" she screams.

Rose laughs, flicks off her Dunlops, slips down her shorts, and wades out too. The stones are smooth beneath their feet. They are so close to the falls they can't hear each other speak.

"I love it," she thinks she hears Pearl say again.

"What did you say?" Rose asks.

But Pearl only smiles at her and closes her eyes against the sun.

They climb from the water and dry themselves on the rocks. They explore. The boulders are bluish gray and pockmarked. Each crater fills up with rain like a cup. They walk among the boulders and dip their fingers into these places, which collect many things: leaves, vividly green, newly caught, or others almost blanched of their color; pods and seeds; smaller pebbles; the tiny fragile skeleton of a baby bird, the perfect drowned body of a lizard, both lying protected behind the clear water glass. They lie on the sun-warmed rocks and watch the clouds drifting past. The alternating shadows and dazzling light make them drowsy.

"I'm burning," says Rose, looking at the pale skin on her legs turning pink.

They head back up through the trees. The forest is loud, full of chatter, the creek babbling, the birds talking, but in the hut it is quiet, a sudden crushing silence that makes their ears ring.

"I'm so tired," says Pearl.

"We shouldn't sleep," says Rose.

But they do.

They lie curled on the floor, side by side, smelling of the mountain and the creek. Rose's hair, unbound, has curled in the sun and Pearl winds a strand around her finger in amazement. Closes her eyes. They wake that way, the strand of hair still coiled around Pearl's finger but the sun almost gone.

"Shit," says Rose, sitting up. "We should have gone earlier."

At night it will be the darkest place in the world.

She knows it's too late. They'll never make it down. Not through the gully, where the hard climbing is, not in the dark.

"Are we going to have to stay here?" asks Pearl.

"I think so," says Rose. "I don't know what else to do. It's my fault."

"My mum will go crazy," says Pearl. "She'll call the police."

"Shit," says Rose.

"We'll need a fire," says Pearl.

"I don't have any matches."

"Can't we rub two sticks together?" says Pearl. "Or something."

They try, but when nothing happens, they give up almost immediately and find themselves laughing. The light is draining from the jagged strip of sky above the falls; everything has become indistinct and blurred at the edges. A soft rain has begun to fall.

"We shouldn't get wet again," says Rose, "or we'll get cold."

They go back inside the little hut, where it is even darker.

"What time do you think it is?" Pearl whispers.

Neither of them has a watch.

"I don't know."

They sit close together, knees drawn up to their chins. The smell of the creek on their skin is very strong. Pearl's stomach growls in the darkness and it makes them both laugh again.

"Mum will be going out looking for me," she says. "She'll probably go and see your dad."

"Dad will tell her not to worry."

"Won't your dad worry?"

"I don't think so," says Rose. "He's not much of a worrier."

"Mum will be having kittens."

"Did she know we were going bush-walking?"

"I'm not sure, did you tell her?"

"I didn't tell her anything, I just said hello."

"Anyway," says Pearl. She offers a chewing gum stick.

In the dark there is nothing else to do but lie down. The darkness is like a tide; it rushes into the clearing and leaves them breathless. They lie curled side by side and don't speak. They listen to the forest, its scraping, snapping, moving sounds. Once, they hear the footsteps of a larger creature, a rock wallaby perhaps. Pearl's fingers wrap around Rose's wrist hard. Rose sits up; the floorboards move and whatever it is crashes off through the undergrowth.

The forest breathes around them. There is the rhythmical chanting of insects and the myriad small rustlings and chimings. Owls sing their hunting tunes. Rain falls on the old tin roof, sometimes a tiny whisper, suddenly a drumbeat. The sound of the waterfall grows huge, filling up the hut and Rose's mind; other times it recedes, leaving other, smaller sounds, Pearl's breathing.

Pearl's fingers, still holding Rose's wrist, relax.

Up close Rose can smell her chewing gum breath, her creek-scented hair, the sweat dried out on her white dress.

"Pearl?" Rose whispers.

Pearl doesn't answer. It's just like her to be so terrified and then to just as suddenly fall asleep.

Rose wants to talk. She, Rose Lovell, wants to talk about herself.

"Pearlie," she whispers.

The wild bickering of flying foxes.

"I'm thinking I'm going to run away after this. When my dad wants to leave, which he will. I'm old enough now; there's nothing keeping me here. When I climb, I feel really free. I mean it, I mean it like the word sounds, do you understand? Like I'm made of air. I feel like I understand it and it's the only thing I'll ever be any good at."

The house groans and tut-tuts.

"I don't mean I'm going to be a mountain climber; I don't mean that, I don't know what I mean. When I was on the boat with Murray Falconer, I think he wanted to kiss me. He kept looking at my lips. I don't know, maybe I had a pimple there."

Pearl shifts against her.

"My mum didn't mean to die. It was an accident. She really loved the sea. She was an Aquarian. I never got to see her, like in her coffin or anything. I know it sounds like she was terrible for putting me to bed and then doing something like that, getting drunk and going swimming, do you know what I mean? But it wasn't like that. It was just a spur-of-the-moment thing. My dad, he used to say, "She loved you, Rose. She loved you, Rose. You were her everything." That was when I was smaller. I can only just remember it. He doesn't say it anymore."

The night inches by with its thousand scratchings and scrufflings. Rose thinks she hears footsteps once but it's only the rain. Sometimes the sounds join together to make one mass of noise, a violent thrumming living heartbeat; other times she can separate them: raindrops, birds' wings, something moving through the leaves.

"This house was built by Jonathan Baker," whispers Rose. "He loved this lady called Florence, who was a dressmaker. She sewed a secret love letter into a suit she made for him. It said, MEET ME AT THE FOUNTAIN."

She thinks about them then, Jonathan and Florence. The many times they must have walked up into the forest, swum at the base of the falls, kissed right here in the hut, lying on the very same floor. How Edie was conceived right there.

"I can come with you to Russia if you like," Rose whispers.

She's unsure if she sleeps. If she does, she dreams she's awake, lying there listening. A slight change in the light arrives, a change in the darkness to a gray, a glistening gray, a gray filled with stars.

She reaches her hand out to touch it. Pearl turns farther on her side, and Rose watches the dim outline of her.

Sometime before dawn they sit up in the gloom. They go out into the forest through the gauzy mist and without speaking begin the long walk home. They go down through the trees, clamber down into the gully, where Pearl does not complain, she listens carefully instead for where to put her feet, where to put her hands. They rock-hop across the creek, the water higher, flowing faster, scramble up the other side. The sun is just up, the first glimmer of it proper, when they make their way through the open sclerophyll and into the stand of butter-colored gum trees.

"Shit," says Rose.

She has run straight into Pearl's back because Pearl has stopped still on the track. Picking her way up the path before them is Edie.

"Good God," says Edie, "I'm so glad to see you."

Rose sets her face into a stone mask, crosses her arms.

"Hi," says Pearl.

"Hello," says Edie.

"I'm Pearl," says Pearl when Rose doesn't introduce her.

"Edith Baker," says Edie. "Rose has told me about you."

"No I haven't," says Rose. "I've never even mentioned her."

Pearl smiles. Edie smiles.

"Look at the pair of you," Edie says. "What happened?"

"We left it too late to come down, that's all," says Rose. "We were never in danger."

"I knew it," says Edie. "But I couldn't rest until I knew for sure. I saw you go up yesterday but not down."

"You shouldn't spy," says Rose, and immediately regrets her words because Edie flinches as if she's been slapped.

Standing there on the path, she's so small and deflated in her sundress and gum boots. She holds a large stick in her hand. Surely she couldn't have gone much farther. Surely she wouldn't have tried to climb down into the gully.

"Come to the house and use my phone," says Edie. "Are you hungry?"

"God, I'm starving," says Pearl.

Edie makes them toast and pikelets. She cuts up mango. The two girls stand in the yellow kitchen. All the windows are shut and the house is night-cool. The sweat dries on their skin. They watch the bluebirds on the wall, the first line of light glimmering on their wings.

"Your dress?" Pearl gasps.

Rose turns to where Pearl points. There by the long bank of louvres stands a dressmaker's mannequin and on it the midnight dress has been pinned. Edie must have done it the Wednesday that Rose hadn't come. The skirt falls in a river, the bodice is perfect, the black mourning lace sleeves pinned into place.

"Something felt wrong," says Edie, "so I pinned it together to make sure. I think I solved the problem. It was the way the skirt fell at the front in my mind."

"It's so beautiful," says Pearl.

Edie looks at Rose. Rose returns her gaze. Edie's eyes don't ask, Will you come back? Will you make the dress with me? She doesn't need to ask these things.

* * *

Pattie Kelly's eyes are swollen and her mascara is running. She jumps out of the car and grabs Pearl into an embrace, not letting her go.

"Jesus H. Christ," says Pattie. "I mean, really, Pearl, Jesus bloody Christ."

"I'm sorry," says Pearl, "we didn't mean it. I mean, we just went up to this place and then we were swimming in this waterfall and then we couldn't get back down because it got so dark. I was always safe."

"Well, I was just about to call the police," Pattie says.

She thanks Edie. Edie says she did nothing except feed them and let them use her phone.

Rose slips into the backseat soundlessly, hoping she'll escape Pattie's wrath, but Pearl's mother turns to her as well and shakes her head.

"I went and tried to find your father but he wasn't at the caravan and I didn't know if that should make me more worried?" She sobs out her last words.

Rose's heart skips a beat, then races at breakneck speed. Pattie Kelly puts the car into reverse and turns in a circle in Edie's backyard. Rose watches Edie and Edie watches Rose; neither waves. Rose looks up at the shimmering mountain; the mountain looks back at her.

"Do you girls have any idea how dangerous it is up there?" says Pattie. "I mean, for shit's sake, you could have slipped on a rock and broke your neck or got washed away if a creek came down; those gullies fill up in seconds."

Rose whispers, "Yes."

Pearl says nothing but Rose sees her looking up as well.

The place they found is in both their minds, she knows it, that place where the shadows of leaves tremble on the walls and the sunlight fills up their skin to the brim and the night rolls in as huge as an ocean. That place is apart from everything and she knows, Rose Lovell knows, they will both go there again.

$\mathcal{L}$adder Stitch ━━━━━━━━━

Detective Glass is interested in Paul Rendell's weeping right eye. It's red and swollen. Tears fall from it in a steady stream.

"I've been to the doctors about it," he says. "The private doctor and the hospital doctor. They can't see anything in it at all."

"Someone scratch you?" asks Glass.

They're in the cramped little flat above the shop. Mrs. Rendell's footsteps have started away down the stairs, then stopped, so he knows she's listening.

"Someone trying to fight you off?" he says when Paul doesn't answer.

"Told you I got it at work. Ages ago. Before the parade. The light kills it; it's driving me insane."

It is true. Everything shines with a chandelier luminance if he closes his good eye. At home, again and again, lying in the bedroom of his childhood, he has taken Pearl's note, ripped clear from the book, and unfolded it. He looks at her childish hand. Closes his good eye so the words read as if they're written in diamonds.

"*I think it must have been just a splinter, a sugar splinter; it must have blown up from the drying pans. I had to go home from work. There'll be a record there and at the hospital.*"

"*So why were you up the hill at the hut with two teenagers?*" Glass asks into the silence.

"*I wasn't,*" Paul Rendell says.

Glass laughs.

"*She asked me,*" Paul says. "*Pearl asked me. It was just a bit of fun. Nothing happened.*"

Glass watches him. Paul Rendell, for the first time, wipes at the stream from his swollen eye.

"*You'd have to be twice her age, wouldn't you?*" asks Glass.

"*You've got it all wrong,*" Paul Rendell says.

"*Well, you can explain it all to me at the station, Mr. Rendell.*"

It isn't a good sign. Her father still isn't home. The caravan is tidied, the dinner cooked; hers is stored away in the fridge. The dishes have been washed and dried. She approaches his bed, opens the curtain. His bed is made up. Unslept in. She sees his sketchbook beneath the bed, his pencils beside it. When she opens it, she sees the drawings of Pearl; she flips the pages, he has tried to draw her again and again and failed. He can't get her right. She shivers and puts the sketchbook back again.

He'll be at the pub, his art having failed him, what does it matter. It was bound to happen sooner or later. It's the way things are. No point getting upset. Steel yourself. Hold on tight. Don't show any emotion.

She takes a towel and walks to the bathroom, showers and washes her hair. She puts in a load of washing. Sits on her little bed. Stands up again. Even washed, she can still smell the mountain on her. She holds up her forearm to her nose and breathes. Not there; it's an aura, a cloud.

When her father doesn't drink, he calls it his disease, but when he does, he says, "Oh, Rose, keep your wig on, it's just a couple down at the pub with mates. There's this great bloke called Frank, old-timer, lived here since he was a boy. He knows the sea like the back of his hand, said he could take us out fishing next Saturday."

Once, when she was eight, he had disappeared down the track in some town. The caravan had been parked in a campground by a dry riverbed. "I'll be back in an hour or so," he had said, but he wasn't. All night she had lain awake in the caravan waiting. She listened to every noise, divided them between good and bad. Someone putting their tea on, someone sweeping out their annex, a toilet flushing, a washing machine chugging in a faraway laundry. Crickets singing in an ominous tone, the crack of twigs underfoot, the sudden flurry of wings.

What if he doesn't come home? she had thought. What if he was in a fight and was punched in the head and someone was dragging him to where he wouldn't be found? She thought these things because these were the things her father told her happened. "Once there was this man called Pep," he said, "who got into trouble with some big men and one night they just came into the pub and picked him up off the stool and carried him away. No one did a thing. Everyone just sat there as if it was normal and no one looked at the carrying men. That was the end of Pep." "Where did they take him?" she had asked. "Who would know?" he had replied.

What would I do? she had thought that night when she was eight. She would have to walk into town in the morning and go up and down the streets looking for him. She would go to the hospital and then to the police station. She would have to say, "Excuse me, I'm looking for Patrick John Lovell," and behind the counter the officer would put down her pen.

But she never had to do these things because her father always came home. That night late or the next. She would hear the caravan door swing open. The sound of the crickets singing would recede like some terrible tide and all the bush noises would become just the normal every-night cracking and springing of twigs. His parka would rustle. A match would flare. He would bump into the table and swear.

That morning by the dry river his face was puffed up from the drinking and he was covered in dirt and grass from where he'd slept.

She said, "I thought you weren't coming home."

He said, "Well, I did."

She said, "I thought I'd have to go to the police station."

He said, "If you do that, we'll be up shit creek; they'll take you off me and put you in an orphanage."

The orphanage. She imagined cold wooden floorboards, porridge at a long table, bunk beds, dirty-faced kids.

Now, in a caravan in Paradise, she hears him come home late in the night. He smells of the sea, sweaty, briny; she squeezes her eyes closed in the dark. He smells huge; he fills up the caravan with his odor. She hears him singing softly, a lilting low tune. She waits for him to stumble, but he doesn't. She waits for the bloody beer-sodden stench of his clothes to reach her, but it doesn't.

She sits up when he opens her curtain a fraction.

"Where have you been?" she says.

"Where have you been, more to the point," says her father. "Elaine reckons Pearl's mother was here last night looking for you both."

"We got stuck on the mountain in the dark."

He raises his eyebrows approvingly. Excuse accepted.

"I've been fishing," he says. "That bloke called Frank. Night fishing. What a crack. Caught fifteen."

"They stink."

"But they'll taste good," he says, smiles in the dark like a boy.

After he has finished in the kitchen, after she hears him shed his clothes and climb into his bed, she pulls her curtain shut. She turns on her bedside light, opens the bedside drawer, brushes out her hair to calm herself. Seventy-one strokes. Seventy-one strokes. Presses her fingers to her eyes. What did her mother look like? It's such a simple thing, to remember your mother's face, yet there is nothing there in her mind but a clean blank space. She takes the pillowcase sampler from the drawer, holds it on her lap for a long time, and then slowly, carefully begins to sew. Each stitch for a memory. Here's the stand of gums, here are the leaning turpentines, here's the space where the gully begins, here's the house among the trees. She sews the small neat stitches, a whole line of them, until she feels her eyes begin to close. Here's the dress, the midnight dress, the beautiful midnight dress, then she turns on her side and sleeps.

Rose leans the rusted bike against the railing and takes the pillowcase sampler from her bag. She holds it out to show Edie in the late-afternoon light. She holds it out without saying anything as though it will settle something between them.

"You've improved," says Edie.

Inside, Edie begins the window-opening ritual and Rose helps. The midnight dress rustles on the mannequin ever so slightly.

"Do you think you're ready, then?" Edie asks.

She doesn't ask Rose where she's been. Or why she's stayed away. She unpins two panels from the skirt and hands them to Rose. She searches through the sewing basket for the blue thread. Chooses a needle from the needle box. She shows Rose the seam width. She sits down herself and begins beading the bodice, intricate work, tiny stitches attaching each little black bead.

That work looks exciting. Much more exciting. But Rose picks up her needle, threads it, begins to sew all the same. She sews with her new hand-stitch. Stitch after endless stitch. It feels as if she will never make it to the end of that row. Edie glances at her work from time to time and Rose puts it down on her lap so that she can see. Nothing, just a nod, keep going. The thread makes a soft noise in the taffeta. Ah, yes, it says, again and again. Edie takes a hankie from her bra strap and wipes her forehead; the night is close. No rain yet.

"We're having a late wet, you know," says Edie. "It's usually drying up by now. Have you seen any rose walnuts on the ground up there?"

"What do they look like?"

"Small, long shape, lovely shiny."

"I don't know."

"What about the porcelain fruit? That's bright pink or white, you can't miss it, it's the most beautiful thing."

Rose takes the pink nut from her pocket. She's carried it there for a week.

"Is this it?" she asks.

Edie holds it in her palm, a prize.

"I only saw two of them," says Rose.

"We've still got some rain to go, then," says Edie.

"You can have it," says Rose.

"Well, thank you."

When Rose finishes sewing the first two panels, she slumps back in her chair and Edie laughs. She shows Rose how to finish off the piece, the knot inside the knot inside the knot. An elephant beetle flies in through the open window and crashes against the lamp. The old woman heaves herself up and throws it back out the window.

"Silly bloody thing," she says.

She unpins another panel from the mannequin and hands it to Rose. Rose doesn't know the time but it feels late. Her fingers ache.

"So did you fall in love and marry that boy?" asks Rose.

"Boy?" says Edie.

"The one you kissed for the magpie food," says Rose. "That's how it always happens in romance books. The woman doesn't like the man at first but later they fall in love."

Edie puts down her beading.

"I fell in love with someone altogether different," she says. "Did I tell you the magpie stayed with me three whole years?"

"Yes," says Rose.

"Three years," says Edie. "Wherever I went, it went. If I walked to town, it hopped along, tree to tree, and when they put in the telephone wires, it hopped along on those. When I went up the mountain, it came as well, through the trees. It had a beautiful song. It sang outside my bedroom window every morning while all the other magpies were caroling down at the front of the drive. My mother said, 'Better be careful, you know how your father hates singing birds.' In the end she was right, he got rid of it, must have, it disappeared when he went away. It had the blackest of black eyes. Have you ever looked into a magpie's eyes?"

Rose shifts in her chair. Rethreads her needle.

"Not really," she says.

"Well, it's the same as with crows, I suppose; they look right inside you. But there was something about that magpie; I can't explain it. You understand, I suppose. I never gave it a name. It followed me to school. Was the cause of much . . . discussion."

Rose wipes her sweaty hands with a tea towel, the way Edie has taught her, so she won't mark the fabric.

"But when my father went, the magpie went too, so he must have done something with it. Or it accompanied him; sometimes I like to think that too. Because he would have been so lonely on the road. He left when I was fourteen, nearly fifteen, and we were making wedding dresses. Now things had changed with the dresses; the Great Depression had come. Girls wanted their mothers' dresses altered, or their sisters', and we did that sort of work, which is not as exciting but work all the same. And sometimes in those old dresses, in the silk satin that had turned the color of rancid cream, I saw other dresses struggling to be free. I looked at the woman and saw the dress she should wear; I looked at my mother and she shook her head ever so slightly and I said nothing.

"My father, before he left, sometimes he touched these dresses.

He drifted past them and stopped, felt with his very fingertips, gently, and I saw some of his gentleness, which I'd never known. His voice was very quiet, you could hardly hear him speak, and he was always trembling with a quiet rage, but when he touched those dresses, well, I can't explain. He got up one morning and went and joined the ranks of men who walked past the front gate; their numbers had swelled, the drifters, the men with no home. He woke one morning and put on the suit my mother had made him all those years before. His good hat. Stuffed a few coins in his pocket. He didn't say goodbye, although he came to my door and looked down at me. I know he did but I kept my eyes closed. He just walked off and never came back. And that morning the magpie was gone.

"That first night my mother waited up for him but not after. She seemed to know he wasn't coming home."

Rose sews. Edie will get to the part about love soon, she always does, she just takes strange circuitous routes. At first these detours angered Rose but now she settles back into them, waits. The rain comes at last, a monumental downpour that makes the floorboards tremble beneath her feet.

"I fell in love with someone else altogether the year my father left," Edie says when it has passed. "His name was Luke Grace and he was the only son of Mr. Grace, who owned Grace Fabrics. Very handsome, Rose, black hair, blue eyes, very tall. He was not stooped at all like his father, who'd spent his life bent over the counter cutting and counting buttons into paper bags and writing receipts. I can still remember how that shop smelt. Each fabric contains its own scent, you know; it's true, satin like eggshell, linen like freshly mown grass. But the top note in that shop was gabardine suiting; that shop smelt like a newly made suit, like the inside of a pocket. I would go there, Rose, to collect my mother's orders.

"I would buy five buttons for myself or ribbons or a certain-colored embroidery thread. Luke Grace, if he was home from boarding school, might glance at me and I might glance at him. Yet at home I could lie on my bed and open the paper bag containing the ribbons and the whole shop would be inside. At night I would sleep with that paper bag and those small bone buttons and it would be as though he was lying beside me.

"Mr. Grace taught his son everything there was to know about the shop. He'd say, 'This lovely lady wants the floral dimity and Dresden blue; see, she has chosen a color that is most compatible with her eyes; remember how we must cut fabric with a pattern, Luke?' Luke watched very solemnly. He did exactly as his father told him, spilling eyelets into packets and wrapping ribbons into figure eights. Or, said his father, 'Now, these buttons that this young lady has chosen are, I believe, among the most beautiful buttons in the world; they are made in Italy, yes, that is right, Italy, and see, on the side of the jar there is even the address; isn't that wonderful, Miss Edith Baker, see, you can smell Rome when you put them to your nose.'

"These things made me blush and Luke also.

"I don't recall when he suddenly grew up. One day he was home from boarding school almost a man. 'Can I help you?' he said. 'I'm just looking,' I said. 'Are you making something special?' 'No, nothing special.' 'You're all grown up.' 'So are you.' He cut me an extra length of ribbon when his father wasn't looking and winked. He walked with me sometimes out of the door into the sunshine and I would forget to breathe and later, walking home, would take huge breaths to make up for it.

"Mr. Grace at first did nothing to stop our courtship. He'd always been very kind to me, nothing like the old Mrs. Rendell, who kept the post office and wouldn't say good morning and whispered under her breath, 'Well, look what the cat dragged in.' And the women at Coolibah Café, where my mother sometimes took me on Saturday mornings, they stopped talking as soon as we entered and didn't start again until we left.

"Mr. Grace encouraged us in a way, when he thought it was all very harmless: he called us the lovebirds and his laugh floated down from the high shelves. He thought, perhaps, it was just a fleeting thing. Sometimes on a Saturday, Luke and I would walk a ways to the creek. No, he never went up the mountain with me, Rose, just to the creek, and it was there he asked me to marry him. I was sixteen and he was seventeen.

"Do you know what love is like, Rose? It's like having a sky, a whole sky racing inside of you. Four seasons' worth of sky. One minute you are soaring and then you are all thunderclouds and then you are deep with stars and then you are empty.

"Once, in the shop, he put his hand up to my face in the button aisle when his father wasn't looking and kissed me on the lips. It was nothing like that kiss from Peter Hansen. Luke Grace's kiss was delicate, gossamer light, sweet.

"'Don't be stupid' must have been what Mr. Grace said, or something like that. I tried to imagine it. Not because I was dirt poor. My mother did well enough with the dresses, enough to keep us fed and clothed. Not even because I'd once had a pet magpie. Not because we lived in a house that was once splendid and now ruined. There were certain things being said, since my father left, and I was only just becoming aware of them. They were things said about my mother, who was good and kind and who never in all her life hurt a soul."

Edie stops then, places the beading in her lap. Rose looks at her face and quickly away again.

"What kind of things?"

"Terrible things."

"Like what?"

"Can you imagine?"

"Was it because of your father going mad?"

"Yes," says Edie. "And because he left, just walked out, they said she can't have been a very good wife and all in all she must have been a very wicked wife, she must have done something to him, and to Granny too. Everything had been good at the big house until Florence Baker arrived."

Rose bites her bottom lip.

"'We'll run away,' was what Luke Grace said to me. 'Do you mean it?' I said. 'Yes,' he said. 'I swear on my heart.' We arranged the time. The bend in the road beside Hansen's corner. I went there in the morning just after the sun came up. I left a note for my mother saying goodbye, and she must have woken, read it, felt very sorry for me, yet she didn't come looking for me. She knew I'd be home. I waited all day. First when the sun was high in the sky and baking and later when the afternoon rains came.

"Finally I went home, drenched. My little suitcase by my side. I came in through the back door right here where my mother was and she was sewing just the way she always did. I had the whole day inside of me. The whole day.

"'Now, now,' she said, catching me in her arms.

"I was ill after that, grew very thin, black rings beneath my eyes, coughed and coughed and coughed. I could hardly sit up, I was so weak. My body was almost destroyed by love.

"'Some people are built for love,' said my mother. 'Some people are not.'

"'They say you're a witch' was what I shouted.

"'Edie' was all she said; my words hurt her terribly; she bent down her head and began to cry.

"And it was a stupid thing to say, because if she was a witch for loving the mountain, then I must have been one too."

When the story is done, Rose has nearly finished attaching the third panel of the skirt. The floor is littered with money beetle jewels. She opens and shuts her fingers and counts the needle pricks. The rain thunders on the roof, pauses, thunders again.

"It's after midnight," Edie says. "You can't ride home in this. I'll clear the daybed and you can lie down there. Will your father worry? Should you phone him?"

"He won't be worried," says Rose. "And we don't have a phone."

Suddenly Rose is so tired that she yawns into her hands. Edie looks at her, shakes her head kindly, and goes about removing boxes from the daybed, newspapers in piles, several toilet dolls in crocheted skirts, some cracked ceramic figurines. She motions for Rose to lie down, takes the embroidered shawl from the back of the chair and spreads it over her.

"I'm sorry I took someone else there; it's just Pearl is my best friend and I wanted to show her," says Rose.

She's surprised to find her cheeks burning and the nettle of tears in her eyes.

"Don't worry," says Edie. The shawl smells strange, like old dried lavender, just the ghost of a scent remaining. "It doesn't belong to me, that place, Rose."

Rose is asleep before Edie leaves the room. She wakes once during the night; the rain has paused and the sound of the mountain comes into the house, the magnified whispering of trees and the creeks speaking in tongues. She opens her eyes and sees a family of possums have climbed through the kitchen windows to graze on crumbs and eat the fruit left out on shelves. They stare at her brazenly with glowing eyes.

The cool air Edie speaks of? It drifts down off the mountain, unraveling itself through trees, dipping its fingers in the streams. It comes in through the back door and through the windows cast open for it. The fat possums shiver and return to their meals. It lifts up the months on the calendar and leafs through the newspaper pattern in a pile on the table. It fills up the yellow kitchen and overflows into the hallway and spills into the rooms.

Rose closes her eyes again and smiles.

$\mathcal{B}$uttonhole Stitch ━━━━━━━

People see him being taken in. He's beside the big detective from out of town who's camped at the Raindance Motel. The big detective has his hand on Rendell's back, a protective, fatherly act; he's talking to the young man as they go in through the front door and down to the tiny interview room.

"Sit down, Paul," says Glass. "I'm glad you've agreed to come and talk to us."

One of the officers, Williams, knows Rendell. They went to the same boarding school and played football together. He avoids Rendell's face. Rendell's fidgeting with his shirt. Scratching his chest. Wiping at his eye.

"We just want you to have a bit of a chat to us about all this. So we can get it right in our heads, your involvement with these girls. Okay?" says Glass.

"There isn't any involvement," says Rendell. "Am I under arrest?"

"No, Paul, you're not under arrest," says Glass.

"Just say what you know, Paul," says Officer Williams quietly. "And you'll be able to go home."

"I don't know what you want me to say," says Paul. "I can't say anything if I don't know anything."

Out on the street Mrs. Fanelli has seen him taken in. The Albert brothers. The council gardener pruning. Everyone who works or is shopping at Hommel's Convenience Store, right next to the station. Mrs. Rendell is seated behind her news agency counter, fanning herself furiously, her face burning.

It takes off, the news; there is nothing she can do to stop it. While her son is questioned, the story is whipped up into eddies along Main Street. It accelerates, steamrolling into shops, careening through the school yard, plowing through the mill yards and out into the fields.

Pearl Kelly undoes the top button of her uniform and tucks one side of the skirt into her knickers. She has rubbed coconut oil on her legs so they glisten and then untied her hair. She bends over, runs her hands through it, makes it big. She does all this in the mirror of the takeaway window. Pouts. Poses. Laughs.

"Jesus," says Rose.

Pearl looks in her bag for *Ashes in the Wind*.

The problem with Pearl Kelly is that she thinks everyone is good.

When Rose tells her what Vanessa said about Edie, it's "Vanessa wouldn't have meant it really. She's very pretty but very stupid, you know that, Rose."

On Paul Rendell, it's "He's lonely. Can't you feel it? He's restless. He's just like me, stuck here in this stupid town. He wants to go traveling again but he had to come home when his father died. He's meant to be exploring the world. He's been to South America, he's been to India, he's seen the Taj Mahal. He's been to Paris."

Rose doesn't see it like that at all. Paul Rendell isn't lonely. Paul Rendell seems apart from everything. He's there, right there in his little suffocating shop, but his heart is somewhere else. Rose can't explain it.

"He's dangerous," Rose says, although that word doesn't seem right either. He doesn't look dangerous. He looks pale and bloated with big words. He looks tired. He looks, under his calm erudite surface, angry.

"Angry about what?" Pearl says.

"I don't know."

When Pearl is happy with her reflection, they go into the news agency, where Mrs. Rendell stops them and asks about their dresses for the Harvest Parade.

"I haven't decided yet," says Pearl.

"Well, you've got less than a month, Miss Kelly. You're leaving it a little late."

"I know," says Pearl, smiling. "I'm going to Cairns this weekend, maybe."

"And what about you?" says Mrs. Rendell, looking with disdain at Rose, her eyeliner, her deep purple lips, her freckles, her oversized uniform.

"Edie Baker is making my dress," says Rose. "It's midnight blue."

"Edie Baker," Mrs. Rendell says. "Well then."

That's all she has to say on Edith Emerald Baker.

"When I was sixteen, I wore a green gown," says Mrs. Rendell, getting up and walking over to the magazines. "Chiffon, it was, and it was just the most heavenly thing you ever saw and I danced every single dance with Mr. Rendell Senior; we were married the very next year. Many romances have started at the parade."

"Green," mouths Rose behind her back, puts her finger in her mouth and pretends to vomit.

When Mrs. Rendell stands up, she leaves a mark behind on her vinyl chair and a hot musty odor trails her whispering nylons.

"Green would have suited you," says Pearl.

"Look at these," says Mrs. Rendell, holding out a magazine full of dresses. "I got it today. It might give you some ideas."

"Thanks," says Pearl.

"Actually, Mrs. Rendell, I'm more interested in making out with your son," says Rose under her breath as they walk toward the book exchange.

"Shush," says Pearl.

Paul isn't behind his desk. That seems to unnerve Pearl. She giggles, whispers, "Hello." Rose watches her, the way she clutches the book to her chest.

"Pearlie," comes a voice from the far aisle. "It's been days and days."

"I've been busy," says Pearl.

Rose rolls her eyes.

"Doing exciting things like getting lost up at Weeping Rock, I heard."

"Who told you that?"

"Small town," he replies.

"I hate this town," says Pearl.

"Tell me about your adventure?"

Pearl doesn't go toward his voice. She stands where she is, leans back against the books, closes her eyes, a conversation through a confessional. Rose sits on the floor and starts to pick through a box filled with ancient magazines.

"We didn't get lost," says Pearl. "It was just we left it too late to come back down. There wasn't a very good path."

"At the Rock?" he asks.

"Not exactly," says Pearl.

"Where, then?"

Rose shoots her an angry warning glance.

"A secret place," says Pearl.

"A secret place?" he says.

Rose hears his footsteps in the shop; he looms up at the end of the aisle, glances at Rose, swallows up Pearl with his eyes.

"Tell me," he says. "I might know it. I used to walk up there a lot when I was a boy."

"It wouldn't be a secret place, then, would it?" says Pearl.

She's tucking her big hair behind her ears, looking away from him. Rose watches Paul Rendell's face break open into a smile. His huge white teeth appear.

"I always liked Weeping Rock; I go there a bit still, just for the walk, good exercise." He gives Pearl a book. "I found this one for you; I think you'll like it, lots of castles and brooding princes, et cetera."

"Et cetera?" says Pearl, this time returning his gaze.

She hands *Ashes in the Wind* to him.

"Thoughts?" he asks, holding it up a little.

"I liked Cole," says Pearl. "He turned me on."

Silence. Rose turns the pages of a gardening magazine from 1966, Pearl laughs and Paul laughs in return. He has backed away from her. There is sweet relief in the air.

"You're a rascal, Pearl Kelly," he says, and he is a man again and Pearl is just a girl.

"See you, then," says Pearl.

She's gone so quickly that Rose, surprised, is left piling the magazines back into the box. Rose doesn't catch up with her until she's past fat sweaty old Mrs. Rendell, who looks over her glasses, shaking her head. By the time Rose makes it outside, Pearl is already on the footpath in front of Hommel's, trying to slow her breathing. She has a hand over her heart.

"What?" says Rose.

"I've done something," says Pearl.

"What?"

"Remember you told me that story up at the house? The one about the secret pocket and the secret letter."

"I thought you were asleep," says Rose. Then it dawns on her. "Oh God, you didn't, Pearl?"

"I did," she replies.

The problem with Pearl Kelly is she thinks the whole world is one big romance novel. She thinks love is the only important thing. She thinks everyone is just waiting for the one big moment when they fall in love. Fall. Why is it falling in love? Falling implies an injury or a trap. Splatting, slamming, plummeting. Rose thinks she couldn't stand to feel like that, all nervous and butterfly fidgety, all pale and swooning.

"Rose," says Pearl on the street, still hardly breathing.

"What?"

"Do you think I've done the wrong thing?"

"Of course you have," says Rose, and leaves her there.

But even when Rose says these things to Pearl, even when she is as mean as she can be, Pearl just chews a nail and smiles back, says, "Oh, Rose." Calls after her, "Ruby Heart Rose, don't be like that."

$\mathscr{B}$lind Hem Stitch ⸺⸺⸺⸺

Glass is trying to catch him up. He's circling him like a shark with his words. "So you're hanging around these two young girls, right, and you go up the hill with them for what, for a bit of exercise? I know you like to keep fit? So is that what you are trying to tell me, you're in it only for the bush-walking?"

"It's not like that," says Paul Rendell.

The two other officers are motionless in the room. One leaning against the wall. Another seated. The seated one has pressed the play button on the tape recorder.

"Anyway, then later, dance night, what, you're feeling a little jilted, are you? Harvest Parade, all the girls sparkling and pretty but not one single one of them for you. So what did you do? Follow her? Is that what you did?"

"No."

"Did you drink? Smoke a few cones? It hurt. It hurt, didn't it, to be dumped like that? Made you feel terrible. Were you feeling terrible?"

"Am I meant to have a lawyer or something here?" asks Rendell.

"We're just having a little chat, aren't we? Man to man." Glass looks to the other officers for their agreement. They nod. "I know what these young girls are like," Glass says, conspiratorial. "They don't know their own power. They're sending out all these signals. They smell, they smell so fresh. They're giving you the come-on, then turning you away. They're driving you crazy."

Paul Rendell, he's putting his head in his hands.

"You've got it all wrong, mate," he says. "You've got it all wrong."

"Yeah, yeah, yeah," says Glass.

He's heard it all a thousand times before. He's close. Glass can feel the fracture line beneath his fingers; he's nearly got him, nearly broken him, it won't be long now.

"You were gone again last night," says Rose's father when she gets home. He's gutting a fish, his hands trembling slightly. "That's twice in a week. I'm getting worried."

"Yeah, right," says Rose.

"No really, I'm serious. I'm thinking this dressmaking caper might just be some kind of cover for a boyfriend."

"It's not."

He looks at her. She hates it when he looks at her like that, as though he cares a fig. It will be such a relief when he drinks again. Why is it taking him so long? It will be like taking a step back from a cliff edge. She will relax. He won't be wound so tight.

"What I'm trying to say is, if it's a boyfriend, there's stuff we should talk about, that's all."

"I know what you're saying and I don't need any of those talks."

"Rose," he says.

"What?"

"Nothing, I just like saying your name sometimes."

"Well, don't."

They're treading water. That's what it feels like.

Inside she opens his sketchbook and moves through the pages. There are no more drawings of Pearl. There's a fish, a caravan with dragon wings, the drawing of a hand.

"Not drawing Pearl anymore?" she says by the campfire.

"I couldn't get her right," he says.

He shouldn't have been trying. Rose doesn't say it; she sits in her canvas chair and begins to reapply black paint to her nails.

"I think it's the heat," he says after a while, "and the rain that drives you a bit balmy here."

She would like to keep needling him except there's the sound of high heels on gravel and Mrs. Lamond is coming toward them in her best Lycra, her face painted up like a clown. Mrs. Lamond comes almost every night. She brings a thermos and two coffee cups. Her mouth puckers like a drawstring around her smokes. She looks pleased as punch.

"How's that dress of yours going?" she asks.

"Good," says Rose, standing up. She picks up her backpack, climbs onto her bike.

She keeps her face motionless as a mask.

"I'll stay at Miss Baker's tonight," she says.

"Suit yourself," he says.

"They've started burning the cane," says Rose.

From the rusty bike she saw a whole field of it ablaze. The

evening air was alive with the chatter of parrots; black ash fell like snow.

"I saw it," says Edie. "It's the McDonalds; they're fools, go too early each year. We've got more rain to come."

"How do you know?"

"Ants," says Edie.

"Okay," says Rose. "If you say so."

She opens the windows for Edie, then takes her chair at the table.

"Will the dress be ready in time?" she asks.

Only four skirt panels have been sewn; the rest is in pieces.

"If we work hard, yes," Edie replies.

Rose threads her needle to begin on the skirt panels while Edie takes up the bodice again. She's making bones from wire coat hangers, which she cuts with tin snips, the wire hidden inside secret pockets, cotton wool at either end. Rose watches Edie work and is amazed at the deftness of her fingers, which are old and liver-spotted and swollen.

"Did it take long to get over that boy?" Rose asks. "The one you were going to run away with."

The house creaks, groans, strains, listens.

"Yes," says Edie. "It took a while."

It seems an unnaturally short answer for Edie, whose stories unravel into the kitchen hour after hour.

"And?" says Rose.

"My mother, she fed me, helped me wash, made me do small jobs, little things like hems and buttonholes. When you are in love, you think nothing will ever be the same, but then the tide rushes out and there it is, everything, just as it was. I didn't go back to school; my schooling was finished. I'd never felt very good there. I wasn't really like the other girls. I hadn't been and now I certainly wasn't. Somehow they all knew, all of them, they whispered it: 'She thought she was going to marry Luke Grace.

"'Remember the house,' they would say, 'the magnificent house, before that dressmaker came and married Jonathan Baker and brought the whole place to ruin?' My father, it was said, had been spotted from time to time on the roads down south, yes. Mrs. Adsett, who had family in Melbourne and went there once every two years for three months, said she saw him near the turnoff to the Goodnight Scrub, thin as a whip, just standing there, swaying in the breeze, and when they stopped the car, he had peered in as though he'd never seen humans before. Yes, that would be my father. That was exactly how he looked. Mrs. Adsett had squeezed five bob into his hand, quite a lot in those days, and said, 'God bless you and keep you safe.' This was just one of the stories. Why should my mother sit in the old house and make wedding dresses while her husband was off wandering the countryside, a swaggie?

"My mother didn't take her supplies at Mr. Grace's shop anymore; she had to order them from away. At first there were still dresses to be made but not as many from the town. One wedding dress in the whole of 1934. It had a rayon underskirt, white lace with matching veil. The sweetest thing you ever saw. We thought the curse might be broken but it wasn't. There were confirmation dresses; I could do those myself with my eyes closed. Then they petered out. Word spread, I suppose.

"One yellow party dress for Miss Elizabeth Sharp at the beginning of 1935. She was the new schoolteacher from away so didn't know the town stories yet and saw our advertisement on a card in Hommel's window. Soon after that it was taken down. She was happy enough with the dress but it was the last.

"My mother had taught me everything there was to know about the making of a dress. She showed me pin tucks and box pleats, she taught me standard yokes and double yokes, and she taught me the many ways of sleeves. We sat all day, every day, sewing. We had a Singer treadle then, and when there were no more dresses, she took a job making ham bags for the Olssons' piggery and also patchwork, she was very good at that, and she could make curtains out of feed sacks and dresses too, so that you wouldn't even notice; she was clever that way and enough to keep us in food. All the while I practiced. And all the while the forest spoke to us into the long empty silences of the afternoon.

"There is a place, it said, a creek with a glittering edge, where the sun falls down off a rock in the late afternoon.

"There is a waterfall, it said, that weeps into an endless pool. It's known to very few.

"Go away, we thought, can't you see we're busy?

"The sun crossed over the house, and sideboards cast long shadows across the floor. The sewing machine said *dig dig dig dig dig* and the treadle counted the endless seconds of the long minutes of the long hours. Until finally we couldn't wait anymore; we jumped up and threw whatever we were working on across the back of a chair and ran down the back stairs through the waving paddock.

"'It has a hold on us,' I remember my mother saying. 'It has us.'

"Which is one way to put it, I suppose.

"The forest sighed high up in the canopy and cast down its leaves. We breathed in the watery air as though we had never breathed before, listened to the barrel and thud of water on rocks like hearing a great heart.

"'We're coming because we choose to come,' I said.

"We never walked the well-worn paths taken by the day-trippers from Cairns, with their sun hats and picnic baskets, who shouted over the edges of falls, loud and exaggerated cooees, we walked the old ways to the hut and other places. We walked on leaves and climbed over rocks and picked our way along creek beds. We followed them upward until they disappeared into stone.

"We found places, sudden places, where the sun lit up the leaves like silver snow, a stand of gums with trunks like the legs of giants. Hidden valleys, solemn and hushed.

"These were the things we collected, Rose. Red leaves. The topaz tamarind, the white passion fruit. The black shells of the rhinoceros beetle, the golden shells of the scarab. Feathers, the emerald-green feathers of the wompoo pigeon, were our prized possessions. Not the kind of things we could speak of in polite company.

"These are the jewels we kept without ever saying why we did—we didn't talk of such things—and we saw sleeping snakes as long as two men, and we saw places where the sun shone straight down in a prism of light, and my mother once stood in such a place and said, 'What if I could just disappear?' and she was half gone from the place before I pulled her out.

"When we came down again, it was always dusk and the house would be in shadows and filled with atlas moths that burst from the walls and flapped madly when we arrived. We would light the hurricane lamps and open up the windows to hear the mountain, as though we couldn't bear to be apart from it. We would sit down, wait for the full breadth of darkness to come.

"We smelt of green, the spiky scent of sap, the tickle of flowers. My mother put the kettle on and combed the leaves from her hair. I washed myself, standing naked beneath the tank stand.

"Rose, we were already turned half wild."

"Do you want to try something a little more exciting?" Edie asks, holding up the black mourning lace sleeves.

"What do I have to do?"

"Sewing lace is difficult but I'm sure you can do it. I'll show you how."

The lace is patterned with roses, heavy in her hands, lustrous even after all the years. Edie shows Rose how to match the pieces, allowing a seam. She must follow the motif and then they will trim the excess.

"Do you understand?"

"Not really."

"Wait, we'll practice on some old lace curtains first."

Rose would have argued once. She would have touched her hair angrily, checking pins. But instead she feels an escaped tendril of her hair tickling her cheek; she blows at it absentmindedly while Edie disappears down the hall looking for curtains.

"Joining lace always makes me think of spiders spinning webs," says Edie when she returns.

Rose is starting to see the dress now. While she practices, Edie pins the skirt panels back onto the mannequin and attaches the front and back of the boned bodice. The dress shines by the light of a hurricane lamp, it's coming alive, it had been nothing before and now it swings dangerously dark against the night, against the window, it hushes against the floor.

Edie looks at the girl looking at the dress.

She looks softer. Her eyes are not so huge or sorrowful. She's not so skinny; her cheekbones have filled out. Climbing has been good for her; she knew it would be.

"What?" says Rose, catching the old woman's gaze.

"What?" says Edie in return.

"You were staring at me," says Rose.

"I was just thinking, that's all, how healthy you look. You've put on condition."

Rose shrugs.

"You'll be the belle of the ball," says Edie.

"Unlikely," says Rose.

"Do you know that when I first held this taffeta, all those years ago, yours was the dress I saw inside of it, but I didn't make it."

Rose shivers.

"You still never told me about the dress you made, how it got so ripped."

"Well, we're nearly up to that bit."

Rose joins the two pieces of lace curtain. It's a mess. A horrible mess.

"You're not following the petals," says Edie. "Start again."

"Tell me the story," says Rose.

"One day a telegram came," says Edie into the quiet. "It was from the police in Brisbane asking what to do with my father's remains. My mother went to the exchange and made a phone call to find out the conditions of his death, which were reported as exposure. They gave the number of the funeral parlor where he was lying and she phoned them to arrange the costs of his burial and to ask if a suit was needed. She asked for his measurements; he was thin, terribly thin, nothing but skin and bones, less than thirty at the waist and thirty-six at the chest, despite his height. That was my father, who I never knew, who never held me in his arms, not once. And all the while the telephonist sat in the corner pretending not to listen.

"'She didn't cry a tear, the old witch,' I can imagine she said, or something to that effect. 'Not a single tear.'

"But she didn't see how my mother made that suit. How she spent all day patternmaking and cutting, then sewed the whole night. She wouldn't let me do anything to make that suit; I just waited, and when it was sent in the parcel at the post office, the word had already spread that the man of the old Baker house had died, been found dead in a park, and that his wife had only asked for his measurements. The women turned away from her on the street. She was served in shops without a single word.

"'Perhaps you should go now' is what my mother said to me. 'Go to a bigger town and learn things your own way. You could get a job as a seamstress anywhere.'

"'I don't want to leave you' is what I said.

"In Brisbane, I had trouble with my hearing. I was dizzy with all the commotion, the scrape and screaming of the trams and the ferries' slicing up of the river. I had a little room above a draper's, and each time the trains passed through Central Station, the walls shook and the bed rattled. I stayed there for two months and then went to work at the munitions factory at Rocklea. It was boring work but the women there were good and they took me under their wing. I went to the dances at Cloudland to keep them happy and I danced with the soldiers. I wrote letters to my mother and she didn't often write back to me. It was as she said it would be.

"She'd said, 'Edith Emerald Baker, we have started something here that needs undoing,' and she pointed to the house that was falling down around us and out the window at the mountain. She meant a spell, a spell that place had cast over us; that was what she wanted broken by turning me away.

"But these things aren't easily undone, Rose.

"I didn't marry, although I was asked again, by Peter Hansen himself, who was serving in the navy and actually didn't look too bad in his sailor suit. Now, it was him who ripped my dress. It's a strange way for someone to ask you to marry them, I know.

"I made the dress at Lowood House, which was a hostel for country girls, and there was one old machine on the second floor. I made all the girls dresses there. They brought me the fabric and the patterns.

"I held the stuff in my hands. The daisy-print voile, the green poplin, which was very popular in those years; I think there must have been whole warehouses somewhere filled with it. I held the fabric in my hands and saw other dresses, magnificent dresses, but I didn't mention them. I followed the patterns and made the dresses they wanted.

"I found this material in a small shop in Ipswich, touched it, saw your dress shimmering there. 'Navy,' said the girls, raising their eyebrows when I arrived home. 'Indigo,' I said. 'Unusual choice,' they said. 'There's something about it, that's all,' I replied.

"I used Vogue pattern number 6601 with the cape collar, of course. Ignored the dress I saw.

"I borrowed another girl's black heels.

"Peter Hansen danced with me half the night. He had desperate eyes. He was due to leave in two days. He said, 'Come outside with me, I need to talk to you.' So I did.

"'We'll get married,' he said. 'Tomorrow. The chaplain can do it.'

"I said, 'I don't want to get married.'

"He said, 'Don't be stupid.' Couldn't believe his ears. I went to leave but he grabbed me by the skirt. That was the first rip, right there. He was always very strong. It's quite hard to rip silk taffeta, you know. 'Look what you've done,' I said. He said, 'Marry me.' I said, 'Don't be stupid.' He said, 'Who else is going to marry you?'

"I went to go inside but he caught me and I fell on the grass, which was wet, and that was the top separated from the skirt. Two other men came running when I screamed. I had to go home like that. He drowned, you know, went down with a ship, which I'm sorry for. No one deserves that type of death.

"After the war we danced in the streets. I was over thirty by then. I took the Sunshine Express from Roma Street to Leonora. The land unfurled, the towns raced past and disappeared.

"In the house there was only silence. Moths flew from the cupboards, shadows the size of birds. My mother was so small and faded I barely knew her. She didn't have long to live. She touched my face with her trembling hands.

" 'Yes' was what she said.

"All she could say was 'Yes.' "

Cross-Stitch ━━━━━━━━━

I can't show you the tree where Paul Rendell hanged himself. There are no pictures of it, not in the Post or anywhere else. It's not the sort of thing they display. In the articles the tree is only mentioned in passing, an extra in the drama, a bit player. "A thirty-year-old Leonora man was found hanging from a tree branch on the main track to Weeping Rock," it read. The headline was MAN IN MISSING GIRL CASE DIES.

There would be certain criteria for choosing a tree for such a job. It couldn't be just any tree; it needed to be climbable, it needed the right sort of limbs. In the rain forest, trees stretch themselves all the way to the canopy, thirty, forty, fifty meters or more, before laying out branches. Paul Rendell needed a reachable limb, something sturdy, straight, reliable.

Did he take his time deciding such things? Did he walk this way and that searching? Does a tree stand out in these situations, present itself to those despairing eyes? It must have been lower, that tree, somewhere near the first car park, one of the introduced camphor laurels, in clear view of everyone.

He felt cold. That was what he said to his mother after the splinter entered his eye. "What do you mean, cold?" Mrs. Rendell said. "I mean cold, like my bones are cold." "Well, that just doesn't make any sense," she replied.

By the time he came home from the police station in the night, there were already several news reports that in a far north Queensland town a man was assisting police with their investigations into the missing girl case. Outside the doors to the tiny station a crowd had gathered.

"Get out of here, you lot," Officer Williams had snarled at them while Paul hung his head.

They had not jeered or shouted, that crowd, but their whispers droned, a nest of angry hornets. Someone threw a Coke bottle, hit Paul square on the nose.

"Jesus," he said.

His mother had waited up for his return, was certain he'd return. She came huffing down the stairs when she heard the back door open but he walked past her as though she wasn't there at all. Put his keys on the counter. He went and sat behind his desk in the Blue Moon Book Exchange. Put his head back in his hands.

Car Park No. 1 can accommodate forty cars. It says that in the brochure Walks Around Leonora. Although there are never that many. It's always nearly empty, a desolate sort of car park where car doors shutting echo and voices seem louder than they really are. There is parking space for one bus. It was exactly seventeen days after the Harvest Parade.

The bus was from Townsville, chartered by the Twin City Rambling Society. It would have been a terrible thing for them, most of them being old, ready with their gaiters and their aluminum walking poles. Their thermoses, their lightweight backpacks. It was a tree at the edge of the car park clearing; yes, it must have been. Maybe he looked higher, went on the paths, that would have been more romantic, but then came back down and did what was practical. Still, the car park always seemed such a tawdry choice.

He wore his Leonora Lions jersey and jeans. His sandshoes. His hands hung by his sides, choice made, palms hidden. The rope, heavy-duty nylon cord, yellow, festive-looking, available from any hardware shop. He swung slightly. He turned his purple face to the car park, then away again, purple face to the car park, away again, some terrible tree ornament.

"Lord," said one of the first to alight from the bus.

There was no note. Not in his jeans pockets, not in his car, which was in the car park, a small blue secondhand Sigma, locked. Not in his bedroom in the house of his childhood, his football trophies still on the wall, not in the small book exchange filled with dusty romance novels. For all his words, his honey-smooth, carefully chosen words, his radio-announcer voice, in the end he had nothing to say.

It's a summer of air, a summer of toeholds, a summer of trees. Rose knows each of them as she goes, touching them with her hands. She knows all the rocks as well, their slightest movement beneath her sandshoes; crossing the gully is like dancing, she knows each stepping-stone. She thinks about Edith Emerald Baker. How she must miss it now, long for the singing creeks and the secrets of the trees. Was that why she collected and kept so much from the place? All the leaves rotting in boxes and white cedar flowers pressed behind paper. All the powdery remains of firewheel blossoms and climbing lilies, like dying stars, withering. The quiet vases filled to the brim with quandongs, gully walnuts, startling flashes of crimson berries.

Rose stops and looks down at her face in the water, her hair tied back in two long ponytails, that's all, not a single pin. Fire red. Pearl smiles at her reflection. It is the second time they have been there together.

Pearl wears a feverish intense expression. Her face has been this way for the last week, permanently flushed, permanently lovesick. She flings herself back into chairs, weak-limbed, stares right through people when they speak. Her notes as secretary of the Harvest Parade Float Committee of Leonora High have grown sloppy. At their last meeting she sat at the head of the table but her mind kept drifting.

Weekend: working bee to paint canvas fruit?

Organize trial run on back of Mr. Harvey's truck?

Question: will fruit even fit?

Everything was unsolved. Everything unsolvable.

She seems puzzled by her own actions. "I can't believe I did it," she says, "put that note in the book, handed it to him. Stared at him right in the eyes. He knew, I know he knew. He mightn't find it," she says. "Of course he'll find it," she says. He would find it. He mightn't find it. He would find it. What if someone else found it? There it was, her name, Pearlie, signed in fluorescent highlighter, lemon sorbet.

"What the hell did you write to him?" Rose asks after they have navigated the fallen tree. She really doesn't want to know.

"I wrote him a poem," says Pearl.

"Oh God," says Rose.

Pearl is good at lots of things, netball, softball, cross-country, doing her hair in a way that looks as if she hasn't done it at all, peeling minty wrappers into tiny ribbons, shading eye makeup, making large fiberglass fruit; Rose doesn't think poetry is one of them.

"I didn't write it," says Pearl. "Don't worry. I copied it out of a book."

"Okay," says Rose, wondering which one she might have chosen. Hoping she didn't dot the *i*'s with love hearts.

At the hut Pearl takes a small dustpan and brush from her backpack and sweeps the new leaves out. She holds up a Jif bottle and sets about recleaning the glass windows. Rose shakes her head, goes and sits at the edge of the falls.

"You know how I like things to be," says Pearl once they are sitting on the blanket that she has brought.

"Just perfect," says Rose.

They sit on the blanket and the shadows of the trees move on the walls. The water barrels over the waterfall.

"I think we'll be leaving soon," says Rose.

"Don't say that," says Pearl.

"I know it; it's the way Dad gets. He's wound up."

"But you said you wouldn't go with him," says Pearl. "That night we stayed up here."

"I can't believe you were awake but not answering me."

"I just wanted to hear you talk. You never talk."

Rose doesn't know what to say to that.

"Why doesn't he just go and you stay?" says Pearl. "You could stay with us until the end of the school year and then he could come back and pick you up."

Rose tries to imagine herself living in Pearl and Pattie's little house behind the shop. All the tinkling of crystals and wind chimes and the cane trains shunting all night in and out of the mill yards.

"We could make up the trundle next to my bed," says Pearl. "You can't go, Rose."

"I'm only saying, that's all," says Rose. "It's just a feeling."

"You said it yourself you didn't want to stay with him."

"I can't imagine my dad on his own."

"He'll have to be one day," says Pearl. "I mean, you won't live with him forever, will you, going round and round the country?"

"No," says Rose.

"Rose," Pearl says breathlessly.

"What?"

"I need you to do something for me. You have to go to the book exchange and see what he does. See if he asks where I am."

"I have to?"

"Please," says Pearl. "You know I'd do anything for you."

Rose can't think of anything worse. Paul Rendell's book exchange by herself. Walking past old Mrs. Rendell with her Japanese fan in her left hand, pushing open the bamboo-print curtain, entering that sticky, lonely space.

"I couldn't," says Rose. "Really, I just couldn't stand going there by myself."

Pearl is silent for some time, and when she finally speaks, it's the angriest Rose has ever heard her.

"You don't understand anything, Rose," she says. "You've never even kissed a boy."

"Fuck off, I have," says Rose.

Pearl ignores her. She puts the dustpan and brush back in her backpack, the bottle of Jif. She undoes her hair and twirls it in a loop on top of her head, looks out at the falls.

"You haven't," Pearl says.

There is nothing left to say; they sit in silence. Finally Pearl smiles.

"I'll do it," says Rose.

"Promise me," says Pearl. "Promise me, I'm dying."

The day is airy, blustery, a big southeaster rattles the storefronts. The streets are busy, busier than Rose has ever seen them, with the arrival of workers for the crush. The barracks have been opened, the rooms swept out, the mill has grumbled to life and belched a dark plume into the sky. Cane ash spins in eddies on Main Street.

Rose doesn't want to go in. To leave such a bright day and go down the aisles in the news agency, past scowling Mrs. Rendell, through the curtains, it's like climbing into a snake hole.

Paul Rendell is perfectly respectable to look at, perfectly clean with shining white teeth, but inside he is the color of a toad. Everything he says is perfectly measured, teaspoon after teaspoon of perfect words, not a single *um* or a single *ah*.

Rose doesn't look at any magazines. Old Mrs. Rendell watches her as she goes past. Rose feels her eyes. She goes into the book exchange and straight to a row of books, not looking around, concentrating on the spines, breathe, breathe, breathe.

Something has changed.

There is something different in the mold-speckled romance-novel air.

"You're Pearl's friend, aren't you?" says Mrs. Rendell right behind her.

"God, you scared the life out of me," says Rose.

"You didn't hear me say the exchange isn't manned now," says Mrs. Rendell. "Paul's gone to work at the mill. It's that time of year. Everyone works there. I said it but you just kept walking right past me."

"Sorry," says Rose. "I didn't hear you."

"You young girls can't hear anything nowadays. No, there's no one running the place; Paul's at the mill. He started Monday. His father wouldn't believe it, he'll be jumping up and down in the grave. Paul, who said he'd never do a crush, too below him. He hurt his eye, he got a splinter in it, but the doctor wouldn't give him a certificate. Anyways, that's why I have to ask you to leave your bag at the front if you're coming in here. You'd be surprised how much gets stolen. Oh, nearly forgot, he left something at the front with me in case Pearl came in, says it's one she'll probably like. Will you be seeing her?"

"Yes," whispers Rose.

"What?" says Mrs. Rendell.

"Yes," says Rose.

Pearl is lying back on her bed when Rose enters. She has flung herself there and cried into her hands.

"Oh God," she says when she sees the book Rose holds. "Oh God, oh God, oh God."

Rose gives her the book. Pearl takes it and holds it as if it could easily shatter into a million pieces, as if it isn't just *The*

Captive Heart, which looks old, tattered, which should be trashed. Rose turns to go.

"Don't," says Pearl.

She goes through the pages one by one. Slowly. Looking. When she finds the message, she gasps, lies down holding the book over her face, kicking her legs.

"What does it say?"

Pearl reads, "'Come to me in my dreams, and then by day I shall be well again. For so the night will more than pay the hopeless longing of the day.'"

Rose takes the novel, looks at the words printed in pencil in the margin of page two hundred and one. He has very plain handwriting, for all his suave words; his handwriting is like simple wooden furniture. He hasn't signed his name. There is no *PAUL* written after the poem. He isn't game to sign his name. There's nothing else.

"Maybe he didn't write it," says Rose.

"Oh, he did," says Pearl.

"I think you have to stop this now," says Rose.

"Why?"

"Because it's freaking me out."

Pearl laughs.

She doesn't say it's a game this time.

"I can't," she says.

"Please," says Rose.

$\mathcal{D}$ouble Cross-Stitch ━━━━━

Afterward he crouches beside her, black. It's impossible that she's dead. Impossible. He has pulled her back as she tried to leave. That's all. Once. She's so light. That's what surprises him, as if she's made of nothing; the dress slips through his fingers and she starts to turn again. She's laughing.

Then again. He's laughing as well but he's angry too. Not surface anger. There's a towline, suddenly snapped taut, inside him. If she'd just stop still, he could explain it to her. Who he is. What he means. But none of it makes sense. She's moving faster now, starting to run; he's grabbed a handful of her dress and she's falling. Heavily to earth, head to stones, not moving. The dress settles around her, a dark cloud. That's all it takes.

He thinks in frantic bursts. She isn't dead. She can't be. "Are you asleep?" he asks her. He looks into her eyes but they look past him at the sky.

He carries her. She's not easy to carry. She melts over his arms. He wants to scream but he doesn't until he is in the car with his windows rolled down, out on the beach road. He howls. That's the word for it. He doesn't want to leave her out in the elements. It seems wrong. He tries to shut her eyes but cannot shut them; it's nothing like in the movies. He's sobbing then. "Oh God. Fucking Jesus Christ, oh God." His words ring through the trees. He carries her on the tracks in the dark.

"Come on," he says. "Just wake up."

He slides with her, tumbles down through the vines. There are two rocks close together with a tight space between them, dark. He shoves her head up into that space and tries to push her body in after. "Come on, come on," he says. It's the dress. It's slippery fucking stuff, whatever that dress is made of. He really didn't mean it. Not any of it. "I didn't mean it," he says to her, smoothing back her hair. Giving up with the little cave.

He piles up sticks. He can see in the dark. He has carried the girl farther through the brush. Slung over his shoulder. He has never felt so strong. He keeps spotting more and more branches he can use. He builds a cairn of sticks over the top of her. He wants to protect her from the light rain that has started to fall.

She'll stay dry under the sticks until she is found. All he cares about is that she stays dry. He laughs lying on his side, at that irrational thought, then sits up. But when the sun starts to rise, he presses the balls of his hands to his eyes and cries like a little boy.

"Hello, Tolstoy," says her father. He's taken to calling Rose that. "What you writing?"

"None of your business."

That makes him laugh.

"You're either off sewing with your fairy godmother or writing in that little green book," he says. "Must be a good story."

"It's not a story."

"This harvest thing sounds like a bit of a caper," he says. "They do it in all these old towns, Elaine says, floats and everything, dancing in the streets."

"I'm going to be on the bowl-of-fruit float," says Rose.

"I'll have to get a photo," he says.

They have an old Fotomatic, have had it for as long as Rose can remember. It sits above the fridge, spews out photos that develop slowly in their hands. Photos of the sky and of cemetery headstones and blurry photos of her father, which Rose must have taken when she was small, standing in some now-indistinct place, his eyes closed against the sun. There are pictures of Rose, small Rose, red hair looping across her face, Rose in a range of school uniforms, sullen Rose, angry Rose.

"Are you going to come, then?" she asks.

"Of course," he says. "I wouldn't miss it for the world."

She narrows her eyes.

"What?"

"Nothing," she says.

"Why isn't a father allowed to watch his daughter in a nice dress on a float and in a parade or whatever the hell it is?"

"I didn't say anything," she says.

Pearl gives nothing away of her plans. Pearl, who can never keep her mouth shut. Pearl, who can never keep a secret. In French she dreamily highlights whole slabs of text in aquamarine.

"Do you want to go to the house," Rose whispers, "tomorrow or Sunday?"

"I can't," says Pearl. "I have to go to Cairns for a fitting and to pick up the shoes. And then we're staying the night."

"Oh," says Rose.

"Promise me you won't go without me, Rose, swear it."

Rose looks at her for a long time.

"I won't," she says.

"Promise," says Pearl. "You have to promise."

"I promise," says Rose.

After Ancient History, Murray says he'll take Rose out in the boat again. He knows other places. He knows the islands like the back of his hand. "We could even go out to the reef. Do you like snorkeling? We'll go out there on Saturday."

"Do I look like I like snorkeling?" says Rose. She's wearing a black crucifix with her uniform. Her lips are painted a deep mauve.

"You don't have to come," he says. "I'm just saying, that's all."

"And I wouldn't go out to the reef anyway, not in that thing; we'd drown for sure. It's a heap of shit."

"God, you're a moody bitch."

"Don't say that," she says. "I'm not."

"You're so dark," he says in a vampire voice, "and so dangerous."

Yet on Saturday she trails her fingers in the water as Murray steers the boat out into the open water. The sea holds the sky, or the sky holds the sea; it's difficult to tell. On the water the whole world is slippery, shiny, made of glass. When they are stopped at the perfect cove, she looks at her own face there, very solemn, hideously freckled. After the cove he takes her to another beach, a long slice of perfect white sand.

"They're going to build something here," Murray says. "Some bloke's bought all the land. A resort or something."

"Is there a road?"

"Not yet, but there will be. They just have to buy a whole heap of cane farms and bulldoze some rain forest."

Just the thought of it hurts her. All those cool, calm places she has seen. She can't imagine those places crushed, split open, exposed to the sun.

"What?" he says.

"Nothing," she replies.

He takes the boat up into the shallows and they climb out onto the stretch. It's a white-hot day; she pulls her hat down hard over her eyes. Murray is wearing a terry cloth hat; he takes it off and wipes his face with it. They climb up into the shade of the palms.

"What are you going to do after school?" he asks.

"What do you mean?" says Rose.

"I mean what do you want to be?"

"Shit, I don't know," she says. "Free?"

He shakes his head.

"I'm going to do science," he says.

"That'll be fun."

"Shut up."

She likes him. She really does.

"What's it like to have a bird in your name?" she asks.

"Once we were, like, the king's men that kept the hunting birds," he says, "a long time ago."

"I'd like to have a bird in my name. I'd be Rose Blackbird."

"The fairest girl in all the world," he says.

"Don't say that," she says.

"It was only a joke."

Is that the sky she feels inside her? The trembling of the seasons? Would she wait all day in the heat and the rain to run away with him? She looks at him from the corner of her eye. He looks at her. Then they both smile out at the sea.

PROMISES, that's what Rose writes in her notebook as the sun comes up. It's a stupid word. The first part round and pompous and plummy, the second half a hiss, a snake whisper. She writes the word three times, then: PROMISES ARE IMPOSSIBLE TO KEEP WHEN THE DAY IS GOOD FOR CLIMBING.

Patrick Lovell is up already. She hears him rifling through his fishing stuff. He hardly sleeps when he's on the wagon. Last night Mrs. Lamond visited and they laughed into the small hours, laughter fueled by coffee. Rose wonders if Mrs. Lamond stays in the caravan when she's at Edie's house. She thought she caught a whiff of her the morning before. Her fish-and-chips scent mixed with floral eau de cologne. She wouldn't put it past her father. There've been others they've left behind in other towns, their faces fuzzy now in her memory. Tina with her hippy handbag. Jo with her bare feet, the old purple scars on her arms, her worried expression as though she'd forgotten something. Something important, like who she was.

They'd left them all behind. Flown the coop.

She puts the notebook away. Opens the blinds beside her bed with two fingers. There isn't a cloud in the sky. She slips out of bed, slides into her climbing shorts, sticks her feet into her Dunlops, throws a T-shirt over her head. Maybe she'll stop to say hello to Edie and maybe she won't. It's perfect climbing weather, no matter what she promised Pearl. Anyway, she'll never know. She'll be too busy worrying about Paul Rendell's love note, holding it close to her, pressing it to her lips.

In Edie's back paddock she doesn't stop. She looks at the house and the ruins of Granny Baker's chair, which still sits in the middle of the sloping field, the newly dried-off grass waving through its frame. She wonders if Edie is watching her; she always seems to know if anyone is there. It's as though she has roots herself that stretch out beneath the house, up the hill, into the forest, sensing whoever comes that way.

Rose shrugs away the thought.

In the first stream she finds a pink pebble and she reaches through the clear water to retrieve it. It's perfectly round and smooth. She decides almost immediately that she'll give it to Pearl. It's a Pearl kind of stone. Pearl will hold it in her hands, say, "What made it this color? I'll show it to Mum, it must be some kind of mineral, but how did it end up there, there aren't really any other pink stones, I love it, Rose, it's just so beautiful." She will add it to her box of beautiful things, necklaces that boyfriends have given her and friendship bands and invitations and now Paul Rendell's love note torn from the romance novel, folded, pressed into a perfect square.

Rose hears the voices as she carries the pink stone up through the trees.

There is another thirty minutes of climbing before she will reach the hut but already she can hear them, snatches of their conversation, a scrap of laughter drifting down. She stops still on the track. A fragment of something deeper, a man's voice, reaches her ears.

It can't be.

She starts to walk again. Quietly. Her heart thudding in her ears. She can hear the water a way off, the voices disappearing and reappearing, the forest playing games with her. It holds the voices, then throws them down like confetti through the trees. Pearl's clear voice, suddenly magnified. Her laughter, the echo of her laughter.

When Rose finally rounds the corner, she sees them there. Paul Rendell sits on the flat rock beside the hut, where he should not be. He's a blight on the landscape. He is shirtless, his pale skin stretched tight across his shoulders and chest. He is staring at Pearl, who stands in front of him, her hair unbound. He is dipping his head to her breast; Pearl is leaning away. Rose's foot touches a twig. The pink pebble falls through her fingers.

"Oh my God!" shouts Pearl, turning. "What are you doing here?"

It's a terrible question. It was Rose who had shown her the place, given it to her like a gift. Pearl is pulling down her tank top, wrapping her hair up, crossing her arms, shaking her head in disbelief.

Paul Rendell is the calm one. He looks at Rose, smiles. He looks, Rose thinks, disappointed, unsatisfied, but also a little scared. He is calculating ahead. Fucking stupid spotty ugly girl with the red hair; see, she can almost read his mind the way he looks at her. Then he smiles his broadest smile and reaches for his shirt.

"What are *you* doing here?" whispers Rose finally. Later she is not even sure she spoke.

"It's not just your place; you don't own the whole forest, Rose," Pearl says.

She has started gathering up her things; she has brought food, and in the hut, through the door, Rose can see the sheet spread out very neatly.

"We better go," Pearl says.

Paul Rendell keeps watching Rose, thinking, Will she be the sort to tell? Will she keep her mouth shut? He seems huge in that clearing. He slips his shirt on, slowly, as though he has all the time in the world.

"You've ruined everything," Pearl says when she passes Rose, who is stuck to the ground, motionless, yet Pearl can't meet her eyes.

"Rose," says Paul very quietly.

$\mathscr{F}$lame Stitch ━━━━━━━━━━━

What if everything could be changed? What if the girl in the midnight dress could walk backward, through the mill yards, backward through that night that smells of molasses and moonlit sky? Back through the cane bins, back across the train tracks, back across the stubble of rocks, the butterflies tumbling over and over in her belly, back across the dew-wet grass, away from the end?

What if that could really happen? If there was some way.

What if Rose and Pearl could stand together beside the bathrooms, laughing, listening to the band playing "Edelweiss" out of tune, the reflection of the swimming pool dancing on their skin? There is a red paper flower in Rose's hair. Pearl has placed it there. What if they made a different decision right then?

What if Rose could go backward? Back to the caravan park, backward in the car, backward through the cane fields until they dissolved, backward through the moonlit scrub, backward through the small nameless towns and backward through the city until it too faded, all the graffiti and brick walls and train stations, houses petering out to nothing but fences and billboards and then empty land again.

She would touch each place she remembered, kneel down and touch it with her hand. She would touch the roads at every corner she and her father had turned. She would touch the doors to motels and hotels and the gates of caravan parks and the faded signs in campgrounds. She would touch the statues and the stone angels in cemeteries and the mountains and their favorite trees. She would cross the desert and cross the mountains and cross the strait. She would keep going until she arrived back at the beginning, at the place where they took their first steps away.

What if Pearl could start again with the letter D? Dimitri Orlov. What if she could write a letter to him and he could open it in Russia one frosty gray morning and read with astonishment of the existence of this beautiful daughter? What if she could go back to Jonah? What if Jonah could take her in his arms? She could take back everything she ever said about his kisses.

What if they could stop right there that night? Rose breathing hard, Pearl laughing, standing together in the shadows. In that moment they are nothing but their skin and breath and whispered words.

Rose has just kissed Murray Falconer; the kiss is still blazing on her lips.

"I can feel it here," she says.

Pearl places her fingers on Rose's mouth.

"Was it good?" she asks.

"It was okay," says Rose.

It was sudden but not unexpected. The moment lubricated by Passion Pop, which Murray had decanted into a soft drink bottle. He was

full of platitudes. His breath smelt of cigarillos and his hair of blue food
coloring.

"He said I was beautiful," says Rose.

"But you are," says Pearl, "look at you."

"I think this dress is magical," says Rose, and it makes them both
laugh so that they hold each other.

"I think it is too," says Pearl, and then she is deadly serious.

She opens her mouth to speak.

Rose is shaking. A real trembling in her hands. She holds them
together to stop it. She sits on the rock at the edge of the waterfall, leans right out and then back in, wishes she could fall. If Edie
sees them going down, she'll know. She'll know the place has
been desecrated. The place of love. The place of refuge.

She touches her eyes to see if she's crying.

Betrayal. That's the word she's looking for. She never under-
stood it until right now, this very minute; it's a sharp emotion,
hot. It hurts her; she feels scoured. She stands up to vomit and
finds she can't, crouches down on the earth, rubs her face over and
over. She puts her hands open-palmed on the forest floor. Gets up
again. She paces like an animal around the small clearing.

Other words for betrayal?

Disloyalty, unfaithfulness, treachery. Pearl.

Her skin is burning. Her skin is burning long before she lights
the fire.

Rose Lovell is not an arsonist. She doesn't sit there, pace
there, think of burning the place down. She thinks of Pearl's
honey-brown back and Paul Rendell's cool white skin. She thinks
about the letters, the handfuls of letters to Russia, the way she got

Pearl down the gully that first day. How she talked to her all the way up the fallen tree when she was stuck with fear. She thinks about the rock pool where they swam and Pearl's finger twirled in her hair, how the night held them in the open palm of its hand.

There is no pleasure in the burning.

She is surprised by it. Its brightness shocks her, all the golden embers and the wildness of the flames.

In the hut Pearl has left a box of matches. Rose realizes she must have been planning to stay with him. They were going to have a campfire. That's what Rose thinks. Girl Scout Pearl. She hasn't taken the sheet with her or the biscuits. A packet of them. Chips Ahoy! chocolate chip. They must have eaten a few, sitting there on the rocks. That was the best she could do. How romantic. She's a joke. She's a child.

Rose stares. The four walls, the colored casements that listened to their quiet conversations, all their plans, creaked and ticked with satisfaction. Rose pushes Pearl's cushion into the corner and sets it on fire. It takes two scratches of a match. It looks as if it won't burn but suddenly there is a small explosion in the cushion, a flare.

She is surprised how the fire quickens and grows and has a soul. She has to stand back from it then. The windows explode one by one, the amber glass showering. The roof slumps to one side.

All the way down the ruin smolders inside her.

She feels rain on her face. Where has it come from, that rain? It had been such a perfect day. Now there are storm towers and the sky is a deep storm blue.

She is angry until she reaches the open forest and then a new feeling takes over, a startling fear. Her heart comes alive and she's running. All the sounds roar back into her ears. She can hear everything, the side of the hut caving in, the rain touching her skin, the clouds moving out to sea.

Near Edie's house there are flying foxes spilling in a fountain from the mango trees. Right there she bends down and vomits in the grass, and when she looks up, the old woman is watching her at the bottom of the steps. Edie looks up at the mountain and then back at Rose, an emotion spreading slowly across her face. Rose expects horror but sadness is all she sees.

"Come on, then," Edie says. "You better come inside."

Rose follows her up the steps, washes her face in the shadowy bathroom with the grumbling taps, rinses her mouth.

"You're as white as a ghost."

Edie takes the shawl from the daybed and wraps it round Rose's shoulders. The midnight dress sways in the shadows, deep, deep sorrowful blue.

"I don't know why I did it," says Rose, sobbing. She's never cried in front of anyone. It's a shameful thing. Like standing naked. "I saw them there."

Edie doesn't say anything, doesn't touch the girl, just waits.

"He's disgusting. She's doing this disgusting thing. He doesn't even love her. He's just tricking her. She's so stupid. Really stupid. Like she thinks she's not but she is, and we went to that place, that was our place, and he doesn't even love her and she took him there. I know I shouldn't have. You can call the police. It's just it was ruined, that perfect place was ruined."

Edie moves forward, drags the chair. She takes the hankie

from her bra strap and wipes at Rose's eyes and nose. Smooths the girl's hair back. Rose cries with her eyes closed.

"I'm sorry."

"Hush, hush," says Edie. "There's nothing to be sorry for."

"But I burnt it down, don't you understand?"

"Tell me," says Edie.

"There was this cushion and these matches. And the flames, they turned the rocks orange. All the glass on the ground was gold. It was your mother's place."

"And yours," says Edie.

"I've never had a home," says Rose. Wiping her nose. "You don't understand, I've never had a home."

"This is what my mother always said to me when I was feeling blue: 'Sew some chain stitch and it will cheer you up. Or some daisies. That brightens everything.' If my father was going from room to room spitting and stamping and thumping the walls because his head ached, she said quickly, 'Sit beside me and finish these buttonholes. There is nothing as calming as buttonhole stitch, everything so neatly enclosed.' Did you know, once, my father grabbed me in the kitchen and said, 'Edith, my eye was eaten by a crow, what do you think of that?' My mother said when he had let me go, 'Don't think about it, Edie. Help me with these pin tucks. Look at me. Don't think of it. He's lying. Don't think of it again.'"

"I can't remember my mother," says Rose.

"At all?" says Edie.

"Only pieces," says Rose.

"You can collect up all the pieces," says Edie. As though it's that simple. Like collecting blue quandongs. Or red leaves. Or passion fruit flowers.

"How can you miss someone you don't even remember?" says Rose, spilling fresh tears.

"I missed my old father," says Edie. "The one I never knew. The one before the war."

"My mother had freckles," says Rose. "And small hands."

"That's a beginning."

"She had long hair, crinkled; I don't know, I know that just from a photo, I think. She put me to bed."

Edie waits.

"She put me to bed."

"Yes," says Edie.

"She shouldn't have put me to bed. Just like that."

Dogs barking in the street, the smell of wet grass. Dishes. The sound of dishes. The clink of glass.

"I fell asleep. She had a sad mouth. She had a sad mouth even when she was happy. That's how I remember it. She drew eyes. She was really good at drawing eyes. She hated doing the washing up. Someone took me to the beach afterward, I don't even know who it was, and put me down on the sand. People had left flowers there. The flowers were all wrong. They were like cake-icing flowers. Artificial. My mother wouldn't have liked them. I knew that. Even if I was small."

"What would she have liked?"

"I don't know. Nothing. Just the sky. Not flowers. I'd like to see her again. Even just for one minute. Even one minute would be enough. I'd take anything."

"Yes," says Edie. She finds the hankie again and gives it to Rose.

"I feel better now," says Rose.

"I feel better too," says Edie.

She stands up, knees creaking, and goes to the kitchen dresser and takes a teacup from the top shelf. She puts it down in front of Rose.

"While we're putting ghosts to rest, what do you think I should do with this?" says Edie.

Rose looks into the crazed teacup at the haunted glass eye.

"Smash it," says Rose. "With a hammer."

Edie laughs. The laugh makes Rose smile.

Rose carries the teacup outside and Edie finds the hammer beneath the house. The first hit and the thing jumps away into the grass, which makes them both laugh, Edie bending over to catch her breath when she's finished.

"Here, I'll hold it."

"But I'll hit your fingers," says Rose.

The blue eye looks up at them wildly.

"I'll let it go just in time."

Rose swings the hammer, smashes the thing into a thousand pieces, a small colorful pile on the bottom step.

"What should we do with it?" asks Rose.

"What do you think?"

"Maybe just scatter it," says Rose. "Somewhere nice. He deserves that."

They bend down to the grass then, picking up the pieces, placing them into Edie's cupped palm.

"It's lighter. I feel better. Maybe one day you could take the pieces back up to the house," says Edie, looking up at the mountain. Then Rose sees the sadness spread across her face. The realization that the place is gone. "I'll keep them until then."

"I'm sorry," says Rose.

Edie shakes her head.

"I've got something to do too," says Rose. "Can I come back later?"

"Not today," says Edie. "And I know what you want to do, but you have to be careful with men like that. You should go home now. Rest. Don't do anything this afternoon. Come back later in the week and we'll finish the dress."

"Later in the week," says Rose. "I don't think we'll have time to finish it if we leave it that long."

"You can't make a dress with angry hands," says Edie.

"I'm not angry," Rose sighs.

"Come back," says Edie. "In a week's time."

$\mathcal{P}$lain Running Stitch ━━━━

Here's the morning after the Harvest Parade and Patrick Lovell is packing up. He's moving, moving, moving. He folds up the deck chairs and shoves them in under the corner lounge. He puts the plates and cutlery away, locks the drawers for the trip. His cigarette drops clods of ash on the floor. He pulls down the kitchen venetians. Stores the kettle, the frying pan. The gas stove is folded and placed under his bed. The sketchbooks, he flips through the pages, sobs, the way he wept against the caravan in the first light.

He stinks of drink. It's oozing from his pores. It's in his tears.

There are his banana-picking clothes. His very own knife. His snake gaiters. He'd seen a brown, two and a half meters long, just a few days before. It was passing, unhurried, through the field, then it coiled itself tight in a space at the base of a banana palm. Filled the space like a ribbon, squeezed itself in, squeezed and squeezed until all that showed was a finger-sized glint of copper. He thinks about that, holding his sketchbooks and his cutting stuff.

"Big night?" asks Mrs. Lamond when he is outside taking down the clothesline.

He doesn't answer.

"Leaving just like that?" she says.

"Just for a week or so, might as well see the top end while it's dry. Can you keep some stuff here for me?"

"You're already six weeks behind," says Mrs. Lamond. She's speaking quietly but there's a tremor in her voice, as if she might explode. If she builds up speed with her words, she'll disintegrate.

"You know I'll make it up," he says, knowing this.

He leans forward, touches the locket at her throat.

"I thought," she says.

"What did you think?" he says gently.

It takes her a while to answer. She's like a schoolgirl now, embarrassed, tears in her eyes.

"It doesn't matter anyway," she says.

He gives her the sketchbooks. A pile of art books, his paints.

"Stuff that's important to me," he says.

"Don't want to lose any of it," he says.

"Elaine," he says.

Rose doesn't confront Paul Rendell on the day she burns down the hut. She does exactly as Edie says and goes home to the caravan. Her father isn't there. His fishing gear is still gone. Everything is the same as she left it that morning, the beautiful morning for climbing, only the day is now ruined. She pulls the curtain around her little bed. The flames jump inside her. She can't smell the mountain on her skin, only ash. She closes her eyes, covers her face with her hands until she sleeps.

"Tolstoy," says her father at half past six.

She doesn't answer him.

"What's up? You sick?"

"I'm okay," she says.

She doesn't confront Paul Rendell the next day either, the Monday. She doesn't leave her bed. She lies, curled in a ball, blazing.

"I'm getting worried now," her father says.

Truth be told, she's not afraid of walking up to Paul Rendell and punching him in the face; it's not about that, she doesn't want to go into town in case she sees Pearl. The news agency and Crystal Corner are only three doors apart. Rose doesn't know what she'll do if she sees Pearl. Her true emotions might be unleashed; she might spontaneously combust, right there and then; there might be a tsunami of tears. She's not sure which. It's safer to stay in bed.

But by Tuesday the smoldering ruin of the house has cooled inside her. She sits up, braids her hair. She paints on her eyes, her lips, puts on her crucifix, her shirt with the devil riding a horse. She takes an apple to eat on the way.

She rides the bike into town, against the afternoon sun, goes to the Blue Moon Book Exchange even though she knows he won't be there. Old Mrs. Rendell watches her go up and down the aisles of the shop. The curtain to the exchange is pinned back so that Mrs. Rendell can see inside; there's a new sign: PLEASE LEAVE ALL BAGS AT DOOR.

"Back again," says Mrs. Rendell when she catches Rose's eye.

Rose tries to think of something to say. She looks at Mrs. Rendell, who raises her eyebrows.

"How's your dress coming along, then?" says Mrs. Rendell.

"It's good."

"How's Miss Baker?"

"Good," says Rose.

"Funny old thing that she is," says Mrs. Rendell. "Harmless enough, I suppose. She had one of the Hansen boys wanting to marry her when she was well past marrying age but she turned him down, you know, and then he went and died in the war."

Rose sees the ripped dress, the magpie, the sky.

"My mother always said beggars can't be choosers. I was fortunate, of course, lucky when I found Mr. Rendell; there never was anyone else. Did you know there was also once a story that Edie's old mother, Florence, was a dabbler?"

"What's a dabbler?"

"A dabbler in the dark arts," says Mrs. Rendell.

Dark arts sounds stupid when Mrs. Rendell says it. It almost makes Rose laugh.

"I thought she made wedding dresses," says Rose.

"Oh, she did, all right, but all the while she was up to other stuff, running around the rain forest half naked."

That does make Rose laugh. Mrs. Rendell looks shocked; she fans herself a little harder.

"Anyway, were you looking for something, love?"

"No," says Rose. "I was just . . ."

Old Mrs. Rendell raises her eyebrows again; she has her proof the girl is there to nick something.

Rose goes out onto Main Street and stands in the sun, looks across to the park. Perhaps she'll sit in the shade there and see if he passes that way, coming home from a shift maybe; she isn't sure of those times. Her stomach growls; she places one hand there. She's about to step off the footpath when a cane train grumbles past, lamenting, wheels wailing, in a diagonal across the street. She counts forty bins raining stalk. The street is full of the stuff. She bends down to pick a piece up that has landed near her foot, and when she stands again, he's there.

He is with another man, older, bearded; they're talking.

"Paul," she says. It's a foreign word. Like a stone in her mouth.

Paul Rendell laughs. He is going to ignore her.

"Paul Rendell," she says, louder, the way a bailiff reads out the name of the accused.

"Hello?" he says.

He isn't going to stop; he's going to walk right past.

"Don't go near her again," says Rose.

Much more loudly now.

"What?" he says, laughs, looks back. Pretends he doesn't understand.

"You heard me," says Rose. "Don't touch her again."

"Beg your pardon?"

"Don't touch her again!" shouts Rose.

Paul Rendell shakes his head, looks at the man next to him, shrugs.

"Do you know her?" the man asks as they turn into the shop.

"Never seen her in my life."

"Was that the girl, the redhead?" she hears Mrs. Rendell ask. "She was just in here looking to pocket something. I've got a bad feeling about her."

Rose feels tears then, shakes her head, rubs her eyes. Stupid, stupid, stupid. Paul Rendell doesn't look back at her.

When she turns to go, she sees Pearl has come out of Crystal Corner and is standing on the one step. Her hair is undone, she's shoeless, she has anger in her dark eyes, as though she might stride across the seven meters that separate them and slap Rose across the face, but she doesn't. She just shakes her head and goes back inside.

She feels deflated then, Rose Lovell, like a hot-air balloon, crumpling, plummeting through the blue. The problem is, the sky is inside Rose when it comes to Pearl.

Rose dreams of black tulle petticoats. She's attaching them to a skirt just the way the dream Edie shows her, only the stuff has a life of its own. It's slipping out of her hands, lifting, floating. She grabs it, fistfuls, but it keeps escaping. As soon as she gets one layer down, another wafts free, until she gives up, lets the whole dark mass of it rise, trembling slightly, propelling itself like a jelly-fish toward Edie's casements. When she wakes, she keeps her eyes closed, doesn't want to let that dream go.

She's waited longer than the week, isn't sure if she'll go back. It's only three nights until the parade. What's the point of the dress? She doesn't want to sit on a bowl-of-fruit float. They mightn't let her anyway. They might ban her because she hasn't been back to school. There are probably rules to these pagan rites. Pearl might make use of her secretarial powers. She doesn't want to think about Pearl.

Patrick Lovell is edgy; she writes that word in her green book. Not edgy cool but on edge. It's exactly the kind of word she hates, blunt, thick around the middle; it grates against her nerves. She wants a better word to describe him. To the untrained eye, he looks just the same, but she knows better.

He trembles faintly. He laughs too loudly.

He has painted the gates for Mrs. Lamond, a mural, it took him the whole week; every afternoon when work was over, he covered them in fish and reef and something that was meant to be the rain forest, although to Rose it is just a green smudge. It's tacky, the whole thing; she doesn't want to comment on it.

"What do you think?" he asks.

"You've sold your soul," she replies, which makes him laugh all the more.

Everything they say to each other is like a script they're reading from; and underneath, everything unsaid simmers.

Simmering, that's the word she needs to describe her father. He's simmering away to nothing. Soon he'll be dry, just a dehydrated skin, like a five-day-dead blue-tongued skink squished on the road. He is nothing but bluster. He is nothing but hot wind. He can't exist much longer this way.

Not long to go now, she thinks.

Edie is glad to see her. She's waiting on the back steps in the cobalt evening. She smiles when Rose comes around the corner.

"I knew it would be today," she says.

"Have we still got time?" asks Rose.

"Of course, of course," says Edie, standing up, limping inside.

They open the windows along the back of the house. The louvres creak, the casements protesting; Rose knows the sound of every one. Always opened in the same order, they sing a song.

"Have you made up with your good friend?" asks Edie.

"She's no friend of mine," says Rose.

Edie hums her disapproving hum.

They sit at either end of the kitchen table and sew. Edie shows Rose how to attach a band to the tulle and sew two lines of stitch so that the whole thing can be gathered up. Rose is going to tell Edie about the dream but stops herself, although she can't say why. She knows Edie will only nod and hum. But she's frightened she might say something else, something about the dress, its true nature, something about dark clouds.

Sewing black tulle *is* like wrestling with a cloud. Rose puts the petticoat on and Edie checks the length.

"Did it burn right to the ground?" she asks.

"Don't," says Rose.

"I want to know, that's all," she says.

"Almost," says Rose.

"It's just as well," she replies, kneeling down at Rose's feet to pin where the tulle will be trimmed. "Sometimes when we went there, my mother and I, we never wanted to come back."

I know, says Rose, only she doesn't speak.

"My mother, she was buried in her wedding dress, although she had lost so much weight that she swam in it. She had sewn leaves into the lining: satin ash and sandpaper figs and of course the bleeding hearts. The green billy goat plums and the porcelain fruit. Into the coffin I put blue quandongs and the black bean pods. It raised eyebrows at the funeral parlor. But I didn't care. I remember how young she looked, unlined; I brushed out her hair.

"I wear mine very short," she continues. "There'll be no one to brush out mine when I'm gone."

She explains how to attach the petticoats, which stitch to use, then attaches the sleeves to the bodice, sews the black pearl buttons at the neck. The night creaks slowly past. Rose, hands numb, gives thanks for every stitch. Here's my mother painting. Here's my mother showing me rock pools, here's my mother brushing out my hair, seventy-one strokes.

"Edie," says Rose.

"Yes?"

"Thank you."

"It's all right, my dear."

"Will we finish it tonight?" says Rose.

"Tonight?" says Edie. "You're too tired. Way too tired."

"No I'm not," says Rose.

"Yes you are," says Edie. "Look at you. You're swaying there like a tree about to fall."

"No I'm not," says Rose.

Rose pricks her finger then, places it in her mouth, closes her eyes.

"Look at you," says Edie. "You're going to fall asleep where you're sitting."

"I know," says Rose. "I am tired, I've never been so tired."

She lies on the daybed and Edie comes and spreads the shawl over her. The hurricane lamps are turned off. She hears the old woman's footsteps disappearing down the hallway. The house sighs, the mango trees touch the roof tenderly. Possums come, back and forward, running errands on moonlit claws. She sleeps and does not wake. Not when Edie leaves in the morning for her walk, not through the morning as the sun crosses over the house, not when the velvety shadows begin to fall. She wakes in the evening and Edie gives her food, damper and hot butter, which she gobbles, licking her fingers, not speaking, before lying down and sleeping again.

She sleeps the way a girl who is preparing herself for the ball should sleep.

*B*eautiful and Easy Rose Stitch ━━━━━━━━━━━━━━━

Glass wasn't expecting the man to kill himself. It floors him. He wobbles for a while like a planet thrown from its axis. He'd been about to go round to the newsagent's and pick him up again for another little chat when it was called in. A man hanging up on one of the tracks. Main suspect. All he had to go on. "Stupid bloody prick" is what he says. "Stupid bloody prick. Why'd you go and do a stupid thing like that?"

The two officers stare at Glass from across their tables. We're not getting anywhere, is what their eyes say. We'd like to get back to Cairns soon. Why'd you let him go home? Do you know what you're doing?

"What are you fools looking at?" he shouts. "It wasn't him anyway."

Stupid bloody prick. He'll have to talk up the line now. Explain.

"Go on, go and do something useful," he shouts. "Go up and see where he is. Did he leave his confession?"

They grab their hats and shuffle from the room, unsure. When they're gone, he rests back in the office chair, puts his hands behind his head. He lets the thoughts come and go.

"*Stupid bloody moron,*" he says out loud every now and again.

Of course he'll have to go up there too. He'll have to go up and see the body taken down. He hates these things, the dismantling of suicide scenes. The tidying up, the zip of the cord spinning free, the crackling body bag laid out on leaves. The way the birds will go on singing and the sky will go on being blue the whole while. The way nothing will be left behind afterward. Such a loud and theatrical act leaving not the faintest echo.

Miss Edith Baker, the witch, glides through his thoughts. He's not expecting her. She's holding something in her hands. He can't see what. She's gone just as quick. He sits up in his chair, shakes his head, touches the drawing of the dress in his pocket.

While Rose sleeps, Pearl comes to the back door. The kitchen is funeral-parlor quiet, not a sound except Miss Baker's needle and thread running through the black lace. She stands there, watching Miss Baker sewing, the crumpled silhouette of Rose sleeping on the daybed against the louvres.

It's afternoon; the sun casts a slant of light over the reclining figure, cuts her neatly in two; the bottom half of Rose in shadow, the top half in light. Her flame hair blazes.

"I don't have it in me to wake her," says Edie.

"How long has she been sleeping?"

"This is the second day."

"Is she all right?"

Pearl takes a step closer to Rose, examines her pale freckled face, looks at her mouth, lips slightly parted.

"I should think so," says Edie. "Just tired. She's had a hard time."

Pearl looks anxious then, she can't turn back to face the old woman.

"I came to say sorry to her, that's all," she says.

"Well, you can," says Edie. "Why don't you try and wake her? I'll give you some peace."

She puts down her work and starts out of the room into the creaking hallway before Pearl can protest, leaving her there with the bluebirds on the wall, the king brown snake floating in its jar, and the shadows of the mango leaves rocking against the louvres. The midnight dress touches the floor with its sighing skirt.

"Rose," she whispers. Takes another step forward.

Rose keeps sleeping.

"Rose?"

Pearl can hear a door open and shut a long way away, deep in the house.

"Come on, Sleeping Beauty," Pearl says, laughs self-consciously, kneels down beside the bed.

Rose sleeps on.

"I just wanted to say sorry. I really wanted to say sorry. I should never have done what I did, I mean take him to our place, I mean what was I thinking? I can't believe I did; you know me, Rose, you know me; hey, sometimes I don't think. He's so vile anyway. I told him. I gave the last book back. I didn't write a poem. I told him exactly in my words: 'No more. It was a mistake. It's over.' My mum always said you need an exit strategy. I said, 'You're way too old for me.' I'm sorry, Rose. Then he saw me in the park and he came right up to me and said, 'What do you think, you're just finished with your little game? Just like that, game over?' He freaked me out. But then he just laughed and went away. I mean of all the places to take him; I can't believe how much I must have hurt you. Do you understand, are you listening?

"You have to accept my apology.

"I've never had a friend like you. Jeez, Rose, now I'll have to say all this when you wake up as well. Anyway. Jonah Pedersen asked me to be with him on the parade night. He's got a little surprise for me. He said he's willing to forgive me dumping him; he said he likes me that much. I mean he didn't say it, of course, he sent one of the others to say it. I don't know what the surprise will be. I think he's getting a car or something, that's what the rumor is, that's probably all it is. What do you think? I think it's good. I think it's meant to be. You know how in all those books you always end up loving the one you didn't like in the beginning.

"Rose? I hope you wake up soon. You're freaking me out. Please say you'll forgive me when you wake up. Maybe you're dreaming this, maybe I'm reaching you in there."

She laughs again, wipes away her tears. She leans forward, brushes the flaming curls back from Rose's forehead, kisses her there. Edie comes back as she's getting up. Pearl has an idea she'd been eavesdropping but all the old lady does is smile.

"No good?"

"She's out to it," says Pearl, "but I said sorry to her anyway. Can you tell her again when she wakes up that I'm sorry and that I love her?"

"Yes," says Edie. "Yes, I will."

* * *

When Rose finally wakes, her hair spills over her shoulders. Ringlets, perfectly coiled, have formed while she has slept. She runs her fingers through them, feels their caress on her cheeks; she puts her feet on the floorboards gingerly, smiles.

"I feel like I've been asleep for a year," she says.

"I was beginning to worry," says Edie. "I thought I'd have to call the doctor."

Rose stretches, yawns, shakes out her ringlet hair, stands before the midnight dress.

"You finished it?" she gasps.

"I needed something to do," says Edie. "While I waited for you to wake up."

"It's beautiful," says Rose. She touches it, the beads, the black lace, the silk taffeta skirt.

"Tonight is the night," says Edie.

"What do you mean?"

"Tonight is the Harvest Parade."

"What?" says Rose. "How long have I slept?"

Edie smiles her small wry smile; her eyes glitter.

"Pearl came," she says. "Wanting to beg your forgiveness."

"Why didn't you wake me?"

"Tried. I let her in; she watched over you awhile. I don't think you should be angry with her. She left a kiss, right here, on your forehead."

"But that's three whole days!"

"Yes," says Edie. "That'd be about right. Enough time for me to finish the hems and sleeves and check all the seams."

Rose looks out the back door; night is coming already. It takes her a moment to realize the sensation, the whirring, shimmering, somersaulting knots of butterflies.

Rose Lovell is beautiful, thinks Edie.

"There's no doubt about it," says Edie. "Go and wash your hair beneath the tank stand. There's nothing like rainwater."

She gives Rose shampoo, a bottle in the shape of a doll. It looks very old.

Rose washes her hair, sits on the steps to let it dry. She looks up at the mountain, which is turning to a solid dark mass with the night. It's growing indistinct, cloaking itself, holding in all its streams and secret places. Years later, when she is older, she will still dream of the places she discovered there, the gully, the secret rose gums, the house beside the waterfall. These places will appear to her clearly in her dreams; the perfume of rotting leaves, of moss, will fill her nose. She will wake breathing, swallowing air, as though they are her first breaths.

There is an uproar of frog song as the night descends.

Edie disappears down the hallway and returns with an ancient powder puff in her hand. Rose dabs at her freckles, and with an old lipstick she paints her lips the color of rubies.

"Do you think I should leave my hair out?"

"Of course you should," says Edie.

A halo of curls. Murray Falconer will fall, crash, plummet in love with her this night, she knows it when she looks into the strange cloudy mirror in the bathroom, half overgrown with vine.

The dress. The dress. The glass beads twinkle by the light of the hurricane lamps. All the windows have been flung open to the night. It breathes against Rose's bare skin as she steps into the dress.

The dress speaks softly against her, in whispers and sighs.

"Yes, you look a great beauty," says Edie. "There's no doubt about it."

"Don't," Rose says.

"I'm only speaking the truth."

Rose doesn't know if she can sit in the dress, doesn't know if she can stand. She's dizzy with the feel of it against her. The rose lace holds her arms, her throat; Edie lifts her hair, fastens the hook and eyes, the three buttons at her neck.

"Now, I don't want you to complain, but I found these in a drawer and I knew I saved them years ago for a reason," says Edie. She holds out a pair of blue diamanté shoes. "Have you ever worn heels?"

"No," says Rose.

She hazards sitting down. When the shoes are on, they peek out, just the toe, from beneath the dress, a perfect fit.

"Lovely," says Edie. "And this."

It's a small black satin handbag with a love heart lock.

Rose wobbles her first few steps down the hallway to a room with a full-length dusty mirror.

"What do you think?"

"I don't seem like me," says Rose. "I am someone else."

$\mathscr{S}$imple Thorn Stitch ━━━━━

When Glass climbs the back steps, she's sitting at her table with a teacup in her hand, as if she's waiting. The whole time he's there, she doesn't raise the cup once to her lips, and it's only late, when he's leaving, that he sees it's filled up with tiny pieces of colored glass.

"I think you know more than what you're letting on, Mrs. Baker," he says by way of greeting. Softly. He feels far too big and ugly in that kitchen. He doesn't want to scare her.

"Miss Baker," says Edie. "I never married but I was asked. Not in a traditional way. He didn't get down on one knee."

"Do you know where Pearl Kelly is?"

"No," she says.

"What about Rose Lovell? We haven't had any luck tracking her down. She was seen around, though, those first few days."

He looks at the half-dark hallway.

"Rose?" says Edie. She looks at her cup. She's smaller, frailer, much more faded, even in a week. "Yes, I know where Rose is."

* * *

There are red and yellow ribbons and crepe-paper flowers deco-rating the light posts, and all the girls in their dresses are lining up in front of the town hall. From where the taxi sets her down, Rose can see their dresses are every color of the rainbow and they wear flowers in their hair. She touches her own hair, realizes she has none of that.

She is midnight blue and flowerless.

She feels the scratch of the black mourning lace against her throat, and she fingers the glass beads on her bodice, tries to re-member to breathe.

The backstreet is filled with the shrill whistling of recorder players, a disheveled marching band struggling to find a rhythm; several clowns, all loitering; a confusion of floats: the Leonora High bowl-of-fruit float, a sorry collection of sagging pastel ap-ples, pears, and grapes; the Leonora Karate Club giant banana split float, truly a sight to behold; the belly-dancing float; the mill float, which features Mickey and Minnie Mouse, both their cos-tumes a little threadbare. Mickey has his head off, is smoking a cigarette, which he grinds out when the drivers shout that it's time to go.

The lead driver blows the truck horn and a clamorous cloud of flying foxes rises from the great fig trees in the park. The streets are filled with people and in the sky the clouds have opened in one great and jagged tear and the stars shine through.

Rose hears a voice close beside her, turns to see her father.

"Home is the sailor, home from the sea," he says, which makes no sense, but, oh, how the rum fills him out.

He's tall, there on the street, a full sail, eyes lit up, obsid-ian glass.

Straightaway she can see it has happened. He is swaying slightly, trying to keep himself still like a man on a rocking boat.

"I've been sleeping," she says. It's the truth.

"Sleeping?" he says. He's angry. He puts his hand out, as though noticing the dress for the first time, but says, "Sleeping, that's plain stupid."

"I've got to go, Dad," she says, already turning.

"Rose," he says. "We'll be packing up in the morning. We'll be leaving this shithole."

She stops, a fraction of a second, then keeps walking.

"Rose!" he shouts.

Shannon sees Rose first; she turns and whispers into Vanessa's ear.

"Well, well," says Vanessa, "look what the cat dragged in."

Vanessa is beautiful in her golden gown with its Barbie doll puffed sleeves and sweetheart neckline trimmed with silvery sequins. Her perfect blond hair is laced with perfect white flowers; huge curls bounce against her perfect tanned shoulders. She smiles with her little white razor-sharp teeth.

"Please tell me," she continues, "that you are not going to get up onstage in that."

Rose looks at her own dress again then.

Of course, beside the others it's old-fashioned. She holds the skirt out with her hands and something about the action makes Vanessa laugh. It looks handmade suddenly; it looks like something she has sewn herself.

"See what happens when you get a witch to make your dress?" says Vanessa.

When Rose left the house, she felt beautiful, transfixed by

herself and the dress, with its waterfall of twinkling glass beads, the solemn loveliness of its mourning lace. Is the dress she's wearing a monstrous thing? She stands like that, holding the skirt, looking down.

"Fuck off, Vanessa," says Pearl, moving from behind the others. "Rose's dress is gorgeous."

Pearl is wearing tangerine. There's an explosion of tangerine flowers across her bodice. She looks beautiful in a way that suggests she hasn't even bothered, she's just stepped out of the sea and straight into that dress.

"It is," says Mallory, moving out of Vanessa's golden corona. She's in flowing fuchsia, beaming.

Vanessa narrows her eyes.

"You look stunning, Rose," says Shannon.

Vanessa goes to flick her hair but remembers the basket weave of baby's breath and stops. She turns away from the group and moves toward the back of the float.

"All aboard," says the driver, and the girls have to climb up to assume their positions among the fruit.

"Stand near me," whispers Pearl. "Please."

They sit together on an apple.

"I'm sorry," whispers Pearl as the truck lurches forward. "I came to the house; did you know I came there when you were asleep, did Miss Baker tell you?"

"Yes," says Rose.

"I'm sorry I took him there. It was the worst thing I ever did in my life."

"It was ours," says Rose.

"I know."

"I burnt it down," says Rose.

Pearl is going to speak, looks away into the crowd instead.

"Wave at the crowd, *belles filles*," says Madame Bonnick. "Smile and look pretty."

Pearl waves, nudges Rose. Rose waves. Vanessa has a fixed smile; she is standing by the banana, waving like a robot.

"Jesus," says Rose. "Look at Vanessa."

"And it's finished," whispers Pearl. The star pins sparkle in her tousled hair. "He's no good. Mum made me see it. She made me understand. She said my aura was changing color. He had cast a spell over me. I told him I never wanted to see him again."

"Good," says Rose.

"I'm back with Jonah."

Rose looks at her then.

"It was always meant to be," says Pearl. It's part apology. "He's got a surprise for me tonight. Hey, there's your dad."

She shouts the last.

"Mr. Lovell," she calls.

"Shit," says Rose. "Don't encourage him."

But her father has seen them. He's putting his fingers in his mouth for a God almighty wolf whistle.

When the street parade is over, the mayoress speaks into the microphone and the feedback sets off the flying foxes again.

"Shall we parade the girls now?" says the mayoress when the noise has died down.

The crowd cheers and the girls begin to line up beside the stage. The older girls go first, with their huge hair-sprayed bangs and stiff curls and dresses with long revealing splits. They know how to pose at the end of the short catwalk. Men on the second story of the pub shout out scores and whistle until the mayoress holds back the queue and reminds the crowd it's a family evening.

Before each girl walks onto the stage, the mayoress introduces her; she says, "This is Corrine Black in a yellow chiffon gown with yellow sequin detail. Corrine likes to water-ski and hopes to be a vet nurse. This is Amber Marchetta in a hot-pink satin dress and matching pink elbow gloves. Amber likes horse-riding and wants to be a marine biologist.

"This is Vanessa Raine," says the mayoress, and the crowd goes wild. "She's in a golden gown with a sweetheart neckline and an intricate bedazzle. Vanessa likes to do all sorts of aerobics and wants to be a swimwear model."

Vanessa struts down the runway like a professional. She stands at the end with one hand on her hip, smiles at the crowd.

Rose knows she could leave the line. She knows it but her feet won't move. She stands where she is, paralyzed. Mallory, in fuchsia, says, "Move forward, Rose. You'll be all right."

Rose moves forward as though she's on stilts.

"I haven't got your details, honey," the mayoress whispers, waiting for Shannon Fanelli to finish her turn. "Did you put your slip in?"

"No," says Rose.

"Who are you, honey?" says the mayoress.

"Rose."

"Rose who?"

"Rose Lovell."

"What do you like, honey?"

"What do I like?" says Rose, trying to think.

"Come on, darling," says the mayoress.

"I like climbing mountains," says Rose.

"Gorgeous," says the mayoress. "And what do you want to be?"

"A writer," says Rose.

"Even better," says the mayoress.

"This is Rose Lovell wearing an absolutely stunning midnight-blue dress with antique— Is that antique lace, honey? With antique lace and antique beading. Rose loves climbing mountains and wants to be a writer."

"Tolstoy!" her father shouts in the crowd. "That's my Rose."

She hears him clearly but can't see him.

The mayoress propels Rose forward onto the stage with one hand on her back. Rose holds up her skirt like an old-fashioned lady because it's too long, much longer than all the other girls' dresses. She totters down the runway.

There are one hundred, two hundred, three hundred faces in the crowd, she can't tell, a moving, blurring rush of faces, all with the same strange fixed smile. They are all exactly, identically, horribly the same person until suddenly, like a lightbulb exploding, a face jumps out at her from the sea. It's Paul Rendell. He's throwing his head back, laughing, wiping his eyes.

When Rose makes it to the end of the catwalk, there is a much fainter, politer round of applause. A man from the top of the bar sings out in the quiet, "Why don't you give us a smile, love?" Rose tries. She smiles. The smile sticks her lip to her top teeth; she looks like a grimacing bear, or that's what she thinks. Someone, somewhere, laughs again. She tries to find Paul Rendell's face again but can't; it's lost in the swell. She turns and walks back past the mayoress.

"Good work, honey," says the mayoress. "Now here is Maxine Singh in a green off-the-shoulder design with an interesting rainbow sequin border. Maxine likes scuba-diving and wants to be a fashion designer."

There are tears, Rose feels them, a huge painful lump of them behind her eyes and another in her throat.

Vanessa says, "Don't worry, Rosie."

Rose says, "I'm not."

Two tears spill down her cheeks.

"You look pretty," says Vanessa. "Really you do. I was only joking."

Another two spill and follow the same path. Rose doesn't hear what Vanessa says next because Pearl has gone down the runway.

"This is Pearl Kelly wearing a tangerine affair in chiffon," says the mayoress. "Pearl loves French and wants to live in Paris."

Rose moves through the crowd, careful not to meet anyone's eyes. The mayoress is announcing a short break to choose the Harvest Queen and princesses. Rose passes the food stands and the balloon stands and the church craft bazaar. She'll just keep walking, she thinks; she'll walk all the way back to Paradise. She'll strip out of the dress and throw it from the rocks into the sea. She'll swim naked out into the ocean. She'll never look back.

Someone touches her shoulder.

"Rose," Murray says. He has his blue hair back.

"Oh," says Rose, setting her face into a mask.

It looks as if he is trying to think of some stupid voice he might use; he's trying real hard but nothing comes.

"Where are you going?" he says.

"Just for a walk."

"Can I come?"

"I'd rather you didn't."

"I have refreshments," he says, and opens his badly fitting tuxedo jacket.

In the inside pocket there is a hip flask.

"Wodka," he says in a bad Russian accent.

He walks beside her through the crowd toward the park. They go to the rotunda and sit side by side on a bench. He unscrews the cap and gives her some. She swallows and it burns.

"I knew you were only kidding me about not drinking," he says.

Another mouthful.

"You look so beautiful," he says.

"Don't say that," Rose says.

"But I mean it," he replies.

Afterward they can hear from where they lie who is chosen as the Harvest Queen, to wear the tinfoil crown and carry the orb and scepter. It isn't Vanessa or Pearl but a senior girl, as it always has been. But Vanessa and Pearl are both chosen to be one of seven princesses, to wear the tinfoil coronets and walk in the procession to the church door to lay down the offering of cane.

"Should I be watching this strange cultural event?" asks Rose.

"Don't go," says Murray. "It is really very boring."

He kisses her on the lips again. He has a thin prickle of a mustache that he's trying to cultivate and it makes her laugh.

"What?" he whispers.

"Nothing," she says.

The vodka is burning inside her. Her lips are numb but she can feel it in her belly. It makes her feel taller and stronger and prettier. He moves her hair from her neck and kisses her there.

After a while she presses her hands against his chest and pushes him away. "Have you got any more vodka?"

"Only a little bit," he says, offering it to her lips. "You like?"

She doesn't know what to say. She's in love with it.

Instantaneously, miraculously, head over heels.

$\mathcal{H}$idden Stitch ━━━━━━━━

"Well?" says Glass when the old lady has nothing else to add.

The house is speaking, creaking and rustling around them. It's agreeing, disagreeing, silverfish swimming through paper, possums turning in their sleep. Updrafts of its strange perfume reach him, rising mold, dead flowers, rotting fabric, pages crumbling. The light in that place, in that long back kitchen, the yellow walls, bluebirds flying, shadows falling across their faces, he'll take them with him when he leaves. The light and those blue-gray shadows, he'll carry them with him. Each time he closes his eyes, he'll return there.

"She's here," says Edie. "All the time, but you didn't ask for her."

"Rose," she says, louder, calling. Into the hallway, the long dark hallway, and the rooms with their peeling paint and sagging ceilings.

"Right," says Glass.

He wants to be angry. It's his first instinct but the anger blooms and evaporates when he hears her footsteps.

She's thin, Rose Lovell. Porcelain white.

She holds one hand across her body, resting on her pale arm.

Her face has been polished bright by tears.

"Are you Rose Lovell?" he says.

"Yes. Yes, I am," says Rose.

They swap their dresses beside the park bathroom, the satiny night against their skin. They laugh in the dark. Pearl holds Rose and Rose holds Pearl in return, hands on forearms, heads together.

"But why do you want to wear my dress?" says Rose.

"Because it's magical, you know it is; he won't be able to resist me. Everyone was just awestruck when you walked onto the stage."

"I thought they were laughing at me."

"They were speechless," says Pearl.

"You have to help me undo it at the back."

Fingers and shadows. Rose stands undressed until Pearl releases her own and steps out of it.

"Redheads should never wear tangerine," says Rose, deadpan.

"It's only for a little while, half an hour; go and kiss Murray some more and I'll be back."

"What's Jonah's surprise going to be?"

"I think he has a new car, only he hasn't got a license; he told me to meet him in the mill yards."

It seems so ordinary that the whole magical night almost dissolves into a puff of smoke.

"Gee, don't die of astonishment and excitement."

"Ruby Heart Rose," says Pearl. "Maybe we could all go to the bay. You and Murray could come too. Wait in the park and I'll be back soon."

She can't imagine Murray in Jonah's car. Murray, with his newly blue hair, his avant-garde mustache, his bad jokes.

"Okay," Rose says.

"How do I look?" asks Pearl.

The midnight dress is perfect on her. As though it were made for her all along. She touches the bodice, looks down at her arms in amazement; she smiles at Rose.

"See you soon," she says, not waiting for the answer, running through the park into the night.

Patrick Lovell is standing by a door in the Cane Cutter's Hotel, leaning there, feeling sorry for himself, when he sees Rose across the road in the park. His girl, Rose. Rose, who he's grown up, all by himself, without any help, so many bloody days and nights, endless work. His Rose, who he showed the world to, or the country at least. His Rose. *His* Rose. The place has changed her. His thankless Rose. His Rose, who wouldn't even stop in the street to talk to him.

He wants to tell her something; it's only half formed; it begins like this: "You can't just walk away from me." Or: "I love you, Rose, you're my girl, Rose, you can't just act this way, like you think you can sew up a dress and turn into someone else. It doesn't work like this."

Or: "Rose, what if your mother could see you now?"

He's not sure but he has to say something. She has to understand something. She just has to understand it.

He pushes off from the doorframe, staggers at first in a diagonal to a veranda post. Regains his legs quickly. There are so many people in the street. He didn't know that many people lived in the crappy backwater. Someone slaps him on the back; it's a man from the banana farm. Colin? Trevor? John-oh? His face is the same as that of any other man he's ever worked with. Broad. Gleaming with sweat. Smoke streaming from his nostrils.

"We're going to the Imperial," John-oh says.

"Yeah, yeah, mate, got something to do, back in a while," he says, waving him off like a horsefly.

When he gets to the ornate gates of the park, he can't see her, then catches just a glimpse of her moving way ahead through the trees. He squints; it's her all right, that dress with the huge skirt, the color of midnight. She'll be meeting a bloke. The bloke she's been lying about the whole time. She'll be meeting him in there at the back of the mill yards. Some secret rendezvous. He wants to say, "Hello, mate, how you doing, I'm the dad, nice to meet you." He'll think of something funny to say. He needs to say something. What is it he wants to say? He steps forward across the lawn quietly, is surprised at just how stealthy he can be; he'll have another drink when he gets back, to celebrate.

She's stopped still in the middle of an open space. She's standing beneath the moon. He knows the way Rose stands when she's thinking. She holds her arms a certain way, fingers together, as though she is about to recite a poem to a small audience. She's so beautiful. That's what he's thinking when she seems to sense him there. Beautiful, is what he's thinking when she turns to him.

$\mathcal{G}$athering Stitch ━━━━━━━━

This is the morning after again, so bright with sunlight you'll have to cover your eyes.

"Elaine," he says.

"Don't Elaine me," Elaine replies, but she's taken all the sketchbooks and paints anyway because there's still a chance.

Rose turns on her side, head pounding. The night swims there with her eyes closed, the wet lawn, the torn clouds, the jagged strip of sky. She tries to listen for their conversation outside but it's gone quiet. Perhaps he's leaning forward touching the locket where Mrs. Lamond keeps Mr. Lamond close to her heart. Her father has always been a trespasser.

Rose sits up in bed. Everything she owns is in her little drawer. She's not like Edie, who has kept everything; she only has her brush, seventy-one strokes, everything will be all right, her black fingernail polish, her black lipstick, her black eyeliner, her bobby pins and hair ties. Her flannel shirts. Red one with a tear. Her T-shirts. One pair of black jeans. One pair of shorts. Underpants, two bras. She has her notebook. Words, that's all she's ever kept, just words.

Pearl's dress lies across the bottom of the bed, pale in the sunlight from her little window. She reaches out to touch it. It was wrong of Pearl to not come back. To take the midnight dress just like that and not return. Rose had waited for hours. Murray had kissed her lips, again and again, dripped the last drops of the vodka onto her tongue.

"Time to get up, Tolstoy," Patrick Lovell says when he's back inside.

He's whistling. His own nervous kind of happy whistle when he's ready to get on the open road. Leave everything behind.

She sits up. Pulls the curtain. Puts on her clothes. She empties the drawer into her vinyl backpack, stuffs the tangerine dress into her plastic bag.

"Nearly ready, Rose?" he asks when she opens the curtain.

He can't look her in the face. There's something wrong with him. He's blown up with the drink, his eyes puffy as if he's been crying. He looks around the caravan interior as though checking everything is shipshape. They're about to plunge into the open sea. Let's launch this boat, crack open champagne.

"What's wrong?" she says.

"Nothing wrong," he says.

He still can't meet her eyes.

"I'm not coming," Rose says.

"Oh right," he says, still not looking.

He reaches out and checks a window.

She's never in all her life felt her mother's presence. Her mother has never stood beside her and made her shiver. She has never flown next to her shoulder. But right here in the caravan, Rose feels her for the first time. It starts in her toes and fills her from the bottom up. A kind of liquid spirit, that's what it feels like. A you'll-be-safe, don't-turn-back resolve pouring into her; she's sure it's her mother that morning: Don't go backward, don't touch all the places, stand up now, pick up your bags, let me see your hair now, it's beautiful the way it's falling over your shoulders, you've grown taller and look how strong you are. One foot in front of the next, that's right, toward the door.

There at last, there, he's finally looked at her.

"What have you done?" she says.

"What're you talking about?"

"What have you done?" she can't stop herself asking. She feels sick. Can hardly stand.

"I've done nothing," he shouts, slams his foot into the wall, then he's suddenly crying.

She shakes her head, turns her back, goes out the door. Down the step. She needs to get away from him.

"What do you think you're going to do?" her father sobs.

"I don't know," she says.

"Well, that doesn't sound like much of a plan."

That makes her laugh. He does too. The ridiculousness of it. They've been driving around the country in circles for eleven years.

"I didn't do anything," he whispers.

She walks down the caravan steps into the sunlight. Keep walking, says her mother. Not in words. She says it in Rose's heartbeat.

"Rose," her father calls.

Keep walking.

"Rose."

Keep walking.

"Rose."

There's rubbish everywhere on the streets. Streamers and paper flowers that have fallen from the awnings. Soft drink cans, burger wrappers, straws. She finds a ten-dollar note as she walks, which is good, because she didn't take any money when she left the caravan.

She pushes open the door to Crystal Corner; there's the cascade of tinkling bells. Pattie Kelly looks at the tangerine dress in Rose's arms.

"Where's Pearl?" she says.

There's something about the way she says it that scares Rose. There is a sharp edge to Pattie's voice. Why isn't Pearl inside that dress? she's saying.

"Isn't she here?" says Rose. There's a half-formed realization; it's crouching, rising, growing limbs. She turns her back on it quickly.

"No," says Pattie. "She didn't come home. I thought she was with you."

"Oh," says Rose. She probably slept in Jonah Pedersen's car at the beach. That's all. She doesn't say that. "She's got *my* dress."

Pattie looks at her, thinking. Afterward, for years, Rose thinks that she's seeing her aura. She's seeing its true color, which is black. She looks at Rose with a kind of horror.

"Something's wrong," says Pattie.

"I'm sure she's all right," says Rose. She knows she isn't. Wants to fall onto the ground and scream.

"No," says Pattie. "Something's wrong."

There's a flurry of phone calls first, then a blizzard. Jonah Pedersen says he arranged to meet Pearl but was picked up by the police for driving unlicensed. It's terrible; it might just ruin his professional football career. His father is still down at the police station trying to sort things out. By the time he'd walked to the mill yards last night, Pearl was long gone.

"I just thought she got sick of waiting," he says.

"Look, I got this for her," he says, showing the police officer. He takes a little box from his pocket, shows a sparkling ring. "It's cubic zirconia," he says. "One day it'll be diamond."

She's missing. *Missing*. Now, there's a good word. It's a lamenting sort of word. She was meant to be somewhere but instead she vanished off the face of the earth.

"Why did she have your dress on, and why have you got hers?" the same officer asks Rose. It's the only time she'll speak to them before she herself disappears. Before the search starts. Before the interviews. Before the bigwig detective comes down from Cairns. Before the mountain paths grow crowded with feet.

"It seems strange, that's all," he says, "to go to all that trouble to buy a dress and then just give it to someone else."

"I didn't buy mine, I made it," Rose says.

"Where was she going?"

"She was going to meet Jonah Pedersen. She said she'd be back in half an hour."

"What do you think happened to her? Where do you think she went?"

"I don't know, maybe she ran away. Maybe she got sick of this town."

It's a stupid thing to say.

"I'm sick of this town," she says. "A girl can't even not turn up for a day and everyone's asking questions. Maybe she just went for a walk."

She's on a roll now; she's remembering Paul Rendell in the crowd.

"Maybe you should ask Mr. Rendell Jr.; he has a thing for young girls."

"What makes you say that?" says the officer, offended. He plays Union with Rendell.

"Trust me, I know," says Rose.

"What's your address?" says the officer. "We'll need to speak to you again."

She says Paradise, wonders if her father has already gone; just the thought of him and her stomach sinks: his eyes, his howling against the caravan in the night.

"Anything else you can think of, Rose Lovell?" he asks.

"Nothing," she says. "I think you're all making a big deal over nothing. She'll be back soon."

But afterward, when she's out in the street, she looks up at the sky. It's filled with cloud writing, delicate, swept-up running writing; it's all written there, everything set out, everything that ever happened, everything that was ever going to be. She's crying. She's crying as she starts to run. She knows none of it's true. Pearl has gone and she's never coming back.

$\mathcal{U}$pright Cross-Stitch ━━━━━

I'll show you how her body lies. The sun is just coming up. The bush blushing rose gold. She's on her side, curled; she might be sleeping except for her eyes. There are ants on her arm. A long thin procession. Dewdrops on her eyelashes. She has been rained on. The sun has dried her.

The place is beneath the Leap, on the seaboard side of the mountain, low down. The tracks there are well maintained. There is a curtain fig, quite renowned, with a raised boardwalk and a circuit route to several lookouts, which afford glimpses of the sea.

It's exactly the kind of place Edie Baker would have shunned, full of her day-trippers with their echoing cooees.

There is a star pin winking in her hair in the first light.

The dress. The dress is the color of a dark sea. It hasn't faded, even with the exposure, although the fabric has grown limp. There is the black mourning lace. The cairn of sticks has flattened out, the leaves he piled on top of her have blown away; there is sunshine. The earth, holding her tenderly, is waiting.

These are the things that Edie taught her: how to fly, how to leap out across a swollen creek, all the praying in your feet, knowing that you can make it to the wet rock. How to listen for the falling of the sun: "It's a sound, Rose; if you are listening, you'll hear it before you ever see it in there." The leaves follow it all the way down, then relax, turn inward. The solitaire palm folds up its fronds. A different kind of scurrying begins, quicker, louder, more urgent.

How to sit still. How to breathe.

How to sew a straight line. How to pin a pattern. How to double-stitch a seam, how to make tulle petticoats, how to work lace at a cuff.

Edie is waiting for her at the top of the back steps. Exactly the way she always has. The house is shadowy cool.

"Something happened," Rose cries. "Something terrible happened."

Edie waits.

"Pearl put my dress on last night and then she disappeared."

The old woman's face changes, pales. "Come inside," she says.

She can't stop crying, Rose Lovell, she feels she'll never stop crying. They sit at the kitchen table, knee to knee. Rose sobs into her hands.

"Was it a magical dress? Was it the dress?"

"What do you think, Rose? You made the dress."

She looks smaller, thinner, Edie. Her hands tremble to her throat.

"Oh God," says Rose. She's seeing her father's face. His obsidian eyes. The way he was in the night. The way he looked at her in the sunlight.

She's clutching Edie's hands. She's sliding off her seat onto the floor. She's saying, "This cannot be happening. This cannot be happening, Edie. What have we done? What have we done? What have we done?" She rests her head in the old woman's lap. Closes her eyes but the tears keep coming.

"You know," says Edie. "You know what has happened."

And she does.

Rose doesn't leave. Not then. Not for a while. She is weighted down by the truth, which is a deadweight, an anchor, holding her there. She sleeps in a long-forgotten bedroom on a dusty-smelling mattress under a dusty-smelling sheet. There is a mirror in that room on a huge mahogany dresser and each morning and night she looks at her face there. The blood still moving in her veins. Her cheeks turned dusky red each afternoon when she returns from climbing.

She goes up at dawn. First to the hut. She sees the policemen there once, crouches like a wild thing, watches them through the trees. The place is split open now, touched by too many hands. It needs to be left alone. Given over to the forest. Already things have changed there. A bird examining a sliver of amber glass has left behind the seed of a satin ash. A tiny sapling has sprouted. The forest is already taking a step forward into that clearing. The crumpled house frame will rot. The orange fungi will bloom along its length. A carpet snake will curl itself amid the old blackened floorboards. If only it can be left alone. These are things she wishes for.

She leaves there and climbs higher.

Climbs farther. Her mother is with her still, in her limbs, in her thighs grown strong; she speaks in the pulse jumping at her throat. Keep going. Keep going. Keep going. Rose climbs until she can no longer stand. Until she crumples on the forest floor. Until she is free of the forest on the upper rocky reaches, where she stands in the clouds. She calls out to Pearl. She calls out again and again. Pearl. Pearlie. Pearl Kelly. Persephone. Pearl.

"I love her," says Rose, limbs exhausted, lying curled on the daybed, Edie opening the windows to the evening.

Edie doesn't say anything.

"I loved her, that's all," says Rose.

When she tells Detective Glass, she doesn't feel relieved. No huge weight lifts from her shoulders. She aches inside; it's a terrible ache. When her mother died, she felt the same way, she thinks, although it was too long ago to be sure. She tells Glass about Paul Rendell, about the love letters, about him kissing Pearl up near the hut, about the fire she caused. She tells him all these things and he listens patiently.

She tells him that it's her father. It's her father they should be looking for.

"Why do you think that?" Glass asks.

"It was his eyes," she says. "He couldn't look at me, and then when he did, I knew. He's always making mistakes. Terrible mistakes." She sobs with those last words. When she says it aloud, it sounds stupid. She's aware how stupid it must sound. "I just know," she says. Glass nods. He doesn't look convinced. He's losing interest. He's going to start asking more questions about Paul Rendell. She senses them there, ready on his tongue.

"Mrs. Lamond has his sketchbooks," she says. "They're full of his Pearl drawings. He couldn't stop drawing her. You should go there. She'll have kept them. She thinks Dad is coming back to her."

Rose writes letters to Pearl, hundreds of them. She posts some up among the trees. Leaves them between rocks. In the lovely carved spaces made by the buttress roots. Throws them over the falls, one by one, her words like petals.

Others she keeps. She'll carry them for years. She'll carry them with her between the places she lives. In cities, towns, across seas. The letters are written on writing paper from motel rooms and on the back of beer coasters, on cardboard torn from tissue boxes, on the last pages of books and on shopping receipts. She'll keep these words she meant for Pearl. When she is lost and, later, when she finds herself again.

They find her father before she leaves town. It's everywhere in the papers and on television. He's on some back road to nowhere. Face grown lean and assuming his biblical air. He offers no resistance, answers every question, slowly and carefully.

She stops the traffic when she goes to town. People freeze where they stand. Whisper when she passes. She sees Murray Falconer beside the park gates. She doesn't want to stop, to harm him, to draw a dark mark across him with her presence, but he calls out. "Rose."

"Rose Blackbird," he says when she is close.

"I'm sorry," she says.

He shrugs. His laconic Murray Falconer smile is gone. He looks behind her to see if anyone is watching. He can't think of anything else to say. He's trying. He's exasperated by it, his lack of words, almost angry; she thinks she sees the beginnings of tears. She can't think of anything to ease his uneasiness. Finally his father blows the car horn and he's gone.

So she never goes again to town until she leaves.

.

"Have you got money?"

"No."

Edie stands up, goes down the hallway, comes back with a small yellow purse with a gold clasp.

"Here," she says. The purse is full of money, stuffed full.

"That's insane," says Rose.

"It will come in handy," she replies.

"Do you think I'll ever see you again?"

"You know where I live."

Rose Lovell doesn't cry. Edie puts her hand out and holds her wrist. Old, old hand, feather-light.

"Maybe I'll come back here to visit," Rose says.

"Maybe you will," says Edie.

Still not crying.

"Bring back some fabric," says Edie. "Some buttons. Paris is a city of buttons, I've heard."

"Who said I'm going to Paris?" says Rose.

"I just pictured it, that's all."

She won't come back. She'll catch the bus that night from the service station at the end of town, opening up the yellow purse, counting out the notes for her fare. She'll lean against the window, watch the cane fields and the stars multiplied by her tears. She'll see the mountain go. Her mountain. It will move behind her and she will crane her neck until it is gone.

$\mathscr{F}$inishing
(Cutting Threads) ━━━━━━━━━

He says, "Pearl," whispers it, louder then, when he grabs for the dress.

She says, "Mr. Lovell. Don't."

It's clumsy, horrible, disorganized; he wants only to turn her to face him, reaching out like that, his hands full of night, the dress, then night again. He's lunging, has got her, she's falling, he's falling with her. A trillion stars glittering in a swath.

"How do I look?" she says to Rose.

Tell me I'm here, is what she means.

They're playing "Edelweiss" again. I won't show you more, except maybe this. The part where she's running, see her feet, the way they are hitting the newly dried-off grass, thudding down, toward the park again, the way they are touching the earth, touching the earth, touching the earth, and then they are lifting. She's running but the ground has fallen away beneath her; she's running but her feet are only touching air; she can see all the girls, all the rainbow-colored girls, snake lines of

them, dancing in the streets; she's calling to them but it's nothing, just
a breath; she's opening up her arms like wings; the midnight dress, it's
floating out behind her as she goes above the trees.

It's another wet season when the man finally arrives. The gutters
are filled to overflowing, the creek riding high across the Falconer
land, its brown back visible through the cane. Main Street is almost empty when the bus stops and he steps down, water up to
the ankle of his huge sandshoe, filling his brand-new Singaporean
socks. He has the letter she wrote him in his pocket.

Pattie Kelly still has Crystal Corner. She does a roaring trade
with the tourists, who step into her shop from the buses, right next
door to the takeaway. It's perfect, they say, magical. And there is
something special about the place. It's not so shiny now, not glitzy
the way it used to be. It's dustier, crammed full; she just can't stop
ordering saris, jade elephants, wrought-iron candleholders. But
it's not really the merchandise, it's something about the way it
feels in there. It encloses you, it holds you, sings you a lullaby. Pattie welcomes everyone. "Hello, darling," she says softly, as though
you are entering a church; it's the same to everyone who enters,
even the sort who don't look as if they would like that type of
endearment applied to them. The sort who would bristle and protest. She works harder on them, fusses over them, reads their aura:
"You, sir, have an aura the color of an azure sea. Now, don't look
at me like that, I can see these things, always have, always will.
Did you think you were something different, did you? Something
darker, or was it something lighter perhaps?"

When the letter first arrived, he was married with three
daughters of his own. They lived in a small apartment, two bed-

rooms, off Spiridonovka. There was no picture of the Eiffel Tower. The letter was such a strange thing, infinitely mysterious, the way it dropped through the letter slot and changed his life. It was written in rainbow-colored letters and it was so joyous that sometimes, in the years that followed, he took it out and held it, and laughed and cried openly. It said:

> *My name is Pearl Kelly and I live in Australia. If your name is Bear Orlov, I think my mother might have met you in Paris on the night of July the 23rd, 1970. She was dancing at the Crazy Horse. She would have been small, dark-haired, very pretty; you said she looked like an Arabian princess. You would have known her as Pattie or Patricia. I am enclosing my address and my phone number. If you are my father, I would love more than anything to meet you one day.*
>
> *Love, Pearlie xxx*

In Crystal Corner there isn't a shrine to Pearl the way you might expect. There is just one photo behind the counter of her in the tangerine dress, the way the night began. Not a single flower adorns her hair, only the star pins; she's not laughing, or even smiling, it's like she's thinking, thinking about something, she has that dreamy Pearl look. Not many people comment on the photo; it isn't large, it doesn't stand out, it's just a photo of a pretty girl.

Bear Orlov wipes his feet on the mat provided; the shop doorbell sounds, a cascade of tinkling bells; he fills the door, the sheer size of him. Pattie Kelly begins to say, "Hello, darling," stops. And so it begins.

Acknowledgments

My thanks especially to Catherine Drayton for her much-needed words of encouragement along the way, as well as to Erin Clarke and Madonna Duffy for their insightful suggestions, support, passion, and patience. And of course gratefulness and thanks to anyone who helped mind the baby.

KAREN FOXLEE trained and worked as a nurse for most of her adult life and also graduated from university with a degree in creative writing. She received the Queensland Premier's Literary Award for Best Emerging Author and was nominated for the Commonwealth Writers' Prize for her first novel, *The Anatomy of Wings*. Markus Zusak, author of *The Book Thief*, called the book "so special that you want to carry it around for months after you've finished, just to stay near it."

Lowell School
1640 Kalmia Road, NW
Washington, DC 20012